A Radical Affair

The Darnalay Castle Series Book 3

Louise Mayberry

Louise Mayberry

A Radical Affair by Louise Mayberry

2nd Edition, September, 2023

Copyright © 2023 by Louise Mayberry
Editor: Isabelle Felix
Cover art: by Hallie Zillman

Ebook ISBN: 979-8-9876378-4-5
Paperback ISBN: 979-8-9876378-6-9

This is a work of fiction. Names and incidents are, at times, based on actual historical events, but they are used fictitiously.

A small portion of the stage play, *The Vampire; or, The Bride of the Isles,* by James Robinson Planché (1820) is directly reprinted in this novel. This work is in the public domain.

Dear Reader

Please be aware that the plot of this novel revolves around an unhappy marriage, an illicit affair and an unplanned pregnancy; and it contains themes and topics that are as difficult today as they were two-hundred years ago. This includes discussion of abortion, physical and psychological abuse, infidelity and the terrible prospect of two parents being forcibly separated from their newborn child.

Take good care,

PART I: THE PAST

ONE

THE CENTRAL HIGHLANDS, SCOTLAND. OCTOBER 1820

CYBIL VENTURED INTO THE forest looking for inspiration, and she found it. A high canopy of birch leaves flamed overhead, orange and red against the blue autumnal sky. It cast an umbrageous light on the woodland below, and in the golden play of sun and shadow, leaf and stone, she saw faeries and goblins, gnomes and elves. A world of enchantment that had her fingers itching for a quill.

She'd promised a story to the *Ladies' Weekly* in just a month's time, and though she should have written it before she left home, she'd put it off, thinking the journey through the Highlands would be the perfect thing to stimulate her creative mind—she so rarely escaped the dreary confines of Grislow Park. But after days of being cramped in a coach beside her brother Percy, subjected to hours of Mother and Aunt Cynthia's idle chatter, she'd started to doubt the wisdom of her plan. Her mind was wrung out and dull.

But this wood . . . *oh*, there were stories here.

A small path branched away from the main trail, perhaps leading to the clandestine lair of a noble highwayman, or a band of nefarious thieves. Up ahead, a boulder loomed, twice as tall as she was. Rough stone draped in a thick carpet of moss. Maybe a troll lived inside, his front door accessed through the deep crevice that cleaved the rock's center. Or even better, this was the trysting place for the daughter of the king and her forbidden lover. He was the highwayman, of course. A gallant knight who'd been forced into hiding by the evil—

Cybil's heart stopped.

There was a man—a *real* man—crouched in the shadow of the boulder. He'd concealed himself in the crevice, and he was barely visible. All she could make out was his silhouette.

Was he watching her?

She swallowed, frozen to the spot. The small Highland village where they'd stopped for the night seemed a quaint, happy place, and the innkeeper had assured her that the path through the wood could be safely traversed by a woman alone.

So who was this man?

He was as still and silent as the craggy rock he'd concealed himself in. Surely, if he'd wanted to, he could have attacked by now, demanded her money or jewelry, yet he hadn't. He just stood there, looking at her.

Almost as if he were enchanted himself.

Cybil's pulse pounded. She couldn't see his eyes—they were pools of darkness—but something about them drew her in. Heedless of the danger, or perhaps because of it, she took a step forward. A prickling sensation ran up her spine, through her scalp. The feeling echoed in her chest, her belly, between her legs. Another step. Unbidden, an image flashed into her mind—of his rough hands on her, pushing her against the hard stone, then lifting her skirt. The feel of her bare skin hot on the cool rock. The weight of him as he filled her again, and again. The scent of rotting leaves. Moss digging under her fingernails as she grasped for purchase, and he bored into her without mercy . . .

Cybil couldn't breathe. The man was still at least ten feet from where she stood, shrouded in shadow, but his hair, she now saw, was unruly and dark, his hat a bit threadbare over prominent, looming brows. His lips were soft against the hard planes of his chiseled features—

Dear God. Cybil's hand flew to her mouth. *It was Will Chisolm,* her brother's friend who, along with his two children, was accompanying the family to Percy's wedding in the Highlands.

Heat bloomed on her cheeks. She barely knew this man. He'd ridden in the other carriage and had scarcely said a word to her in the four days since they'd been introduced and set out from Glasgow. How had she let her wanton imagination get the better of her, with *him* of all people?

"Mr. Chisolm, I'm—"

His eyes widened, and he raised a finger to his mouth, commanding her silence. At the same time, his lips curved into a small smile.

What on—?

"Come *out,* Da. This isna fun," a childish voice echoed from up the path, then Rose, Mr. Chisolm's daughter, came into view. She was a girl of six or seven, with a long, blonde braid and pale skin. Her eyes were wide and fearful.

She hastened her steps toward Cybil, talking all the while. "Lady Falstone, have you seen my father? He said we'd play hide-and-seek, but I canna find him and—oh . . . I'm afraid somethin's happened."

From Cybil's vantage point, she could see both Rose and her father. She dared a look at the latter, and he shook his head, his grin growing wider.

"I'm sorry, my dear. I haven't seen him." Cybil smiled at the child. "But I'm sure he's somewhere nearby. Is your brother out looking as well?"

"No," the girl replied flatly. "Nat says he's too old for games. He's gone back." She gestured down the path, to where Cybil knew it looped back to the innyard. "I've looked everywhere. I canna think . . . are there *wolves* here?" She peered up at Cybil entreatingly. Her chin trembled, and she was blinking away tears.

The poor child really was panicked.

"No." Cybil sounded as reassuring as she could, though really, she had no idea if there were wolves. "I'm sure he—"

"*Ha!*" Mr. Chisolm leapt out of his hiding spot onto the path.

Rose shrieked, then burst out crying. "Da!" She rushed to him.

The jovial expression on Mr. Chisolm's face melted as he wrapped his daughter in his arms. Clearly, this was not the reaction he'd hoped for. "Rosie, Rosie, I was just tryin' to have a bit of fun." He stroked her hair. "It's alright,"

Rose pulled away to look up at him, her face streaked with tears. "I thought—I thought you'd been eaten by wolves." Again, she buried her face in his chest.

"No wolf wants me. I'm tough as an old hen." Mr. Chisolm's attempted joke did nothing to calm his wailing daughter.

"I'll just . . ." Cybil began walking backward. Mr. Chisolm's eyes rose to meet hers. There was no heat in them now, and no fun, only resignation and some kind of sadness she didn't quite understand. Nor did she want to. "I'll just be going."

He nodded, then turned his attention back to his daughter.

Cybil turned and walked toward the inn. As she strode away, she heard Rose's muffled voice. "Never do that again, Da. Please."

Her father sighed wearily. "Very well. We'll find other games."

The two coaches arrived at Darnalay Castle three days later, just as the gloom of a murky day darkened into night. A cold rain spattered the carriage window as they turned into the castle's drive, but Percy was so excited to see his betrothed, Lady Jane Dunn, that the sun might as well have been at its zenith. Lady Jane came out to greet them, or to greet *Percy*, as it were. He was out of the coach and in her arms before they'd even rolled to a stop. The auburn-haired Lady Jane barely took her eyes off him to greet Cybil when Percy introduced them, though she *did* have a friendly smile. Cybil suspected once the flush of new love wore off, they would be friends—which was a good thing, as Lady Jane would soon be the new mistress of Grislow Park. Jane's younger brother, the newly dubbed Earl of Banton, emerged just as the passengers from the second coach were disembarking. He proved a more attentive host, smiling broadly then commanding everyone to call him Cameron, before ushering the crowd of guests inside.

They were shown into what must have once been the great hall of the castle but was now furnished as a sitting room—an enormous sitting room. Everything about it was oversized, from the massive logs crackling in the towering fireplace, to the soaring height of the ceiling and impossibly large beams that held it up. It made Cybil feel a bit like a girl in a fairy tale, a wee child in a castle made for giants.

"It's just as I imagined." Aunt Cynthia, a cup of steaming tea in hand, joined Cybil. Her eyes were sparkling. "Like the Castle of Dunbayne, is it not?"

Cybil nodded absently. Her aunt often tried to draw her into conversation by appealing to her literary side, but Aunt Cynthia had decidedly old-fashioned tastes in reading. Cybil had little patience for those aged Radcliffe novels, though she supposed this *was* something like the Castle of Dunbayne. One wouldn't be surprised to find tunnels hidden beneath it, or secret passages threading through the walls.

Her aunt's attention snagged on something across the room, then quickly returned to Cybil. She leaned in. "Mr. Chisolm looks dreadfully uncomfortable. Why don't you go talk to him?"

A nervous flutter rose in the pit of Cybil's stomach. She didn't move her head, but she let her eyes roam the crowded room until they landed on Will Chisolm. He did, indeed, look uncomfortable. He was standing by himself, watching his children who, for once, seemed to have forgotten their father and were chasing each other around the room. Mr. Chisolm's prominent brows were drawn into an expression of wary apprehension, his arms were crossed, and a mirthless smile played awkwardly on his lips. He looked out of place, like a schoolboy too shy to join in a game.

Cybil hadn't said two words to him since that odd episode in the forest. It wasn't that she'd avoided him exactly, but she hadn't sought him out either. She couldn't shake the feeling that he'd somehow seen into her mind in that moment, when she'd let her imagination run away with her. Her cheeks heated at the thought, and the fluttery feeling increased . . . But of course he *hadn't*.

How would he? And anyway, embarrassing encounters aside, she'd had no reason to speak with Mr. Chisolm in the last few days. She'd been preoccupied with her aunt and Mother, and the story she'd finally begun. He'd been busy with his children and in conversation with Percy. And it wasn't as if they shared any interests. His speech and clothing clearly indicated he came from the lower classes, and though Cybil didn't hold that against him—just two generations ago, her own family had been nothing more than tenant sheep farmers—it was clear they had nothing in common.

"Cybil?" Aunt Cynthia's voice cut through her thoughts. "Do go talk to him. You're close in age. I'm sure there's something you have in common."

Cybil resisted the urge to roll her eyes. Her aunt was serious, and one couldn't just say *no* to Aunt Cynthia.

"Very well." She sighed.

She crossed the room, weaving her way through the crowd. Percy, she noticed, had removed himself from conversation and was now circling the room dreamily, taking it all in. Dratted boy—he got to be in love, *and* he wasn't forced into awkward small talk. His eyes met hers, then darted to Aunt Cynthia, then Mr. Chisolm, then back to her with a knowing grin that only a brother would dare. He'd obviously guessed at their aunt's directive.

Cybil *did* roll her eyes at him.

Then she redirected her attention to the man she was approaching. "Good afternoon, Mr. Chisolm." She forced a polite smile.

"Lady Falstone." He nodded, then blinked twice. Even out of the shadows, his features were like chiseled stone. *Rough-hewn*. Yes, that was the word. Like a primitive wall made of crudely shaped fieldstones. Except for his lips. There was nothing rock-like about them. They were soft, pillowy, sensuous . . .

Cybil cleared her throat and dragged her gaze up to meet his. Her cheeks warmed. "'Tis a wonder we made such good time from Inverness, is it not?" She waited for a response, but he said nothing. "The weather's dreadful," she prompted.

"A wonder." Mr. Chisolm stared at her, then blinked again. His brows lowered and drew together, causing two parallel furrows to appear.

"I do hope tomorrow's weather improves," she ventured.

"Mmhm," he agreed.

"At least there's plenty of room here for the children to run about." She gestured to Rose and Nathan, who were now exploring the outer reaches of the room. "'Twas quite a long journey for two so young."

"Indeed."

Another dreadful pause, longer than the last, dilating until it threatened to swallow all pretense of easy conversation.

Cybil caught her aunt's gaze. Cynthia raised her brows and nodded, smiling encouragement.

Then she looked back at Mr. Chisolm, and without warning, something fractured inside her, then relaxed into place. *This was absurd*. What was the purpose of acting like a girl just out of Miss Pugel's Academy? She'd witnessed this man playing hide-and-seek, for goodness sake. Surely, he wouldn't mind a bit of fun. And even if he did, what did it matter if he thought her a ninny? Better that than a light skirt.

"I do hope the dragon doesn't escape the tower tonight." She spoke in the same polite tone she'd used to talk of the weather. "'Twould be a shame if any of the guests were eaten alive before my brother is properly wed." She paused, cocked her head as if in thought, then added, "Or burned to death."

Mr. Chisolm's eyes widened, and the two vertical furrows gave way to a plethora of surprised, horizontal ones. "I—I beg your pardon?"

"The *dragon*." She allowed a tiny smile to slip through. "I said, I hope it doesn't escape..." she leaned in ever so slightly, daring him, "and *eat* someone."

Mr. Chisolm stared, expressionless. His eyes were green, she noticed, but muddied with brown.

She'd just given up on a response and was about to apologize for her silliness when he spoke, as serious as ever. "Forgive me, Lady Falstone. I hadna heard about the dragon."

Cybil willed her face to remain placid, though inwardly she bubbled with glee. "Oh, haven't you?" She batted her lashes in mock femininity. "He's quite fierce, I'm told. His lair is the highest level of the tower." She paused dramatically, widening her eyes. "But woe to him who goes near."

Mr. Chisolm shook his head sternly, lips pressed together. "Couldna compare to the dragon of Strathfarrar. Now *she* is a brute. Too big by far to live in a castle like this one." He snorted derisively. "Hers is a cavern behind a linn . . . she used to fly over my house when I was a lad, breathin' fire in the night sky and makin' all the wee bairns cry out in fear."

"Breathing fire?" Cybil scoffed. "The dragon of Darnalay was never so common. His scales are made of molten gold. They spark flame as he flies, and it rains down from the firmament." She rolled her eyes up to the heavens. "An incandescent blaze of menacing fiery light." She raised her brows, daring him to best her. It was a nice phrase, that, she'd write it down later.

Mr. Chisolm blinked. "You mean . . . 'tis *bright*?"

Involuntarily, Cybil let out a peal of laughter, which she quickly reined in to a giggle. Mr. Chisolm grinned in response, and his smile, it changed everything. She had to check her impulse to lean in, to examine the details of the dimple that marked his left cheek, the sunburst of creases that appeared at the corners of his eyes.

She took a step backward, wrestling her expression into one of polite interest.

"My aunt," she nodded almost imperceptibly at Aunt Cynthia, "asked me to come talk to you. She thought you looked uncomfortable."

"Hmmh." Mr. Chisolm's grin disappeared. He seemed to consider the new information. "She was right. I havena had much practice at . . . *this*." He looked around at the guests, all happily chatting, then he leaned in slightly, cupping his hand to his mouth in an exaggerated whisper. "I'm not the genteel type, ye ken?"

A shiver went down her spine as the whispered brogue swirled around her, rough, as if it scratched an itch she hadn't known she'd had. Cybil swallowed, then pushed the feeling away. *Polite conversation.* That was what she was here for.

"Consider yourself lucky," she said lightly, widening her eyes to accentuate the droll comment.

But instead of an amused chuckle, or a wry smile, Mr. Chisolm narrowed his gaze, almost menacingly. He peered at her as if he could see right through her. "I do," he murmured.

They were close enough now that she could see his eyes in more detail—a rich, dark amber around the irises, giving way to soft green on the periphery, and sprinkled with gold, like stars. His lashes were long for a man's, thick and curled like his hair.

Another silence ensued but of an entirely different nature. It was as if everything around them disappeared, they were back in the forest, and he *knew*. He knew exactly what was in her mind.

Her nipples chafed against her stays. Her belly turned hot, and all she could do was gaze at the man before her, luxuriating in the warmth that flowed between them. She wanted to step into that luscious heat, to draw it around herself like a cloak until it surrounded her, filled her, and she could think of nothing else . . .

But then Mr. Chisolm blinked, and she remembered where they were. Who *he* was.

What was she doing? This was her brother's wedding. Her entire family was here. And he was her brother's *friend*. He knew quite well Cybil was married.

She looked away, searching for an escape. Her eyes fell on the table by the hearth that had been laden with tea, scones, and a decanter of whisky. "I—would like some tea," she stammered. In truth, she wanted the whisky.

"Oh." Mr. Chisolm seemed similarly disconcerted. A flush spread across his cheeks. "Of course. I'll ge—"

"No," she cut him off. "I'll go." She turned and left him standing alone once more.

Two

"LADY FALSTONE?"

Cybil looked up from the manuscript to find Mr. Chisolm standing awkwardly in front of the garden bench where she sat. The man really must not have many clothes. He had on the same coat and trousers he'd worn the day before in the great hall, and all the days of their journey—though she had to admit, his broad shoulders filled out the threadbare coat nicely. He held his hat in his hands, and the sun gleamed off his curly chestnut hair. His face had the paleness of any city dweller, but the chill air had put some color on his cheeks. His mouth was a perfect curve, like a parenthesis turned on its side. And his eyes . . .

Cybil blinked and pulled herself out of her daze. "Mr. Chisolm. I'm sorry, I didn't see you."

"No—you didna." He shook his head, as if to banish some errant thought. "I'm sorry. You're readin'—I'll—" He turned to leave.

"Stay," she called after him. "I'm not as impolite as that. My reading can wait. Sit with me." She set the manuscript to one side and patted the other side of the stone bench.

Hesitantly, he sat. It was a small seat. They weren't quite touching, but she could feel the heat of him through her clothing. She looked down at her lap, trying to compose herself, only to be mesmerized by the firm length of his thigh next to hers. The solid contour of muscle was just visible through his trousers. All she'd need do is lift her hand, place it on his leg, and—

She jerked her head up. Trained her eyes on some flowers across the way.

Silence fell between them, broken only by the trilling song of some Highland bird.

What *was* this? Did he feel it too? Certainly, Cybil was prone to lascivious fantasies, but this . . . this was more. More than she'd felt with Peter, certainly, or *any* man. Not that she'd had the opportunity to meet many men—the separation agreement Father and Ernie had agreed to saw to that. She was interned at Grislow Park and would be for the rest of her life. All she *had* was her imagination.

And wasn't it better that way? Hadn't she learned anything from her affair with Peter all those years ago? These things only led to regret, or worse.

"The weather has certainly improved, wouldn't you say?" She said it only to fill the silence, but it was true. The rain of the previous day had given way to sunshine, the kind of golden afternoon light that could only come in October, crowned by the deepest cerulean sky Cybil had ever seen. Tiny insects danced in the air around them, glowing motes of living gold. It was chill in the shadows, but the bench and the tall stone garden wall behind it were bathed in warmth.

"I want to apologize, Lady Falstone."

"Whatever for?"

"I dinna ken, but I believe I may have behaved . . ." Mr. Chisolm hesitated, then settled on the word, "*improperly* yesterday. I didna mean aught by it."

"You didn't?" She tried, but couldn't keep the disappointment out of her voice. Not completely.

"No. I—I meant no disrespect."

"There's no need to apologize, Mr. Chisolm. Or, I'm sure I have just as much to apologize for—"

"*No.*" he cut her off forcefully, impassioned even, then, softer, "you dinna."

Cybil still wasn't looking at him, but she could feel the heat of his gaze on her skin. Her pulse sped up, and warmth pooled in her belly. Lower. She waited, expecting him keep talking, to smooth his outburst into something resembling politeness, but he didn't. When she could bear the silence no more, she ventured a look at his face. His mouth was held in a firm, controlled line, but his cheeks were flushed and his hazel eyes gleamed at her with—it *was* desire. She was sure of it.

Their eyes held, and she shivered, though the sun was warm on her skin. A verse from Dacre floated into her mind.

> *Sudden she caught the wand'rer's eye;*
> *His cheeks assum'd a crimson dye,*
> *His glance was fierce, impassion'd high;*
> *Dissolv'd he seem'd in amorous fire,*
> *Yielding his soul to soft desire . . .*

Mr. Chisolm was the first to blink. He looked away. "What are you readin'?" His voice was gruff, lower than she remembered.

"A play," Cybil replied, glad for the reprieve. She picked up the manuscript and held it so he could see. "A stage adaptation of *The Vampyre*, written by a correspondent of mine. She plans to submit it to Drury Lane in London, and she's asked me to have a look before she does."

He stared at her, his expression unreadable.

"Have you read *The Vampyre*, Mr. Chisolm? Some claim it's by Lord Byron, but in actuality his doctor, Polidori penned it."

"No. I mean, I *do* read." He seemed intent she believe him. "But I've not heard of that one." Without warning, he shifted in his seat, turning his knees toward her so he could look at her more directly. "I wish you'd call me Will."

"Will." She said, testing the word. It felt easy on her lips. Simple. "Then you must call me Cybil."

"Cybil," he repeated her name softly. The flecks of gold in his eyes lit up, luminescent in the October sun.

She cleared her throat. "*The Vampyre* is a monster disguised as a nobleman. In order to survive, he must prey on innocent young women."

"Prey?"

"Aye. He bites them, just here." She tilted her head back and ran her finger along her neck, from just below her ear to her collarbone. "Then he drinks their blood"—awareness tingled through her as his eyes followed her move-ment—"and achieves immortality." She let her hand drop.

Will's gaze returned to her face. He swallowed. "*That's* what you're readin' about?"

"That's what I'm reading about." She laughed, then suddenly, an idea formed. A daft one, to be sure, but she was so delighted by it that it was out of her mouth before she could stop herself. "Would you like to read with me? I've just come to the part where Lord Ruthven, the vampyre, is claiming a victim. It's perfect for two people." Will didn't respond, just stared at her. Undeterred, Cybil held the manuscript so they could both see, then pointed to where he should read. "You read where it says R-U-T, for Ruthven, and I'll be Effie." She paused, then allowed just a bit of sultry heat into her voice. "And remember, you want to *possess* me. You *need* to. It's a matter of survival."

There was a long silence. Cybil let her gaze drop, then sat, waiting. *What was she doing?* Carrying on with this man in this way was idiocy. It would lead nowhere good. She could only hope she was reading him correctly, that he wouldn't feel it his duty to tell Percy about his sister's indecent behavior—

A hand grasped her arm, just above the elbow, tugging ever so slightly.

"Come nearer, charming maid." His ragged baritone caressed her ear, and a frisson of excitement shimmered through her.

"My lord, I—I dare not." She tugged back, relieved when he didn't let go.

"Fear nothing," Will read slowly, in a commanding tone. "An atmosphere of joy is round about thee, which . . . whosoever breathes, becomes thy slave."

"My lord, what mean you?" She gazed up at him, fluttering her lashes inno-cently.

"My heart ne'er throbb'd but for one woman." He looked up. Their eyes met, then, quickly, he went back to the words. "And you have just her features. This morning the flame of love was extinguished in my soul; but now, now it burns with redoubled ardor."

"But the lady whom you admired, my lord—"

"*She is dead*," he growled, the perfect vampyre.

"Dead!" Cybil gasped dramatically, allowing her eyes to become impossibly wide.

Will blinked up from the page. "Did I kill her?"

"Of course you did. Keep reading."

He nodded, then his expression darkened as he resumed his character. "Yes, *dead*. Effie: but in you she lives again. The bridal preparations are complete; my bride thou art—no power on earth shall tear thee from me! Say, Effie, that you love me."

He paused. The stage directions instructed him to take her hand, and Cybil waited, wondering if he would. Her breath came quickly, almost a pant. Then, thrillingly, his fingers left her arm and grasped her hand. His was warm and work-roughened, just as she'd imagined it would be.

"Mercy on me! My lord, I—I know not what to say. Oh, pray, leave me, my lord." She mimed trying to pull away, but he held tight then drew her closer.

"You weep: those tears are for me," he murmured. He was so near she could feel his breath on her cheek. Just a few more inches and they'd be kissing.

"No. No: indeed, my lord—for pity's sake—" she whispered, allowing her head to list back, arcing her neck toward him.

His eyes followed her movement, then narrowed as he read. "You plead in vain: Effie, thou art mine forever!" The stage direction that ended the scene was—*he carries her away*—and Will didn't hesitate. Before Cybil knew what was happening, he'd wrapped one arm around her waist and the other behind her knees and was rising from the bench, lifting her.

She shrieked as he took on her weight. "Stop! I'm too heavy—" She felt awkward in his arms, worried she might hurt him. But he didn't seem to have any trouble. He took several long strides toward the end of the garden, then at last, grinning, he dropped her to her feet. They returned to the bench, both breathless with laughter.

"I could never play a heroine like Effie." Cybil shrugged. "I'm simply too heavy." *Also much too wanton, and too cynical.*

"Not too heavy at all." Will gave her a sideways grin, his dimple on full display.

Cybil smiled back dazedly, warmth radiating through her entire being. If only she could store this feeling for later, when she was home at Grislow Park wallowing in her solitude.

"How does it end?" he asked, sitting back down beside her. She looked at him in confusion, and he motioned toward the manuscript.

"Oh. The vampyre wins the day. He kills Effie, then escapes into the night."

Will was silent for a few breaths. "Is that the kind of thing *you* write?" His tone was carefully flat. She had no idea what he wanted to hear.

"Well—nothing so *successful* as *The Vampyre*. But what I write is in the same vein, yes."

"Do yours have happy endings?"

"Never."

Another pause. Conversation with this man was more silence that talk, but Cybil decided she quite liked it. His pace was slow and deliberate, and she found herself slipping into his rhythm.

"I think they should—have happy endings," he finally said.

"Why? Life doesn't."

"But, dinna you think—"

"Da! Are you out here?" A voice wafted over the rock wall behind them, cutting off Will's question. "Da! Da-aa!"

Will's expression changed in an instant. He jumped to his feet. "Nat!" He shouted. "I'm here. In the garden." He took two steps toward the door cut in the stone wall, but before he could get there, his nine-year-old-son, Nathan, appeared. The boy was the spitting image of his father, and though usually he'd seemed to Cybil a serious, self-possessed lad, he appeared excited now. His cheeks were pink, his eyes wide. He was out of breath from running.

"What's wrong, lad?" Will seemed almost panicked. "Is it Rosie? Did something happen—"

"No." Nathan waved his father's concern aside. "She's at the castle. But, Cameron said he'd take me ridin' in the forest with him if you'd agree to it—"

"No." Will spoke decisively.

Nathan's expression fell.

"'Tis too dangerous." Will strode to his son and put a hand on his arm. "What if somethin' happened, and you being so far from the castle?"

"Cameron would be with me. And Mr. Burns in goin' too." Nathan's eyes widened entreatingly. Travis Burns was the stablemaster, and Cameron's dearest friend.

Will's lips pursed, considering. Then he shook his head. "On the road perhaps, but not the forest."

"But Da—" Nathan was clearly disappointed.

"Let's go see Cam, shall we?" Will sighed. "Perhaps we can work somethin' out." He looked back at Cybil. "Seems I have business to attend to."

"It seems you do," Cybil replied. Then, on a whim, she lifted her hand, offering it to be kissed. "Perhaps we might have the opportunity to read again sometime?"

Will glanced at his son, who was watching impatiently, then he strode back to Cybil, took her hand and bowed slightly. She held her breath as his lips brushed her bare knuckles. "I'd like that." He looked up, and their eyes met. "Good afternoon, Lady Falstone."

Cybil swallowed. "Good afternoon, Mr. Chisolm."

THREE

WILL COULDN'T SLEEP. IT'D been four days since his encounter with Cybil in the garden, but still, he couldn't get her out of his head.

That wasn't to say he hadn't enjoyed his time at the castle. On the contrary, he'd relished every moment. He'd taken Rosie and Nat to the wee loch to fish, wished the bride and groom a hearty good fortune, and he'd even given into Nat's pleading and taken the lad riding in the wood with Cam and Travis. In all those years lost to the filth and smoke of Glasgow, he'd given up on the idea of ever riding again, of seeing a slope covered with heather or the full dome of a Highland sky. But here he was, enjoying it all. In a castle, no less.

And he'd been offered employment, an escape from the constant threat of hunger, the soul numbing toil in the mill, and the agonizing fear of knowing Nat, working in the same factory, could at any moment fall victim to the machine that had taken three of Rosie's fingers. Sommerbell had offered him fifteen hundred pounds a year to manage the spinning mills the man had recently inherited from his father in Glasgow, with the aim of maintaining their productivity while making them more humane for the workers. It was an astronomical sum for an astronomical task, and though a manager was the last thing Will ever imagined himself to be—one of those smug fucks who lorded themselves over the common people—he'd swallowed his pride and agreed to it. He *had* to, for his family, and for Davey's too. Davey, who was even now locked in the hell of Calton prison, awaiting transport and unable to provide even a pittance for Emily and their lads.

It all felt so far away—Glasgow, the canal, the hussars—like a dream. But even still, Will's stomach hollowed with guilt at the memory of Emily's face the last time he'd seen her, tear-streaked and hopeless, cradling her infant child while her other son clung to her skirts.

But it wasn't that, nor the prospect of a new position, nor the clean Highland air that kept Will up tonight. It was *her*. Every time he closed his eyes, all he could see was the luscious curve of her bosom, her hips, and the smooth round moons of her arse, just begging to be squeezed. The way she'd looked when she floated into his view in that birch wood—rosy-cheeked and raven-haired, like a temptress from a storybook. The way she'd smiled at him when they arrived here, all coy and inviting, and the way she'd felt in his arms, so soft and warm. Picking her up had been foolish. His shoulder—still healing from the bullet he'd taken six months before—had been sore ever since but, by gad, it had been worth it.

She was his employer's sister. She was married. A baroness, no less. It was the height of lunacy to pursue such a thing. Dangerous in so many ways, especially for a man like Will.

But no matter how many times he told himself these things, he still wanted her.

His prick was hard as stone, though he'd already taken himself in hand hours ago when he first laid down to sleep. What time was it? One? Two in the morning? Only a few hours till the sun rose and Rosie would sneak into his chamber as she had every other morning so far.

He sighed and threw back the counterpane. There was no point in lying here. Perhaps a walk in the forest would help. He'd tire himself out, then get a wink of sleep.

He fumbled in the darkness for his trousers—or Cam's rather. The third day Will had come down to breakfast wearing the same threadbare trousers and coat, Cam had brought him to his chamber and insisted he take what he need. Jane had done the same for the children, outfitting them in old clothes and refusing Will's offer to pay.

What he'd done to deserve their kindness was beyond him. He didn't deserve it, not by a long shot.

The moon, just past full, was bright in the sky. He could see tolerably well in his room, with its tall paned windows, but the corridor, he knew, would be as dark as pitch, so he lit a spill and touched it to the wick of a candle. It flickered to life. Holding it in front of him, he made his way into the black interior of the castle.

He padded down the corridor, the leather soles of his shoes silent on the thick carpet. The candle's glow barely pushed back against the dark, but it was enough to light his way.

He came to the chamber he knew to be Cybil's and paused, looking for light beneath the door. There was none.

What was he thinking, that he'd knock on her door and be invited into bed? Danger aside, she was a genteel lady, a rich man's daughter brought up to know the rules of high society. A bit of wordplay was one thing, but to actually follow through—especially with a man like Will—was another entirely. He still couldn't fathom why she'd come to talk to him that day in the great hall, after the debacle she'd witnessed with Rose and the game of hide-and-seek. And that afternoon in the garden . . . well, probably reading plays together was a common diversion of the well-to-do. It meant nothing.

Shaking his head at his own foolishness, he continued down the corridor. If he followed it to the end, he'd come to the wee door Cam had shown him. It opened to a tight, winding staircase that led belowstairs, then eventually to a servants' entrance.

He was just reaching for the brass door pull when the door opened.

Will froze, arm still extended. His muscles tensed, and he watched, heart hammering, as the panel swung inward, then the light of a single flame emerged, a candle, and the vaguest hint of a face.

He stepped back as whomever it was stepped into the corridor. Slowly, features came into focus—a proud nose, arched brows, sharp chin, creamy skin . . . *Cybil.*

Their eyes met, and hers widened in surprise. But then a smile crept across her face. A pleased, knowing kind of smile.

Either he was the world's biggest muttonhead, or she wanted him.

And damn his eyes, he wanted her back.

"Lady Falstone." He forced his tone into something much more assured than he felt.

"Cybil," she corrected him, gliding closer. She seemed to float in the darkness. All he could see was her face, her flame, and the barest hint of a dressing gown.

"What—are you doing here?" he asked.

"Truthfully?" She was close enough to touch.

He nodded, never letting his eyes leave her face.

She laughed self-consciously. "You'll think me daft."

"No. I willna."

She sighed. "If you must know, I've never had the chance to haunt a real castle. I suppose you could call it research, for my writing."

He swallowed.

Her eyes darted to the movement in his throat, then came back to his face. "And why are *you* haunting the castle, Will?" She raised a brow.

He exhaled, and with the release of breath, all his resistance crumbled. She obviously liked to play games. So did he. They'd established that. But this was a game he hadn't played in many, many years, and never with a match like her. He could only hope he understood her invitation, and the unspoken rules.

"I was lookin' for you," he murmured, stepping forward so there were only inches between them.

"For me?" She widened her eyes, then bit her lower lip, slowly letting the plump flesh drag against her teeth.

"Aye." Will didn't even pretend not to be mesmerized. His prick was stiff as a rod, a clearly visible protrusion under his trousers. Holding his breath, he leaned forward an inch, bringing his mouth to her ear. The head of his cock brushed against her belly. "To make sure you were safe from the dragon," he whispered.

"And the vampyre?" She arced her head away from him, laying out the length of her neck. Offering herself.

Without thinking, he lunged, wrapped his free hand around her waist and roughly pulled her closer till their bodies ground together. His mouth landed on her neck, and she moaned softly, leaning into him with her hips as he feasted on her soft flesh. Biting. Kissing. Sucking.

She was impossibly soft. Impossibly yielding, yet solid as the earth itself. She smelled like sweet, fresh soil and ginger and honey. A goddess of the field. Of life. Of everything he craved. His candle flickered, then sputtered out, and mindlessly he dropped it, only half hearing the dull thud of the candlestick hitting the carpet as he threaded his now free hand through her hair. It was loose, flowing down her back in a gleaming wave, just as fine to the touch as he'd imagined it would be. Before he could stop himself, he'd fisted a lock of it and roughly pulled her head back. She gasped, her eyes widening in fear.

Ach, what was he doing? He dropped his hand, then backed away, hot shame rising in his cheeks.

"No. Don't—" She reached for him, grasped at his hands and pulled him back toward her.

"I dinna mean to hurt you," he mumbled. "I'm sorry. I—"

"You didn't." She spoke slowly, brows raised meaningfully. "I liked it." Her dark eyes never left his as she brought his hands to her mouth and brushed her lips—soft as a feather—across his knuckles. "I'll tell you, if you hurt me."

It was a dare, or an invitation, or—Will couldn't think anymore. With a groan, he pulled her to him and crushed his mouth against hers. She was soft and lush, and he was the vampyre, devouring her, claiming her essence as his own. She yielded to him, yet her passivity was aggressive as she used her lips, her tongue, the pressure of her body against him to lure him deeper, further.

He would follow her anywhere. Be willingly led into any trap . . .

But they couldn't do this here. The thought started small, an easily ignorable trickle amongst the roaring need flowing through him, but it grew until finally, with a low growl, he forced himself to back away. Nearly every room in this corridor was occupied, by people they did *not* want to wake. Cybil's mother, her aunt and uncle, Will's children.

"Cybil. I—"

"Will—"

They spoke at the same time, then stopped. Both breathing hard, they looked at each other, daring the other to speak, to make the decision to escalate or retreat. Somehow, her candle was still burning, and perhaps his eyes had gotten more accustomed to the dark because its flickering light illuminated more of her now. The gleaming black burn of her hair. The soft sheen of her silk dressing gown, the pink ribbon tie of her night dress. Her cheeks were flushed, her lips red, her eyes sparkling.

Cybil finally broke the stalemate. "Come," she whispered. She reached for his hand.

He'd thought this impulse was dead in him. Or perhaps he'd just been too desperate and hungry to allow it to surface. But it had surfaced now—and danger be damned—it would not be denied.

He grasped her hand. It was soft and small, yet strong and sure as she led him down the corridor toward her chamber.

She has a husband. The thought snared somewhere in the back of his mind, but he pushed it away as she opened the door and pulled him inside. She'd been separated from the Baron for years, Sommerbell had told him, insinuating some cruelty the man had done to her . . . She seemed to know what she was about anyway. And Will knew better than to do anything that could cause consequence. What harm could one night of pleasure do?

Four

Will regretted his decision as soon as the door closed behind him.

Cybil released his hand, then walked about the chamber lighting candles, and slowly, the room came into view: a large bed with a canopy, a writing desk strewn with papers, a washstand holding a basin and pitcher, a set of plush chairs set by the faintly glowing hearth, and a dressing table decked with a large oval mirror. The more light the room held, the more Will's resolve floundered. It was as if each bit of flame pulled him farther out of the dreamworld of the corridor, and back into the reality of life.

Will Chisolm was a steady, quiet sort of man. Yes, he liked a good game and a good jest, and yes, he had a certain kind of passion—a quick temper, and an innate sense of justice—but this . . . this man who'd stolen into a woman's—a *married* woman's—chamber in the dead of night with the intent of ravaging her? This was outside anything he'd ever known himself to be.

He edged backward and had just resolved to leave when Cybil set her candle on the dressing table and turned to him. Her eyes moved up and down his body, registering his proximity to the door, his awkward stance.

"What's wrong?" She stepped closer.

"I—" Will stammered. "I dinna think this a good idea. I—"

"Of course it's not a good idea." She arched a brow. "But we've made it this far." Her lips quirked into a teasing smile, but Will couldn't match her mood. He didn't smile back.

She studied him for a long moment, then her face slowly fell. She looked away and spoke into the empty space. "I thought you wanted this. But if you don't, of course you need not—"

"Oh, I want it." He couldn't bear her look, the mix of sadness and shame. "I've wanted it since that first time, in the woods."

"Did you?" She returned her gaze to his and smiled, soft relief. "So did I—I mean—I wanted *you*." Her tongue darted out to wet her lips. "And since then . . ." She sighed. "You've been a bit of a distraction, I'm afraid."

"As have you." Will couldn't think straight, even now, looking at her. He raised his gaze to the ceiling. "It's just that—I'm not this sort of man. I dinna do—*this*—on a whim." He brought his eyes back to hers. "Or at all. I never have. Not since my wife."

"Oh." She exhaled. "Neither have I. Not like this."

Her eyes narrowed, and she studied him for a long moment, then she brought a finger to her lips, as if weighing what to say next. "What if—you weren't yourself?" She lifted a brow. "What if you were Ruthven?" There was that wicked little smile again. "And I were Effie?"

Will blinked. "You mean, *playacting*?"

She nodded, her eyes sparkling in the candlelight. "It was . . . enjoyable, in the garden, was it not? We could continue the scene."

Will's mouth went dry. *Ruthven*. The vampyre. The idea struck like lightning. To forget himself and give way to that mad impulse. To possess her, dominate her . . . but—he shook his head to clear the image. "But Ruthven is a monster, and I'm—you're—I'm afraid I'd hurt you without meanin' to."

"If you did, I'd tell you." She repeated her words from the corridor.

"But Effie is fearful already. I wouldna ken if—"

"I'd *tell* you. And you'd stop." She raised her brows again, not teasing this time, but defiant, daring him to cross her. It was clear this woman would not allow herself to be hurt.

Christ, he wanted her. But even still . . .

"If we did . . . play the parts . . ." Will started, not believing he was entertaining this, "and you wanted me to stop, for any reason, you could speak to me as Will, not Ruthven. Then I'd know you mean it."

She considered, then nodded. "Very well."

His pulse sped up. "You promise? You willna just—suffer."

She stepped closer, took his hand. "I promise."

Her words faded into the flickering shadows, then the silence loomed large.

Will swallowed. Cybil was still holding his hand, watching him, waiting for him to do something. But what would Ruthven do? He was such a dramatic character, the opposite of Will's own. Appealing, yes, but— "I confess," he said, forcing a rueful smile, "I have no idea what to do next."

Cybil giggled at this, and Will was glad to laugh with her.

When their laughter had faded, her head tipped to one side, thoughtfully. "If *I* were a vampyre," she mused, "I believe I'd start by telling my victim what I want them to do. I'd have such power over them, they'd have no choice but to obey." Her eyes widened and met his, and her voice took on the helpless breathiness she'd used when reading Effie in the garden. "What would you have me do, my Lord Ruthven?"

Will's prick responded before he did, hardening to rock. He opened his mouth, unsure of what he would say—or if he had the courage to speak at all—but the words came. Not in his voice. but in Ruthven's, the vampyre—sure, commanding and strong.

"Bare yourself to me, Effie."

She stared at him for a long while, and he'd just convinced himself that she'd decided against the whole thing when she lifted her hand, slowly untied her sash and let her dressing gown slip to the floor. Her arms gleamed white in the candlelight. He could see the gooseflesh rise on them, whether from cold or excitement, he would never know.

She stood in her thin nightdress, staring up at him with wide, frightened eyes. "I am but a poor maid, my lord. Please, have mercy. My virtue is all I have—"

"Bare yourself. *Now.*"

Her trembling fingers found the tie that held her nightdress closed. She tugged it, and the panels fell open, revealing the plump tops of her breasts. Slowly, the fabric slid down her shoulders, another inch, then another—

"*Enough.*" Ruthven could stand it no more. "When I tell you to do something, you *do* it." He reached out and yanked the fabric open. The cotton tore slightly, and for a fraction of a second, he regretted his force, but one look at her face told him she didn't care one whit for the nightdress. Her lips were parted, her breaths fast and shallow, her eyes wide and fixed on him, anticipating his next move.

Then he caught sight of her breasts, and nearly forgot about Ruthven, or Effie, or anything . . . *Christ's teeth.* In all his life, he'd never laid eyes on such a perfect pair of titties. They were large, plump and heavy. He wanted to burrow his face in them, squeeze them, suckle them, run his cock between them and fuck them. Her nipples were pointed and hard, dusky against her creamy skin.

His eyes flicked to the mirror on the dressing table in front of them. "Turn around."

She looked at him quizzingly. "But, my lord—"

He fisted a lock of her hair. Pulled. She inhaled sharply, her chin rose, and her body stiffened. "I said. Turn. Around."

She obeyed.

Her pale reflection shown in the mirror, dreamlike in the flickering light. Ruthven's image was just behind her, shrouded in shadow but still grasping her hair. *Ach,* she was gorgeous. Her nightdress was torn and slipped down her shoulders, her cheeks flushed, her eyes glassy and drinking in the view just as thirstily as he was.

He leaned down and whispered in her ear, at the same time tightening his hold. "Now, listen closely." She inhaled, but said nothing. She seemed too dazed to speak. "Are you listening?" he growled.

She licked her lips, then nodded.

"Speak." He pulled just a bit tighter.

She gasped. "Yes, my lord. I'm listening."

He spoke slowly, allowing the words to come without forethought. "I am going to tear your nightdress off you. Then I'm going to touch you, wherever I please. I'm going to devour you, Effie. Your flesh, will be mine." She swallowed, and her eyes in the mirror moved from his reflection to her own, as if imagining what he would do. "Then I'm going to fuck you. I'm going to push you up against that table, and I'm going to fuck your cunny, hard, deep and without mercy." Her eyes widened, but she said nothing, made no objections. "And you are going to watch."

Those dark eyes flicked back to him, then she half turned. "Please, my lord." She whimpered, desperate. "I'll give you whatever you ask for, but take pity. My honor is—"

"There will be no pity." He pulled her hair taught. "You are mine, Effie. Do you deny it?"

She closed her eyes, then whispered, "No, my lord."

Still holding her hair, he brought his mouth back to her ear and growled, low and menacing. "Say my name."

Her breath was ragged. He could see her pulse pounding in her neck.

"Say it." He pulled.

"Ruthven," she whispered. "Lord Ruthven."

"Open your eyes." He released her, and she did as he commanded, gazing at their reflection as he reached around and grasped her naked breasts. They were just as he'd imagined—soft and warm. Two bits of heaven. He squeezed her nipples, and she cried out, then they both watched—mesmerized at the sight of her soft flesh overflowing his hands. His rough fingers squeezing and kneading her.

As if overcome, Effie's eyes closed again. Her head dropped back. Unable to stop himself, his mouth came to her neck, kissing and sucking and biting, and—

He tore himself away. "I said. *Watch*." Roughly, he pushed her head up. She opened her eyes—wide and fear-stricken—and focused on the mirror. Then he grasped the already rent fabric of her nightdress and tore it, viciously and without hesitation. It gave way easily, with a loud, ripping sound that set his blood on fire.

Then it was in two pieces, and Effie was naked before him.

His breath caught. Her curves. The smooth thatch of hair guarding her cunny. The soft swell of her belly, and the flesh of her thighs. It was all as he'd imagined, but better.

Still standing behind her, he ran his palms down her sides. Her waist. Her hips. He grasped the pale moons of her arse, squeezing till she squealed in pain. Then he moved his hand to the front of her, caressing her mound, feeling for the smooth wetness he knew lay within.

"Spread your legs." His voice was rough, and raw, not his at all. Stumbling a bit, she moved her feet apart, then she leaned into him, moaning as he explored her, teased the little nubbin at the top, dipped a finger into her quim. It came out coated with her essence, and he smeared it on her folds, playing in her slick heat. At the same time, seemingly of its own accord, his straining cock ran up and down her arse, each stroke bringing him higher, closer—

And suddenly, like a great wave, his lust overtook him.

He couldn't wait.

Feeling much less a vampyre and more a man, he fumbled with his falls, finally pulling out his hard prick. It was hot to the touch, pulsing.

He'd never been so desperate for a woman. "Brace yourself, Effie."

Following his command, she bent over and placed her hands on the table before her, arched her back slightly and planted her feet farther apart. The pink folds of her cunny were barely visible, peeking out from between her legs—

He couldn't wait another heartbeat. He guided himself in.

"Argh," he shouted, unable to contain the feeling. It had been so long since he'd been inside a woman, and this—this was everything. Hot, and wet, and . . . fuck. There were no words.

He grasped her hips and pounded into her, again and again. Their reflection was wild now. Her breasts swung and bobbed to his rhythm. Her eyes were closed, her forehead touched the mirror's surface, and her mouth was slightly open, her breath fogging the glass. And he . . . Ruthven was like a man possessed. Hair standing on end, eyes gleaming, grunting like a wild animal as he ruthlessly used the woman before him.

"Watch," he snarled, unable to get out more than the one word.

She opened her eyes and watched, staring herself down as he fucked her with abandon.

It seemed they'd just begun when Will felt his balls tighten. "Come. Now. *Now. Come.*" He commanded, thrusting into her with each word, pounding her with all his weight, all the power he could muster, pushing her harder, faster, over the edge . . . She shrieked as she climaxed, biting her lip to muffle the sound. And just in time. He pulled out, stroked himself once, twice and the spend spurted out of him, wave after wave, landing thick on her arse and thighs.

Then it was finished.

Will felt a bit fuddled. He was out of breath, dizzy, and, once again, he had no idea what to do. Cybil still seemed lost. She leaned against the mirror with her eyes closed, little tremors wracking her body.

He stood a moment, watching her, then he remembered the washstand. He could at least help her get cleaned up.

He tucked himself into his trousers, then, leaving her where she was, he went to fetch a towel. By the time he returned, she seemed herself again, if somewhat shaken.

She accepted the towel, then awkwardly reached behind herself with it.

"Let me." He took it back and worked to wipe her clean. "I'm sorry about the nightdress," he murmured.

"Sorry?" Her voice was shaky. "Wha—*no.*"

He chuckled at her lack of coherence, then tossed the towel away and bent to pick up her dressing gown, offering it to her. "I did hope to make it last a bit longer." He scrubbed his face. "But I got—desperate."

She smiled, more sure now. "You have *nothing* to apologize for. That was—" She searched for the word. "Brilliant."

Will grinned. "It was, wasna it?"

Cybil beamed back at him—a new kind of smile he'd never seen before. Warm, and—and *satisfied.*

Then, suddenly, he noticed the black outside the windows wasn't as black as it had been. "I've got to go." He spoke as much to himself as to Cybil.

She followed his gaze. "Yes. The servants will be up soon."

He hesitated, not sure how to end this. What did one say when leaving a woman you've just ravished but barely know at all? "Goodnight then, Cybil." Was all he could come up with.

She grinned. "Goodnight, Will. Or, good morning, I suppose."

"Indeed."

He turned to go, then, on a whim, turned back. "I wonder if you'd give me another chance?"

"Chance?" Her brows rose, confused.

"At—*this*." He gestured between the two of them. "We'll be here a week more, and I—I really did want to go longer." He also really wanted the chance to fuck her titties.

"Of course." An even brighter smile spread across her face. "I'll be here tomorrow night. Come whenever you wish."

PART II: THE PRESENT

FIVE

FOUR YEARS LATER

THE PUTRID SMELLS COMING from the slaughterhouse were too much. Cybil had to get out—now.

It seemed impossible that the odor could be so intense. The stagecoach door was closed, and the low, brick building was at least two furlongs away, across the road and at the bottom of a steep slope. A shelf of rough, pitted basalt was the only thing separating it from the choppy waves of the North Sea. The fresh air should have been enough to dilute any stench at this distance, but somehow, the stink of dead flesh and dung penetrated the carriage. It melded with the briny tang of the sea and was only made worse by the lingering malodor of kippers on the breath of the man sitting beside her and the pressing heat and bodily odors of the seven other passengers crowded into the small space.

The stagecoach had been stopped at the tollhouse for five minutes at least, and Cybil had borne it as long as she could. She'd closed her eyes and took long, slow breaths. But her stomach—

She was going to vomit.

Without a word—she didn't trust herself to speak—Cybil stood and pushed her way to the door. She wrenched it open and ducked her head into the open air, desperately searching . . .

There.

A low stone wall bordered both sides of the turnpike as it came into Dunbar. A peeling wooden gate was cut into it just before the tollhouse. Some scrubby bushes, which might have once been a garden, lay beyond. Ignoring the curious eyes of the men riding on the roof of the stage, she stumbled down from the coach and darted toward the gate. She'd just managed to open it and step into the weedy expanse when a wave of heat washed over her and her stomach began to heave.

Three minutes later, she emerged to find the driver back on his perch. He noticed her just as he was lifting the reins, then glared, obviously annoyed, as he dropped the ribbons and moved to climb down and let her back in.

But Cybil waved him on. There was no way she could get back in that detestable coach. "I'll walk," she shouted. "Leave my luggage at The George."

Jane, her sister-in-law, had told her that things smelled differently when she was carrying a child. But this was not just *different*. 'Twas awful. Scents Cybil used to find tolerable were now detestable, and the odors she'd already disliked made her ill.

The change in her sense of smell had been the first thing Cybil noticed, along with a feeling of bleary detachment, as if she were viewing the world through a smudged window. Then she'd realized her courses, usually quite regular, were late—*very* late. Two weeks, then three, four, five. It was now six weeks past when she should have bled. She'd woken up with intense nausea for the last week, and she could no longer pretend, even to herself, that she didn't know why.

The driver scrutinized her for a long moment, then he nodded, turned and slapped the reins. The stage departed in a clatter of wheels over cobblestones.

Cybil watched the coach disappear. She breathed in the cold sea air, allowing the solitude to spread out around her. A walk would do her good, give her time to collect her thoughts and settle her stomach before she saw Will. And before that inevitable, terrible conversation.

It had been an exceedingly tiresome day. She'd risen at three in the morning, endured the two hours over the rough country roads from Grislow Park to Newcastle, then another nine in the crowded stage to Dunbar. It would've been much more pleasant to be driven in her own conveyance for the entire journey, but she'd needed the anonymity of the public stage, so she'd left her comfortable Brougham and its driver at the Newcastle Townhouse, telling the staff the same lie she'd told her family—that she'd be traveling for two days with Lilian Smith, her friend from Sunderland, to tour Dunstenburgh Castle and investigate it as a possible setting for a novel. Mother, Jane and Percy were accustomed to her solitary outings with her old school friend, the widowed—and imaginary—Mrs. Smith. No one questioned her.

This was always the way when she traveled to meet Will—secrecy and lies, the obscurity of the public stage. But usually, once she was free of Grislow Park, she quite enjoyed it. For it was only among strangers that she was truly free, released—albeit temporarily—from the fetters of propriety and isolation that imprisoned Cybil Bythesea, estranged wife of Baron Falstone. On those anonymous journeys, she could be whomever she wanted . . . and she was a woman on her way to meet her lover. There was something heady about surveying the strangers around her with the knowledge that she would soon be in Will's arms, indulging in clandestine pleasure, and none of them suspected, or even imagined.

But this trip was nothing like those rhapsodic journeys of the past. Instead of excitement, there was only bitter dread—a dull painful misery in the pit of her stomach.

And what came next . . . Cybil's throat ached at the thought. She knew what she had to do, but—but she couldn't see it. She simply could not see past this day. Or the next.

There was a foul taste in her mouth. Her head ached. She wanted to walk away from this town, away from the man who waited for her. She wanted to lie down in the weeds on the side of the road and let herself drift into the ignorance of sleep. But what she wanted was immaterial. She had to face reality. To lift one foot, then the next as she made her way into the town of Dunbar.

It was as grey as one could imagine a day to be. A solid mass of clouds filled the sky without a hint of definition between them. The coastline was dull brown rock, as was the road, the stone and mortar wall that bordered it, the two-story tollhouse and the houses beyond. The vast slate blue expanse of the ocean reached to the Eastern horizon. A chill wind blew in.

Cybil shivered and drew her pelisse closer.

Gradually, the reek of the slaughterhouse receded. She was still lightheaded, but the nausea had subsided, leaving only the ever-present mass of roiling dread in the pit of her stomach. She passed the new red-stone kirk and the burying ground that spread out around it, then the imposing gate of the Earl of Lauderdale's house. She kept her eyes trained on the intricate wrought-iron bars. She would not look to the other side of the street, to the winding path that led to the secluded seaside cottage she and Will had rented for the week they'd stayed here. How happy they'd been. It was only a year ago, but that woman—*herself*—flush with lust and inspiration seemed a ghost. Unreal.

At last, she came into the close confines of High Street, feeling more and more like a specter as she passed each familiar landmark. She tried to do as she always did when despair closed in—step away from herself and observe, carefully cataloging the sensations of hopeless melancholy so she could later depict them in words. But even that trick failed her today.

In just a few minutes, when she reached the plain white Doric columns up ahead, the columns that framed the entrance to the George Hotel, she would have to tell Will that everything—her life as it had been, their affair, their *connection*—was over.

———◦———

Will sat in the corner of the barroom at The George, nursing his second ale. The most recent edition of The *Dundee Advertiser* lay unfolded on the table before him. He'd picked the paper up on his way through Edinburgh and read most of it on the coach to Dunbar. The *Advertiser* was a radical rag, one he dared not read at home in Glasgow. Being seen with it might not only raise the eyebrows of his middle-class neighbors, but of the law as well. But here, no one knew him. He need not fear the association with his past.

He'd finished the last article now, leaving nothing left to distract from the folded note that lay beside the paper.

He picked it up and read it again, though there was no reason for it. He knew it by memory.

19 September

R:

I need to see you. Urgently. Meet at The George on Wednesday. I'll arrive on the early stage.

Effie

It was so unlike any of Cybil's other letters. Her missives were few. She daren't post them from Grislow Park, so she had to wait till she was in Newcastle and send them anonymously. But when they came, they were always long, full of innuendo and big words that Will had to look up in one of the two massive tomes of the Johnson's Dictionary he kept at his office. And it wasn't just the brevity that was odd. It was the contents too. To command him to appear in just two days, with no explanation. It was strange indeed. Usually, their trysts were planned well in advance. But there was no mistaking her cramped tidy hand. And she'd used their pseudonyms. No one else knew those names.

What could she possibly be about? A small part of him was annoyed by the summons. He'd had a devil of a time leaving Glasgow. He'd just taken on the management of two more mills that Cameron had acquired. There were a thousand and one repairs needed on the old buildings before they could begin production, and Will had had to reschedule an appointment with the architect to answer Cybil's summons. Worse than that, he'd had to give a hasty, made-up excuse to his children. Gad—he hated lying to the bairns.

But perhaps this was a new form of seduction Cybil was playing at . . . calling him to her with no explanation, just to see if he'd come. And damn his eyes, he *had* come because, as always, the draw of Cybil was impossible to resist.

I need to see you. Urgently.

His prick hardened at the thought of her walking through the hotel door, his own sonsy lass, all soft curves and raven hair, fixing on him with those dark eyes . . . He'd have her tonight in the small room he'd rented upstairs. Then tomorrow morning, they'd steal away to the ruined castle by the sea and he'd pull her skirts up and fuck her against the weathered stone wall, just as he had that week they'd stayed here. *Ach*, what a week that had been.

His mind wandered back to their last encounter, just two months before. Cybil had been in Glasgow for Cameron's wedding and though it had been almost impossible for her to get away, just before she'd left, they'd sneaked an entire day in the country. He'd chased her through a woodland, fucked her in the sunlight beside a rushing burn, and they'd spent the rest of the day laughing and talking and fucking again, rutting like animals—

The door *did* open then, and Will's attention snapped back to the present. A stream of travelers entered. Men mostly, but a few women too. The early stage must have arrived. He kept his eyes on the door, watching each person who came though, every time expecting Cybil to be next. He counted more than a dozen, then came the coachman, red and puffing, toting the luggage of whichever travelers had elected to stay the night.

But no Cybil.

Will scanned her note again. It was Wednesday. The early stage. There could be no mistake.

The driver passed close to Will's table on his way to the bar. Will waved him over, and the man stopped, bushy eyebrows raised inquiringly.

"You're the driver of the stage?"

"Aye."

"My wife was to be riding with you . . ." Will hesitated. It always felt odd referring to Cybil that way. She was not his wife. Would never be his wife.

"Tall lady? Black hair?" the coachman asked.

"Aye. She would have gotten on at Newcastle. She was there visiting her sister."

"She got off at th' tollhouse," the driver said. "I don't know for certain, sir, but I believe she may have been ill."

Will gave the man a sharp look. "Is she—?"

"Walking, sir," the driver assured him. "Asked me to deliver her luggage here." He held up a valise that Will now recognized as Cybil's. "It isn't far. She'll be here anon. I've no doubt."

Will accepted the valise, stuffed Cybil's note in his waistcoat pocket, then tossed a coin on the table and strode quickly to the door.

It was a bloody dreary day. Grey sky. Cold. He cleared the columns that flanked the entrance to the hotel, then turned left, the way Cybil would be coming if she were walking from the tollhouse. He scanned the pavement. A woman with a basket over her arm. A man hawking meat pies. Two gentlemen walking into the bank, then—a female figure, too far away to make out. He squinted, she was wearing a large bonnet and a pelisse over a plain dress. The wind whipped her full skirt in all directions. He walked briskly toward her, and finally, he was close enough to make out the features behind the wisps of black hair that had escaped her bonnet. It *was* Cybil, but her face was oddly blank, her mouth a flat line. Her expressive brows drew together as if she were in pain. Her eyes were trained on the pavement in front of her, dull and almost unseeing.

He increased his pace.

"Cybil," he shouted to get her attention.

Her eyes lifted and met his, but her expression didn't change. If anything, it became more bleak.

"Hullo, Will," was all she said when he finally reached her. No embrace, no seductive smile or sultry raise of her brow. Not even relief for the end of her journey. She just stared at him with that terrible, flat look.

He reached out to touch her arm, but she grimaced and shrugged him off.

"What's wrong? Are you—"

"I'm pregnant."

The word—blunt and vulgar—hit Will squarely in the chest.

He glanced around, ensuring no one had heard. "What do you—"

"I said, I'm *pregnant*, Will." She spoke louder this time, and the driver of a passing gig whipped his head sharply toward them. "With a *child*," she clarified, as if he didn't know what the word meant.

"But—" A thousand thoughts raced through Will's mind. Far too many to say aloud. One thing was clear, though, this was not a conversation they could have on the pavement.

"Come. I've a room in the inn. We can talk there."

Six

Will offered Cybil his arm, doing his best to ignore the curious looks of passersby.

She looked up at him with a tight, agonized expression, then she exhaled, and everything about her seemed to droop. Her shoulders, her eyelids, even her head lolled slightly to one side. She nodded slowly, then took his arm, allowing him to guide her into the hotel through the crowded barroom and up the stairs. He only released her when they finally arrived at the small room he'd secured for the night and he turned to lock the door behind them.

It took him a few tries to get the key to turn, and by the time he was finished, she'd removed her pelisse, bonnet and gloves and was sitting on the bed, bending to untie her half boots. He had no idea what to say, so he just stood and watched, arms crossed as she pulled one boot off, then the next.

Without looking at him, she reached her hands up and behind to unbutton the back of her dress.

"Let me—" Will moved to help.

"No." The look she gave him stopped him in his tracks. "The ties wrap to the front. I just need to . . ." She brought her arms around and reached down the neckline of her loosened dress, then untied her stays. She sighed as the garment relaxed, then swung her stocking feet onto the bed and reclined, eyes closed.

"Do you need water, or—"

"No." She didn't open her eyes.

Will studied her, trying to determine what to do or say next. This Cybil was a stranger. Every impulse urged him to hold her, kiss her, comfort her but he had no idea if he'd be welcome to even sit beside her. Not wanting to risk rejection, he pulled up the one small chair the room offered and sat, leaning in with his elbows on his knees and his chin resting on his fisted hands, waiting for her to speak.

She said nothing, though her eyes opened to stare at the ceiling.

"Are you—are you feeling ill?"

"Not anymore."

Silence.

"You're sure—that you're with child?"

She closed her eyes and swallowed. "Yes."

"But how could it—"

"Shall I explain?" She turned to look at him, her eyes glassy and hard. "Some of your mettle must have seeped into my—"

"That's not what I meant." He took a long breath. He could feel the heat rising in his neck, but he must not let it get the best it him. It would only make matters worse. "You said you were barren," he spoke slowly and evenly, hoping not to upset her further. It didn't work. She glared at him, her lips drawn into another tight line. But it was true. She *had* said she was barren. It was also true that he'd known better than to assume just because she hadn't conceived with her husband that she wouldn't with him. That was why, at first, at least, he'd always been so careful to pull out before his crisis.

"I'm sorry. I didna mean—"

"I said I *thought* I was barren," she interrupted. "It seems I was wrong." She returned her gaze to the ceiling.

"Have you been seen by a doctor? Perhaps your courses have stopped naturally, or—"

"I'm five-and-thirty, Will, not fifty. My courses are six weeks late. I've been ill every morning for the last week. Everything smells differently, and—" She sighed heavily. "I've never felt this way. Ever."

"But *have* you been seen by a doctor? Or a midwife?"

"No." Her gaze met his. "But there's no other explanation." There was a finality in her tone, a desperation that allowed for no argument.

A band of fear tightened around Will's chest. "Who else knows?"

"No one."

"Not even Jane?" Cybil's sister-in-law was her dearest friend.

"Not even Jane, or Percy or Mother. No one."

The band loosened slightly, leaving Will feeling relieved and short of breath. But his mind ran ahead, seeing all the possibilities, all the inevitabilities, play out. Cybil's brother was Will's employer, and though Percy Sommerbell wasn't exactly a paragon of propriety, Cybil was his *sister*. And it wasn't as if Will could make things right by marrying her. If—or when—Sommerbell found out, Will would be sacked. Then another thought—if Cybil's *husband,* the Baron, found out, he'd have cause to sue Will for all he was worth. And if Nat and Rosie found out, what would they think of him? Their father, who'd been lying to them all these years? Leaving them to indulge himself in base pleasure? And how would he support them if he lost his position? Not to mention Emily and her boys.

But Cybil hadn't told anyone. Not yet, at least. That meant he'd have some amount of time to devise a plan before the inevitable happened—

"Will." Cybil was looking at him mistrustfully. "What are you thinking?"

He blinked. The misery in her eyes bowled into him, stopping his breath. And it wasn't just misery. It was terror. A fear that far outweighed his own.

Cybil carried a child—*his* child—in her womb. As far as he knew, she hadn't seen her husband in years. It was clearly adultery. Even if Will were sacked *and* sued, the consequences would be far worse for her than they were for him. Yet, his first thought had been for himself.

Damn.

"I'm—I'm just," he stammered. "I dinna ken. Just that—I'm sorry, Cybil." He leaned in to smooth her hair, but she jerked away as if his touch were poison.

Will's hand froze in midair, and, not knowing what else to do, he let it drop and pressed his back into the chair, as far from her as he could get. Then he waited.

She lay still on the bed, eyes searching the ceiling. The minutes ticked by. Will breathed, though the air seemed weak and thin.

Then, without warning, she spoke. "Would you like to know my plan?"

"I—I suppose so. Aye."

She brought one hand to her face, pinched the bridge of her nose, then massaged little circles into her brow line. "I'm going to tell my family that I'm traveling to the Continent with Lilian to research old castles, or abbeys or something. I've never gone so far before, but they're used to me leaving. They won't question it."

"The Continent? But—where?"

"I don't know." The certainty in her voice broke. She inhaled sharply, bringing both hands to cover her face as she continued in a choked tone. "I'm not even sure I should keep the child. Perhaps I should just—"

"No." Will couldn't let her finish. "'Tis too dangerous."

She looked at him sharply. "How would *you* know?"

He hesitated. It wasn't a story he'd told anyone, save Cam, and the memory . . . it was one he'd much rather forget.

"What is it?" Cybil narrowed her gaze.

Will studied her. "'Tisn't a pretty tale."

Her brows rose impatiently.

He sighed. What was the use in arguing? If anything would dissuade her from causing a miscarriage, this would. "Before your brother gave me employment, we lived in a shabby little room in the wynds—Rosie, Nat and me. You know where that is?"

"It's the slums in Glasgow, correct?"

He nodded. "A dismal place. There was a woman lived in the next room. She was young, twenty or so. I dinna ken, but I suppose it's possible she'd go it sometimes, for extra coin."

"You mean, she was a whore?"

He winced at Cybil's bluntness. "Aye. But a nice lass. She used to have Rose over for tea sometimes, as if they were fine ladies." He smiled faintly at the memory of the two of them, chatting and carrying on at Sophie's rickety little table, drinking weak tea out of chipped cups.

"Let me guess." Cybil's voice interrupted the memory. "She ended up with child."

Will nodded. "I heard her stumblin' up the steps one night, after the bairns were abed." He could still hear the ominous thump . . . then drag of Sophie's slow footsteps. "She wasna a boozer, and I—I ken'd somethin' was wrong, so I went to check on her." He swallowed, remembering the trail of blood that led up the stairs, shiny and black in the candlelight. The crumpled body he'd found in Sophie's doorway. He'd been sure she was dead. "She was layin' in a puddle of her own blood, on her doorstep. I dinna ken how she made it up the stairs."

"She'd—intentionally miscarried?" Cybil's voice shook.

"Aye, Found a quack doctor willin' to operate on her for cheap."

Cybil shuddered. "What did you do?"

"Picked her up and got her into bed, then I ran as quick as I could to Cam's." Will still remembered the pain that carrying Sophie had brought to his still-healing shoulder. He'd been convinced he'd torn the wound open. "You know he trained as a doctor before he became the Earl?"

Cybil nodded.

"He came quick. Saved her life, as far as I could tell."

"But that was only one instance. Surely—"

Will shook his head. "Cam told me stories of other women he saw in the hospital when he was workin' there. No decent doctor will perform the operation, so it's left to the quacks. Some use poison. Some go in the other way, tryin' to get it out before its time, like with Sophie."

Cybil's eyes were still fixed on him, but her gaze had turned inward, her face taking on a stricken look, as if she were imagining all he described.

"Don't do it, Cybil." Will reached out and touched her arm, bringing her back to him. "Tell me you willna."

Thankfully, this time, she didn't shrug him off. Instead, she sighed resignedly, then nodded. "I'd thought of going to France. I have a correspondence with a woman there. She's English, a writer who lives in Chantilly. She may agree to take me on until—until I can go home again."

"And the child?" It took all his willpower to keep his voice even.

"Perhaps I can find a French family to take it." Her voice cracked. "If you could—" She turned to look at him. "It would require money. I don't know how much, but I don't have—"

"Cybil." Her name was all he could manage. Of course, he was relieved that she wouldn't intentionally miscarry, but the image of her alone in some bustling French town, leaving her child, and his, behind . . . He couldn't take it. And from the look on her face, he suspected she couldn't either. She was simply resigned to the unbearable. "Of course, I'll give you whatever you need, but—there's got to be another way." He brought her hand to his lips, kissed her knuckles, then threaded their fingers together. "I'll think of somethin'—"

"No." Cybil jerked her hand away, then looked at him, tears welling in her eyes. "You can't." She swallowed. "Will. You must know. This thing between us—" She paused, inhaled, then let the breath out slowly. "It's over."

"But you canna just expect me to—"

Cybil continued in a forced, even tone. "I called you here so you'd know why we can't be—whatever it was we were, anymore. And why I'm going away, and—I *do* need your help, with the money, but—it's over." Her breath caught, and her chin trembled. He could see the muscles of her jaw working.

"But—Cybil. It's my bairn you're carryin'."

"Is it?" She stared at him, lips pressed together. She didn't have to say any more. They both knew the truth. He may be the man who'd fathered her child, but he'd never be its father. That title, by law, belonged to her husband.

It struck him suddenly what a stranger this woman was to him. They'd been lovers for four years. They'd done debauched things that Will never imagined he'd do with anyone. Cybil knew a part of him he'd always kept hidden, or hadn't even known existed before he met her. Not even Ann, for all he'd loved her, had known him the way Cybil did . . . But they'd never talked of their lives outside the fantasy they'd concocted. Doing so would have broken the illusion. Ruined it, somehow.

Well, it was damn well shattered now.

Will took a breath. "I canna tell you what to do, or *not* do. So, I'll ask, as the *natural* father of the bairn and as your friend. Please. Dinna go to France. Tell your family what you like, but stay close. When the bairn's born, we can—"

"*Where*?" She glared at him, eyes flashing. "Where would I stay? Glasgow? So Aunt Cynthia can find me?" Her face twisted into a sneer. "Or Leeds, perhaps? A pretty little cottage next door to my husband's estate?" She inhaled. "If Ernie found out, he'd—" She stopped, clamped her mouth shut, then returned her gaze once more to the ceiling, blinking to stop the tears.

"What? What would he do?" Will spoke softly. Did he even want to know the answer?

"Honestly? I don't know." She was quiet again for a long time, her eyes closed. But the cramped, tight way she held her face and her quick breaths made it clear she wasn't asleep. "He threatened once, to lock me up. I don't know if he meant in his house or in—in an asylum."

"Lock you . . . but you're perfectly sane. Surely, your brother wouldna allow—"

"Ernie is my *husband*." Cybil's eyes flew open, and her head rose slightly off the pillow. Her tone was bitter, and hard, "I was given a reprieve, thanks to Father's and Percy's money, but I *belong* to Ernie. He can do whatever he wants with me, and now—" She shook her head. "Reputation is *everything* to him. It's all he cares about. If he found out—" Her voice broke, and she allowed her head to drop back on the pillow.

How anyone could think this vibrant, strong-willed woman *belonged* to anyone was beyond Will's comprehension. But she was right. The law was the law. And Will had read enough in the papers to know that Baron Falstone was a mean sonofabitch, one of the hardline Tories who fought tooth and nail to keep themselves in power, and the common man out. A man like that—Will shuddered to think what he might be capable of when confronted with a woman like Cybil.

Again, he reached out to smooth her hair. She allowed it, but it was impossible to tell if she welcomed the touch or if she was just too tired to shake him off.

"Rest now," he murmured. "I'll order some supper."

She didn't argue, so he covered her with a blanket. Gradually, her breathing slowed and deepened.

Will sat, watching her. It was time he get up and go downstairs to find food, but . . . she was so peaceful in her sleep, the pink curve of her mouth finally relaxed, her brow smooth of worry. *Ach, she was beautiful*. His lover. The mother of his unborn babe.

Christ. A child. His own flesh and blood, his responsibility just as much as Rosie and Nat. There was no getting around it. He'd need to find a way to provide for the babe, and for Cybil. But how the devil would he do that if he found himself without employment? She was right. It had to be kept a secret. Above all else, no one must know—

A secret.

The thought came as a spark, then grew into a flame. She could stay with Emily. Both of his deepest secrets in one house. No one would ever know, or suspect.

Will sat back in his chair as a plan began to form. Surely, if he offered her a bit more coin to cover Cybil's room and board, Emily would agree . . . and no one would ever think to look for Lady Falstone in a humble weaver's cottage in Strathaven. It would be perfect.

His eyes wandered back to the sleeping woman before him . . . all he needed now was to convince Cybil to go along.

SEVEN

CYBIL WOKE TO THE aroma of cooked meat and fresh bread. For a moment, she forgot where she was or even that anything was amiss. Then she opened her eyes to see Will sitting by the bed, and the nightmare returned.

He'd moved his chair so that he now sat in profile to her, facing the glowing fireplace, and he gazed into it, legs stretched out and arms crossed. There were several lit candles on the table by the bed. Night must have fallen.

She studied the man who'd been her lover for the last four years. The dark brows shadowing those golden hazel eyes with their lush lashes. The curl of his chestnut hair. The sweet little cleft in his chin, covered with day-old stubble. He frowned at the hearth now, his brow furrowed, his lips drawn into a grim line. He'd taken his coat off, and she could see his well-muscled arms and broad chest through the linen of his shirt. A serious, quiet, almost shy sort of man . . . that was what most of the world saw in Will Chisolm. But underneath was a playful, fiercely passionate soul. A soul that so perfectly mirrored Cybil's own.

Making love with Will was like being overpowered by a great force of nature—a cyclone, or a tsunami. He dominated her completely. Made her forget all else. In his arms, she was powerless . . . Yet supremely powerful, for within his dominion was worship. She was his goddess. His temptress.

Or, she had been. That was all over now.

Cybil's throat began to ache. She wiped away a tear. *Would she ever stop crying?*

She'd contemplated hiding her condition from Will just as she had from everyone else, an attempt to preserve their attachment. But it wasn't possible. She'd never again be able to abandon herself to passion the way she had, he deserved to know why. And blast it, she needed his money. There was no way to explain to Percy why she'd require so much for a sojourn to the Continent.

She shifted her body on the bed, and Will's head swiveled toward her. "You're up." He attempted a smile, but the bleak look in his eyes betrayed him. He nodded to two covered dishes and a wrapped loaf on the table. "There's supper."

Cybil's attention turned to her stomach. Would food do it ill or good? Good, she decided. She was famished.

She started to rise, but Will stopped her with a wave of his hand.

"Stay. There's only the one chair anyway."

So, she pulled herself up on the pillows while he uncovered one of the dishes, tore off a piece of bread and balanced it on the rim of the shallow bowl, then handed it to her. She dipped it in the savory broth and began to eat.

"Ale?" He held up an earthenware jug.

She grimaced and shook her head. The fermented aromas of wine or ale were one of the things she could no longer countenance.

They ate in silence. Usually, such silences with Will were pleasant—either shimmeringly erotic, or at the very least comfortable. But not this one. She dared not even look at him. She'd said everything. There was nothing left.

"I know a place." Will's voice broke the quiet.

"What?" She was confused.

"A place you can go. Till the babe's born."

"I told you. I'm going to Chantilly." Cybil tried to keep her voice even. She'd hoped he'd drop this nonsense of helping her. It would be easier on her own, without his getting mixed up in things.

"But this plan, I think you'll see—"

"It's not your—"

"Just hear me out." He spoke over her, a serious, stubborn look clinging to his face.

Cybil sighed. There was no use arguing. "I'm listening. But you understand it's my decision in the end?"

"Of course." Will studied her intently, then exhaled loudly, as if he were about to lay all the ills of the world at her feet. "There's many things you dinna ken about me, Cybil."

She peered at him warily. "And there are many things you don't know about me, Will."

He ignored her. "Do you know of Strathaven?"

The name sounded familiar. "That's where you're from?"

"No. That's Strathfarrar, in the North. Strathaven is a village just south of Glasgow."

"Oh. No."

"There's a woman there, who I—"

"Your lover?" The word was bitter on her lips, but, "I've wondered if you had—"

"Gad, no," Will cut in, then paused. "I havena been with any other than you. Not since Ann died." He took her hand, looked her in the eye. "You know that."

Something relaxed inside her, and she nodded. Not that it made any difference now, but Will was such a passionate soul—she *had* wondered.

He drew in another long, slow breath. Released her hand. "What I'm goin' to tell you, you must swear not to tell another soul."

"I'd hope by now you'd know you can trust me."

He shook his head. "But this—'tis different. Tisn't just *me*."

There was something ominous in his look, something Cybil had never seen before. Her limbs felt cold suddenly, and she had the urge to turn away. "If it's such a secret, perhaps it's not—"

"No. You should know. You'll *need* to. If you accept my idea."

Cybil stared at him. *What was this about?*

"You promise?" Will was undeterred by her silence. "Not even Jane, or your brother can know."

"Very well," she shrugged, "I promise."

"The scar on my shoulder," he began, then paused. "I was shot."

The white, puckered scar was unmistakably that of a gunshot wound. Even Cybil, who knew nothing of medicine, had discerned that. It intrigued her, but she'd never asked him how it happened. It was just one more thing from the past they'd never allowed into their affair.

"Did Rosie tell you anything of it?" he asked.

"No." Rose and Nathan had been made godchildren to Jane and Percy, and they came every summer to Grislow Park to visit. Rose was a chatterbox who loved to talk about her father, of whom she was obviously quite proud. Such talk always made Cybil feel uncomfortable, as she had to pretend she knew nothing of Will. "She told me of how you played the hero saving a neighbor from a burning house. And of your life in Glasgow. How your wife died, just after her birth . . . But nothing of a gunshot wound."

"Good lass. She knows she's not to tell." Will nodded approvingly.

A prickle ran down Cybil's spine. She'd finished her meal long before, but she realized suddenly she was still clutching the bowl. She held it out, and Will set it on the table next to his empty dish.

"Who shot you, Will?"

He eyed her for a moment, then blinked, and, inextricably, changed the subject. "What do you know about the movement for reform? Of the men they call radicals?"

Reform? Radicals?

"Not much. I—I've read Godwin. I tried to read Locke, but—"

"What about Rodgers?"

"*Rodgers* . . . ?" Cybil had no idea who that was.

"She's a poet from Glasgow. Wrote for The *Spirit of the Union* before it was banned."

"Oh. No, I'm afraid I'm not familiar."

"Did you follow the goings-on in Glasgow around the time I met your brother? The Radical Uprising, they called it in the papers."

"I remember Percy seemed interested in that, after he returned . . ." She searched her memory, trying to recall the particulars. Mostly, her brother had been a lovestruck fool during those months, but— "Some men were hung? Radicals?"

"Hardie, Baird, and Wilson." Will nodded.

"But what does this have to do with your scar? Or Strathaven?" Cybil impatience was growing. What was he getting at?

Will shook his head, as if to clear it. "I'll just start at the beginning." He sighed. "We came to Glasgow eleven years ago, Ann and me, after we were evicted from the farm in Strathfarrar. Rosie told you about that?"

"Yes, more or less."

"Nat was just a wee babe then. We had some money saved, and we rented a house. I found work buildin' those new houses in Blythswood. Then Rosie was born. It seemed like we'd make it." He stopped to drain his ale, then poured himself another as he continued. "But Ann never recovered from her layin' in. She was taken from us just a few months after Rosie came." He put the cork back on the jug and drank deeply. "An' after that, everything just . . . fell apart. The bairns were so wee, and I was alone. I found a woman to help. She didna ask any wages—I couldna pay any—just room and board. But she was fuddled half the time, and I couldna leave them to her when she was like that . . . and—I lost my place. Then the house. Eventually, I didna have a choice. Either we starved or I went to work, and the only thing I could find was the factories. I left Rosie home with Nat, in just one dirty room." He shook his head, lost to the memory. "She was still so wee—not even walkin', and he only a few years older. 'Twas grim, Cybil."

Cybil stared at him, trying to process what he'd just told her. She'd known the sketch of the story, the eviction, Ann's death, his working in the mills, but to hear it like this . . . Will was such a devoted father. She reached out and put her hand on his shoulder. "I'd imagine it was," she murmured.

Will didn't seem to feel her touch. He stared straight ahead. "Eventually, they got old enough to work themselves, and that helped some with the money. But, gad, the guilt." He stared into the fire for a long moment. "Then I met Davey."

"Davey?" That was a name Cybil had never heard. "Who's that?"

"A weaver from Strathaven. One of the old kind who kept looms in their houses and made their livin' there. His family'd been weavers forever, but with the factories movin' in . . ." Will stared down at his cup. "Davey fought on the Continent, all the way to Waterloo. He was a brave lad. But when he came home, there wasna anything left for a man like him."

"Weaving, you mean?"

"Aye. No money in it." Will shrugged. "Or—not enough anyway. He ended up in the same factory I did, livin' away from his family most the time. He was angry." Will looked up and caught Cybil's gaze. His was fiery, a kind of indignant fire she'd never seen before. She drew her hand away. "People like him and me. We deserve the right to vote, to have men fightin' for us in London. To make change."

"So—Davey's a radical?" *As was Will, it seemed.*

"Aye, but a family man too, with a wife, Emily, and two lads. Davey was the best sort."

"*Was*? Did he die?"

"No." Will set down his empty cup and clasped his hands, steepling his index fingers. "We started goin'—Davey and me—to meetings. Reading things . . . Then when Rosie had her accident—" He broke off.

"Her fingers?" Cybil prompted. Three of Rose's fingers had been crushed beyond repair in the factory where she had worked.

"Aye. 'Twas the worst day of my life. Worse than being burned out of our house in Strathfarrar. I failed her, as her da."

Cybil reached for him again. "But it wasn't your fault—"

He shrugged her off. "A father's supposed to protect his bairns. Provide for them." He opened his mouth to continue, then shut it again. "But it wasna just me. 'Twas the whole system, all of it, that allowed a lass like her to work a job like that. A family like ours to find ourselves in the city in the first place. I felt—" He closed his eyes and shook his head. "I was angry. It made me stupid. Davey and me, we got caught up in somethin' we shouldna."

"This has to do with your scar?" she guessed.

"Aye. There was a man, Wilcox. Worked at the same factory we did. Said he was from Leeds, but got down on his luck and came to Glasgow lookin' for work."

"Leeds?" A chill went down Cybil's spine. Ernie was from Leeds. It was a large city, and her husband rarely visited his estate. Of course, there was no connection, but it spooked her nonetheless.

"Wilcox had a plan, and he was lookin' for men to help see it through. You see, the coal for the factories all comes through the canals. Wilcox had an idea a strike was comin', and he thought to block the canals and stop the coal barges, in support of the strike. The factories would have to shut down. He said there were men in Leeds and Manchester lookin' to do similar actions, and if we were coordinated, we would get the scoundrels in London to take notice."

"Did you . . ." she started.

"Turned out he was right. There was a strike called. Papers plastered all over the city, though nobody seemed to quite know who put them there." He shrugged. "That same day, Davey and I walked out to get a look at one of the bridges, to plan where we'd put the powder."

"*Gun*powder?"

He nodded. "To blow it up and block the canal. Wilcox said he had connections who'd get it for us. He went to see to that, then we were to meet back at a tavern that night to make the final plan."

Cybil realized her mouth was hanging open. She closed it.

"Davey and I were just turnin' back home when the hussars came."

"Hussars?"

"Aye. Two of 'em, on horseback. We didna even see 'em comin', didna ken to run. They rode right up to us, ordered us to put our hands over our heads. But Davey . . . he had a pistol. and he took aim. He didna shoot, but still, 'twas a cracked thing to do. They fired on us." Will sat back in his chair, looking down at his lap. "I was hit, but Davey ran into the woods, and they followed. They left me for dead, I guess. An hour hour or so later, your brother, and Cam, and his sister found me. Saved my life."

Cybil blinked at him. She'd never heard anything of this from either Jane or Percy. "Were they out looking for you, or—"

"No. They were strangers. 'Twas only by chance they happened to be drivin' by."

"But—Percy had met you at the factory. He said—"

"Is that what he told you?" Will's lips turned up at the corners. "I'd wondered."

Cybil stared. "He lied?" *And Jane.* She had been there too. "They'd—they told me Percy met you in his factory, that your work stood out and he promoted you."

Will shrugged. "'Twas to protect me and the bairns." Then he turned and looked directly at Cybil. His deep-set eyes were cast in shadow, but a spark shone through from the depths. "But even *they* dinna ken about the rest of it."

There was more? Cybil lifted her brows, willing him to continue.

"Davey was caught and hauled into Stirling, then Edinburgh, and tried with the others. I dinna ken what he told 'em. But I *do* know they went back lookin' for me, and I've no doubt they asked him about me. He could have named me. Easy. Probably would have gotten himself off, or a lesser sentence. But he didna." Will sighed deeply. "He took the blame for both of us, and—well. He's gone."

"Gone where?"

"Transported. Sat for three months in Calton Prison, then shipped out to Botany Bay." Will's eyes lost focus, as if he were seeing something that wasn't there, then they snapped back to her. "He canna ever come back. But Emily and the boys, their bairns, are still here."

"In Strathaven?"

Will nodded. "I've been lookin' after them these last years as best I can."

"Looking after them?" Cybil repeated, slowly. "You mean, you give them money?"

"'Tis the least I can do, after what Davey did for me."

"And you haven't told anyone about it? Not even Cameron, or my brother?"

Will shook his head. "The sheriff has eyes everywhere. At first, he had men watchin' Emily's house, to see who came and went. If it were known I was helpin' her, it'd only be a matter of time before they realized who I am and hauled me in."

"I see." And suddenly she *did* see. "So—you want me to go *there*. To Emily's in Strathaven."

Will nodded. "No one will look for you. The house isna big, but there's room enough and I'm sure Emily'd have you. She knows what it is to be a mother. She could help you when your time comes, and—" He hesitated. "I'm used to slippin' in and out without bein' seen. I could visit."

Cybil stared at him dubiously. Her plan to go to Chantilly was tenuous at best. She had no idea if Isabel would even welcome her. And if all Will said was true, this village he described might be a good enough hiding place. No one knew of the connection between Will and Emily, or Will and Cybil for that matter, and certainly Ernie would never think to look for her in Strathaven.

But it would mean being beholden to Will. And when the child came . . . Whatever happened, it would be difficult enough on her own, without Will to think about.

"I'll—I'll think on it," she said.

"Thank you."

A sudden thought occurred to her. "Will?"

"Aye?"

"What happened to the other man?" He stared at her blankly. "The one who was to get the gunpowder," she supplied.

"Wilcox." Will's look hardened. "He must of testified against Davey, but it wasn't in public. I never saw him again."

"Did he get a lesser sentence? For testifying?"

Will snorted. "He got no sentence at all. He was an agent, Cybil. A damned blackleg. He set us up." The bitter anger in his voice—suddenly, she had no trouble imagining Will a violent radical, intent on blowing up a bridge.

"But—how do you know? Perhaps he just decided to go along with them, in order to—"

"How else would the hussars have known where we were, what we were up to?" Will leveled his gaze. "There was another man, Oliver, supposedly from

Manchester. He led Hardie and Baird right into the trap that got them hung. Oliver was in it up to his neck, just like the others. But he was never charged. Never even seen after—feared for his life, no doubt." Will's voice took on a steely edge. "I woulda killed him myself given the chance—" He stopped short, took a breath, then continued with forced calm. "They were plants, Cybil. Both of 'em."

This new anger frightened her, but— "But if Wilcox was a spy, surely *he* would have named you," she argued.

"Ah." A small, wily smile appeared on Will's lips. "We werena all daft. We knew Sidmouth had spies in Glasgow in seventeen and eighteen, and Wilcox wasna a known quantity. I called myself Richie, and Davey was Tom, just to be safe."

"*Sidmouth*. The Home Secretary?" The familiar name seemed so out of place on Will's lips. Viscount Sidmouth was a great friend of Ernie's. Ernie had seen him as a mentor of sorts, and Cybil had hosted him at dinner many times.

Will nodded, a derisive sneer on his face. "Vilest man in all England. And Scotland."

"So, he could still be out there—Wilcox, I mean? And he knows you, by sight at least."

"Aye." Will nodded. "I didna dare go back to the factory after. I thought we'd have to leave Glasgow, but then your brother offered me the position and the money was so good—I couldna say no." He smiled grimly. "No one thinks to look for a wanted man in the manager's office."

"But what if—they *could* find you, even now."

He shrugged. "It's been four years. It seems they've given up lookin, but . . . aye. They could."

—◇—

The telling of the story was exhausting in itself. It had been a long while since Will had allowed himself to relive it—the grief at Ann's death, the blinding anger after Rosie's accident, the bond he'd shared with Davey as a father and compatriot. The terror of that afternoon by the canal and the wrenching guilt afterward, knowing Davey was being shipped away in chains while Will's own family was somehow benefiting from a sudden turn in fortune.

Supporting Emily and her boys had never felt like enough, yet what more could he do?

Will stared into the fire, trying to push back the memories. They served no purpose. The current situation was enough to deal with.

He heard Cybil get up and make her way to the chamber pot behind a screen in the corner, then she opened her valise and rummaged through it. On any usual tryst, he'd be at her by now, ripping the clothes off her, burying himself in her soft flesh. But tonight, he didn't even turn around as she undressed.

When she finally settled into bed, he rose with a sigh, stripped, then donned a nightshirt, blew out the candles and lay himself down beside her.

The air was heavy. The inches of space between him and the woman he shared the bed with yawned into a chasm.

"Will?" Cybil's voice, soft and full of vulnerability, floated to him. "Are you awake?"

"Aye."

"Will you . . ." She hesitated. "Will you hold me?"

Wordlessly, he turned toward her and drew her into a tight embrace. She seemed to melt into him, scooting down so she could burrow her face into his chest. A warm feeling settled over him—not a happy one, but a relief. A togetherness.

Then she began to cry. It started small, a slight shaking that grew into great heaving sobs. Her face remained hidden from his view, but he could feel the wetness of her tears as they soaked into his nightshirt.

His own eyes began to sting as he brought his hand up to stroke her hair. "There, lass, it'll come right in the end. I promise."

Of course, in reality, he could promise no such thing. So often, things did *not* come right in the end. Just ask Davey, or Andrew Hardie or John Baird.

But, somehow, his soothing seemed to help. Gradually, she quieted. Her breathing grew steady. She shifted in his arms so she was faced away from him, but he still held her and their bodies were still pressed together.

"I'll go to Strathaven," she murmured.

Thank God. He pulled her tighter, planted a kiss just below her ear, then whispered, "Thank you, Cybil."

She fell asleep in his arms, but Will lay awake for a long time, trying to forget.

EIGHT

HENRI'S EYES WERE ALWAYS mournful, but never had they looked so heart-broken. The spaniel stared up at Cybil, and all she could think was that it was a wonder dogs didn't cry. If they did, Henri would be sobbing, just as Cybil was.

They were curled up together in a pool of light on the oversized chair in her chamber at Grislow Park. It was a beautiful day, but it wasn't. It was the day she would tell her family of her departure, and she'd decided to start with the one who loved her most—Henri.

She'd gotten him as a puppy ten years ago, in those first dark months after she'd fled Ernie's townhouse in London. She'd been so lonely. Percy was off at school. Father was rarely home, and Mother . . . well, Mother meant well, but her stifling presence was one of the reasons that marriage to Ernie and escape from Grislow Park had seemed so appealing in the first place. Before Jane came, Henri had been Cybil's only friend.

"I'll be back before you know it." She hugged the dog against her chest and allowed the tears to fall on his silky ears. "Don't worry."

But he *was* worried, she could tell. Henri was old now. His walk was stiff, and he rarely ran like he used to. He still had that sleek, inky coat that Cybil adored, but his muzzle was going grey. *Would he die while she was away?*

She couldn't bear the pleading in the dog's kind, trusting eyes, so Cybil averted her gaze, looking instead out the window.

A movement caught her eye—Jane, in the orchard. Cybil watched her friend wander amongst the trees, occasionally stopping to peer at an apple or pick one and sample it. Even from this distance, it was clear she was close to her lying-in. Her belly was impossibly swollen, even more than it had been with little James.

It was the perfect opportunity to speak to Jane alone. Cybil had already decided to tell her before she told Percy or Mother, or *asked* Percy rather. That chafed, the asking, as if he were her prison guard. He wasn't. He was her little brother, and she was certain he'd say yes—he'd not denied her anything since he'd taken over as the head of the family—but Mother would be against it, Cybil was sure, and there was no doubt she'd try to sway her son's opinion. It would be good to talk to Jane beforehand, so she'd have an ally in the conversation.

And yet, telling Jane, telling *any of them*, meant she could never go back . . .

Cybil shook herself. *Silly chit.* Back to *what*? It didn't matter a whit what she told, or didn't tell, anyone. The damage was done.

And Jane herself had been lying to Cybil all these years, hadn't she? About how she'd met Will. It was a lie for the good, Will had said. And perhaps he was right, but—it only highlighted the fact that there were already untruths flowing between them, a stream of them running both ways.

They'd easily forded that stream so far. Perhaps this would be no different.

Cybil heaved a sigh and rose from her chair, gently extricating Henri from her lap and placing him on the floor. "Come along." She moved toward the door, her dog on her heels.

Two minutes later, they stepped into a lovely autumn day. It reminded Cybil of that afternoon in Darnalay when she and Will had read together in the garden. Golden light filtered through fall leaves. The air was crisp and fresh, yet the sun shone warm on her back. The ambrosial scent of ripening apples filled the air, along with the sound of Henri snuffling in the damp, rotting leaf mould that Jane had so carefully spread beneath the trees.

Her sister-in-law waved to her. "Gorgeous, isn't it?" She motioned to the sky, the trees, the world around them.

Cybil nodded. It was, but she had no eyes for the beauty. Her stomach was a pit of nerves.

"I'm glad you came out." Jane smiled at her. "I have news."

"As do I."

"You go first." Her friend's blue eyes were sparkling, her skin glowing. She was the very picture of maternal beauty.

Cybil swallowed the hard lump in her throat. She forced her lips to smile, her brow to rise as if in heady excitement. "I've received an invitation from Lilian. She's planning a tour of Italy this winter, and she's asked if I might accompany her." Jane's smile faded as Cybil spoke, but she kept going. To stop would mean allowing the tears to come. "I've an idea for a novel set in an abbey near Florence, but without having some acquaintance with the place and the people, I don't think I could do it justice." She paused, steeling herself. "I've decided to go."

"Italy." Jane's eyes widened. "You're going—to Italy."

"So long as Percy agrees."

"When would you leave?" Jane's voice was quiet.

Cybil looked away, pretending to study an apple that hung from a nearby tree. "Lily is determined to reach Florence by Christmas."

"But—"

"Of course, I'll stay until the babe's born." But Cybil knew that was of little comfort. It was the time *after* the birth that her friend would need her most. James, Jane's first child, had been a fussy infant. He hadn't taken to the breast easily, and during those first few months Jane had been at her wit's end. Mother had been mired in one of her depressions. Percy had done what he could, but he was a man, and men were generally worthless at such times. It had fallen to Cybil to support her sister-in-law, directing the nursemaid to take baby James on walks so Jane could sleep, ordering food when her friend forgot to eat, and, at times, simply sitting and allowing the new mother to cry on her shoulder. Those weeks had cemented their friendship. But this time around, Jane would have no one except her adoring but often absent husband, and her self-absorbed, moody mother-in-law.

"I'm sorry." She ventured a look at Jane's face and found her friend staring not at Cybil, but into the golden space beyond. She'd stepped out of the shade and into the bright sunlight, Cybil could see the dark circles under her eyes. "I—I may not have this chance again. I couldn't say no."

"It's fine, Cyb. Really." Jane wiped a tear. "I'm glad for you. I just—carrying a child isna easy. I'm tired."

The sadness, the hurt in her friend's visage—a desolate, aching pain settled into Cybil's chest. There was no one in the world she'd rather have with her through her own confinement. No one. She met her friend's blue eyes and felt her own well with tears. Then she blinked, looking up into the endless azure of the sky.

Perhaps she should just tell the truth. Surely, if anyone in the world would understand— or at least have the capacity to forgive—it would be Jane. To be able to stay. To support her friend through her trial, then be supported in turn . . .

But Percy. Jane would tell Percy, and Percy was Will's employer. He could sack Will, or worse, alert Ernie. Percy would mean well, surely, but he also seemed to grow more like Father every day, and how he might react—there was just too much at risk.

"Don't feel badly, please." She felt a hand on her arm and turned to see Jane's gaze trained on her. "I'm just—I'll be fine." A wobbly smile flickered across her friend's face. "You're going to have a wonderful time. You deserve it."

Cybil forced her lips to turn up into some approximation of a smile, and Jane mirrored her, though Cybil knew her expression to be just as false. Then her friend swallowed, turned and strode to a nearby tree. It was small, as were all the trees in the young orchard, but it was covered with enormous bright gold apples. Jane picked two and held one out to Cybil.

"Try this. The King of the Pippins, they call it. They're perfectly ripe."

Cybil accepted the fruit. It was beautiful, like a jewel, large and golden yellow, overlayed with streaks and speckles of crimson. But her stomach was churning. She couldn't eat right now. She slipped it into the pocket of her dress.

"Thank you." She looked back at Jane. "Not just for the apple, but for understanding. I really do wish I could stay a bit longer."

Jane didn't respond, perhaps she hadn't even heard. She was too busy considering the fruit she still held. She wiped it with the hem of her apron. "Bring me back some seeds if you can," she murmured. "I've never worked with Italian stock . . ."

"Of course."

But Cybil wasn't going to Italy. She was going to Strathaven. The stream of lies that flowed between them had widened into a river. A rushing, icy torrent, impossible to cross.

"Come. Let's get you in for a nap before dinner." She offered her arm.

Jane took a bite of the fruit. It gave a loud crunch, and she laughed, a ruse of a laugh, but a laugh nonetheless. "'Tis as loud as it is sweet." Then she threaded her arm through Cybil's. Cybil called Henri, and together, they walked toward the house.

⚬

Five hours later, dinner was nearly finished. The third course had just been cleared away—something with chicken and mushrooms that Cybil found impossible to choke down. Three times in the last hour, she'd opened her mouth to announce her travel plans, and three times, she'd closed it again.

The problem was Mother. She was in good spirits tonight, and she chatted on endlessly, scarcely stopping to allow a reply from the three younger people at the table. She had been pondering a name for the new babe and was going through her list, trying them on the expectant parents.

Cybil knew that Jane already had names picked for both a boy and a girl, but she and Percy played Mother's game without argument, good naturedly batting away each ludicrous suggestion. And as Mother was partial to old names, particularly those she gleaned from Arthurian legend, they were *all* ludicrous.

"Ywain?"

Percy shook his head. "I'd never spell it right."

"Leodegrance?"

"Too long." Percy grinned. "And it rhythms with *prance*."

"Mordred?"

"Wasn't he the evil one?" Jane's brows furrowed.

"Yes, but, it's a *strong* name," Mother shot back. "What about Nimue? For a girl, of course—"

"I'm going away for the winter," Cybil blurted out before she had time to think better of it, "and the spring. Until mid-summer, I'd expect."

There was a long silence as her words sank in. A footman came with dessert, pears poached in wine and some kind of spice. He set the dish on the table, then left. No one moved.

Mother's countenance slowly changed from shocked annoyance at being interrupted, to blinking dismay. Percy peered at Cybil over the candles, his dark brows pulled together in an expression of brotherly confusion. As she'd hoped, Jane's face remained placid, her steady gaze lending her friend strength.

"To—where exactly?" Percy finally asked.

"Italy." Somehow, Cybil's voice sounded certain. "Lilian Smith has proposed a visit to Florence. She's always wanted to see that city . . . the cathedral. The artwork. And she asked me if I might accompany her." She plastered on a smile that she hoped looked excited, and sure.

"But *Cybil*." Mother finally found her voice. "What about Jane, and the—"

"I'll stay until the birth. It's not ideal, but—"

"And what about the *Baron*?" Mother's voice was rising.

"What *about* him? I've taken trips before. This is no different."

Mother snorted. "A week is *entirely* different than a full season. A winter *and* a spring. What if he comes looking for you? What would we tell him?"

"He hasn't come looking for ten years. Why would he now?" She'd known Mother would be like this, just like Father always was. He'd never let Cybil go anywhere.

"It's too dangerous." Mother's chin rose stubbornly. "You must think of the risks."

"I *have*, Mother." Their eyes locked.

"I've already given Cybil my blessing," Jane offered, her voice soft. "I think she should go. I've got you, Martha, and Percy." She glanced at her husband, and he gave her one of those tender looks that always made Cybil want to throw something. "Cybil is a grown woman." Jane directed that at Mother, then back to Percy. "She'll be fine, and . . . it will be good for her to get away. She deserves it."

Cybil shot her friend a thankful look.

"Percy?" Mother looked at her son, pleading with him for support. "She *cannot* go. You must see that. It's been hard enough keeping the peace with that man all these years. To antagonize him now—"

"You're sure you'd be alright?" Percy wasn't listening to Mother. He was looking at Jane, speaking in a low tone. "When the babies come, 'twill be so much more—"

"*Babies*?" Mother interrupted. Louder than before. "What do you mean *babies*? There's only one *baby*, my dear."

Percy's eyes widened. He looked at his wife, who was suddenly glaring at him, her lips pursed. "Oh—"

"We've been waiting for the right time to tell you both." Jane moved her gaze from her husband to her mother-in-law, to Cybil, then back to her Percy. She took a breath. "When the doctor was here yesterday, he discovered a second child in my womb."

News. Earlier, in the orchard, Jane had told Cybil she had news. Cybil had forgotten all about it.

Mother's mouth hung open. "Twins?"

Jane nodded, finding Percy's hand. "Aye." She forced a smile. "'Tis no wonder I'm so huge." Cybil was unable to speak, unable even to move, or breathe, as Jane's attention moved back to her. *Twins.* "But, aye, I do think Cybil should go. She'll be here for the birth. That's the hardest part, after all."

Percy was watching his wife intently. "If you're really sure." Jane nodded, then he looked to Cybil. "Very well, you have my blessing. I can give you a few introductions in Florence if you like, but—" His brows creased in concern. "If the Baron *did* come looking, or discovered you'd gone, you must know there's a limit to what I can do. It's a risk."

Cybil nodded her understanding, but she was still unable to find her voice. *Twins.* Jane was having twins. And Cybil wouldn't be here.

She absolutely did not deserve this woman's friendship.

Mother picked up the dessert, all worry for Cybil's welfare apparently gone from her mind. "This means you'll need two names." She spooned a pear onto her plate. "Mordred and Merlin." She passed the dish to Percy. "Or Guinevere and Igraine. We could call her Graine for short, so their names would both start with G . . ."

Percy ignored her. He served Jane and himself, then got up and walked the dish around the table to Cybil. All the while, Mother continued talking.

He leaned down as he set the dish beside Cybil's place. "I'm glad you're going," he whispered. "You deserve to live a bit." Then he stood and smiled—a pure, kind smile with no hint of his old roguishness or sarcasm.

Cybil tried to smile back, but she could feel the tears threatening. Her throat ached. Hastily, she looked down and spooned herself a pear, leaving her brother to return to his seat.

But she couldn't eat it. Her stomach was unsettled, her throat tight, so she sat and silently stared at the fruit on her plate as her family finished their meal.

NINE

Faugh, how Will hated lying. Yet, somehow, of late, it seemed all he did.

The thought occurred to him, as he directed his gig down Gallowgate—nearly empty in the early dawn light—and onto the road to Edinburgh, that there was no one in his life, save Cybil now, and perhaps Emily, to whom he didn't lie to regularly.

It was not the man he wanted to be, but there was no help for it. It was the man he *was*, or, at least, the man he'd become.

He'd said his goodbyes the night before, explaining to Rosie and Nat that he had a few days' business to see to in Edinburgh. Another lie. Rosie had been disappointed and worried—he was always disappointing and worrying his daughter—with her big, sad eyes fixed on him. Nat had just stood there, quiet and sullen. It was impossible to know if his now thirteen-year-old son was angry with him for his frequent absences, or if he just didn't care.

The six hours to Edinburgh went quickly. It had only been a month since Will had traveled this way to see Cybil in Dunbar, but the countryside had changed. The oranges, yellows and reds of autumn had given way to dull browns and greys. But Will barely noticed his surroundings. His mind was elsewhere, thinking through the problems of the months ahead, the trips he would make to Strathaven and how he could get away. With the bairns already unhappy at his frequent absences, what excuse could he devise to be gone even more often? And the factories, the established ones could run just fine without him, but the renovations on the new mills had only just begun. The architect and foreman had questions every day, questions about ventilation and windows, spaces for workers to take their rest, questions he didn't want anyone else answering. And, of course, the biggest puzzle of all, what would become of the child once it was born?

He ate the bit of food he'd brought with him as he drove, and other than to pay tolls, he stopped only once, outside Corstorphine, to put up the gig's top when a light rain started to fall.

It was early afternoon when he reached the hotel that he and Cybil had agreed to, Oman's Tavern Hotel in New Town. It was one of the modern, high-end establishments in the city. A bustling place full of men on government or court business and ladies come to shop in the nearby arcades. It was nothing like the comfortable inn where Will stayed when he *was*, in fact, in Edinburgh on business. But it was a place neither he nor Cybil was likely to be recognized. He'd also thought it might be a nice treat for her, two nights of luxury before she retired to the cottage in Strathaven.

He regretted the choice now. The massive grey stone building and wealthy clientele gave the place an air of pomposity. Smug rich fucks, with their smug rich wives, filtered in and out the front door. It was too polished, too wealthy and self-important. It made Will's skin crawl. He always felt like an imposter in a place like this, and that feeling—like he wasn't good enough somehow—only made him more angry.

He didn't want to belong here anyway.

But he *did* belong, at least in his current station. He was no longer a Highland clod breaker, a destitute millworker or a radical hell-raker. He was the manager of five profitable millworks, with hundreds of people in his employ and plenty of coin in his pocket.

Again, not the man he wanted to be, but again, there was no help for it.

He left his gig, flipping a coin to the boy who led his horse away, then he pulled his hat down a bit over his eyes and opened the shiny new door by its shiny brass handle.

The soft buzz of polite company was the only noise within. None of the raucous laughter of a true tavern or inn, and none of the smells either. This place smelled faintly of perfume and fresh paint. Thankfully, the lobby was nearly empty.

Will approached the desk and was told by a well-dressed older man that Mrs. Oliphant—the surname they always used—had, in fact, checked in the previous evening, *without* a maid. The man raised a brow at this while he inspected Will with barely veiled suspicion.

A woman traveling alone was scandalous at best, particularly at an establishment like this, so Cybil had planned to tell the hotel staff that her maid had taken ill at the last coaching inn and had to be left behind. Will explained this to the desk clerk, feigning annoyance and giving his best impression of an aristocratic nob. It must have been passable because the man nodded and handed him a key for room 306, along with instructions for getting to the stairway that would lead him there.

Will asked curtly that whisky and food be brought up with his bag, and the man nodded again, a look of distaste still on his face. Will's suppressed Highland accent hadn't fooled him one bit, but money spoke louder than breeding, at least in this establishment.

Relieved to be done with the clerk, Will made his way to the staircase, then climbed the three flights of stairs and emerged into a thickly carpeted corridor. Bronze wall sconces with green glass lamps were installed down its length. The muffled sound and tinted light gave the place an empty, almost spooky feel, as if it were removed from the rest of the world. Not part of the hotel below. Not part of the rooms it led to.

He hesitated in front of room 306, wondering if he should knock. If he were truly Cybil's husband, he wouldn't, but there was no one watching and he had no idea of her mood. She'd been like a stranger when he'd seen her last, and since then, she'd attended the birth of twins, left her family behind and, of course, her own condition would have progressed.

He knocked softly. There was a pause, then a muffled voice sounded from within. Drawing a breath, he pushed the handle and the door swung open.

He entered into a well-appointed sitting room. A plush sofa of blue brocade and carved wood. Two armchairs to match. A thick rug and several end tables, one bedecked with a gaudy vase filled with fresh hothouse flowers. A crystal chandelier dangled from the ceiling, and two large bay windows, hung with heavy velvet drapes, allowed in the faint afternoon light. It was the height of refined elegance and wealth—the kind of room a younger Will would have wanted to smash to pieces. For so long, he and his bairns had lived in a room a quarter this size. They could have survived for years on the money that would come from the chandelier alone.

"Cybil?" he called.

"Here."

He followed her voice through the room, then into a bedroom—just as finely furnished—and to a third door, this one ajar. He pushed it open to reveal a small space with a tiled floor and yet another large window, this one covered by a translucent gauzy curtain. In the center of the room was a large copper bathtub, and in the tub was Cybil.

She wasn't attempting a seductive pose. She simply lay in the tub, looking at him with her rosebud lips drawn into an amused pout. Her body below her neck was hidden beneath the water, but he could see the tips of her rosy nipples and the pink of her toes gripping the edge of the tub. Her dark hair was piled atop her head, but several locks had escaped and hung damp, clinging to her nape, curling around her ears. The skin of her neck and shoulders was wet and slick—

"Aren't you going to greet me?" Cybil's amused voice called to him, and he startled, realizing just how blatantly he'd been staring, and also how incredibly hard he'd gotten in just a matter of seconds.

"Good afternoon," he choked out.

Her eyes skimmed down his body, stopping halfway to where he was sure his prick was making a tent of his trousers. She smiled knowingly, then lifted her gaze back to his face. Their eyes met, and it was as if the last month had never happened. As if there were no babe in her womb, no desperate plan, no tears. No aristocratic prigs downstairs. No lies. *This* was the man Will wanted to be. A man alone in a room with Cybil.

He pulled the door closed.

"I was just wishing I had an attendant," she spoke slowly, as if each syllable held more meaning than the word it was part of, "to wash my back." One of her hands emerged from the water, grasping a linen cloth. She held it out. The other hand remained submerged, but from the way her eyes half-closed, the whispered moan that escaped her lips, it was clear what she was doing with it.

He growled, releasing all the built-up tension of the day, the week, the month. "I'm no one's attendant, my lady."

"No?" Her brows rose in an expression that blurred the lines between haughty, fearful and excited. "Then what are you?"

He didn't answer. He didn't have to. She knew exactly what he was.

He crossed the room in two long strides. He had to remember she was with child—but still, they could have some fun.

Roughly, he snatched the cloth away. She let it go, her eyes widening at his force, then slowly, she lowered her hand to rest against the side of the tub. He could see the pulse beating in her neck, and now that he was closer, it was clear exactly what her other hand, still submerged below the water, was doing. He could just make out the thatch of black hair, her fingers lost beneath it, moving, swirling. It took every bit of his willpower to keep from hauling her out of the bath and taking her against the wall. But that would be too quick.

"Enough," he snarled, and obediently, her hand left her cunny and came up to the side of the tub. "You will wait, till I give you leave," he commanded, then he turned his back on her.

He could feel her eyes on him—a hot, heady sensation—as he set the cloth down, then slowly, deliberately, removed his hat, his gloves, his coat. He unwound his cravat and pulled it off, then unbuttoned his waistcoat and shrugged out of it. The rest of his clothes he left on. He enjoyed the power that came from being fully clothed while Effie lay naked before him.

He turned to look at her, and indeed, she was watching him, eyes wide, lips parted, breath coming in short, frequent pants—as a rabbit might watch a wolf who'd cornered it and was now moving in for the kill. Her body writhed under the water, yearning to be touched, yet she dared not. Her hands gripped the lip of the tub, her knuckles white.

He stalked closer, and for almost a full minute, they stared at each other defiantly, reveling in the tension they'd built.

Then, Effie's eyes closed. Her hands went limp, and her head dropped. She surrendered to his will.

He strode behind her, folding the wet cloth several times as he walked, then he tied it around her eyes. She gasped as he cinched it behind her head and the excess water was wrung out, sending droplets streaming down her lips, her neck, the tops of her breasts.

When he was done, he circled the bathtub, taking in the sight. She'd sat up, and the perfect fullness of her breasts, creamy flesh and peaked, hardened nipples, was bared to his view. Her head was cocked to one side as she listened, straining to ascertain where he was, where and when he would touch her.

"Touch your tits." His throat was so thick with desire that he barely got the words out.

She didn't move.

"*Now*, Effie."

She followed the order, cupping one breast. She bit her lip, stifling a groan as she squeezed the soft flesh. Ruthven longed to hold them himself. He loved how they filled both palms and still overflowed his grasp . . .

But he wasn't ready to touch her. Not yet.

"Both of them," he growled.

She complied, then winced, and this time, it seemed more pain than pleasure. "Will," There was no hint of desire in her voice, and she'd called him *Will*. For the first time, in four years. "They're sore. Since I've been—my nipples—" She bit her lip again, either in pain or embarrassment, he wasn't sure.

Will cursed himself. Of course, she was with child.

Cybil's cheeks were growing red. She'd lost her confidence and seemed to be melting into the water. Her lower lip trembled. "Maybe this wasn't a good idea—"

"Enough." He interrupted her, letting his voice rise, then lower to the smooth, low timbre he used for Ruthven. "Your cunny, Effie. Does that hurt as well?"

"No, it—"

"Then touch it. *Now.*"

She lifted her head as if to meet his gaze, though she couldn't see him, didn't know he was silently pacing toward her.

"Now," he repeated, louder, lower. "Do it." He knelt till his lips were nearly touching her ear. Effie stiffened as his breath hit her neck. "Touch it. Bury your fingers in your quim." His tone was neither a whisper, nor a growl, but something in between. "Come for me."

She swallowed, then slowly lowered her head to the lip of the tub as she brought one hand back into the water. Ruthven watched, transfixed, as her titties with their straining, pink nipples bobbed gracefully before him, like two islands of pure, earthly delight. He couldn't see her cunny from where he knelt behind her, but watching her face was almost as erotic, lips parted, eyes unseeing behind the blindfold, cheeks crimson—not from shame now but from relief, excitement, and pleasure. She tipped her head back, panting softly, and he took her earlobe between his teeth, scraping it gently, then letting it fall.

"That's it," he whispered. He nibbled the skin just below her ear, marking her gently with his teeth. "Make yourself ready me. I will *devour* you."

Effie moaned. Ruthven fisted her hair and pulled gently, just enough to let her know he was there, watching. "*Yesss.* That's a good lass. More. Fuck yourself." He bit her earlobe again, harder this time, then scraped a line down her neck to her shoulder with his fingernails, leaving a trail of four red marks behind. "You're mine, Effie . . . Come for me."

Effie's hips were gyrating now, and the water sloshed in the tub, overflowing onto the floor. Her moans intensified as he continued to growl encouragements in her ear, mark her with his fingers and teeth. His cock was unbearably hard, and he stroked it through his clothes with his free hand as she rocked under her own touch in the bath, higher and higher till finally she came with a hoarse shriek, her body convulsing in wave after wave of release.

But he didn't wait for her climax to subside. He needed her, now.

In another time or place, he might have taken her up roughly and thrown her over his shoulder only to drop her against the wall, or on all fours on the tile floor, but not today. Today he tempered those impulses.

He dipped one hand into the tub to circle under her knees, not caring that his shirt would be soaked through. The other hand, he brought behind her waist, then he lifted her. She was still wearing the blindfold, and she shrieked in surprise at the unexpected movement, but he paid her no mind. He gripped her tighter, letting the rivulets stream down his body and soak his shirt, his trousers, his boots. Then he turned, kicked the door open and carried her into the bedroom.

A large oaken bed with green velvet curtains stood in the center of the room. By the time they reached it, Cybil had given up being Effie and was giggling and squirming in his arms.

"Where are you . . . put me down . . . I can't see."

He placed her gently on the foot of the bed, then reached around to untie the blindfold. He cast the wet linen aside, and Cybil blinked at him, smiling. Their eyes met, and something passed between them, something familiar and warm. It wasn't love—they could never have love—but it was more than friendship. A kind of kinship, an understanding. Will hadn't been sure, after everything that had happened, if he and Cybil would ever share such a look again.

"That was—" she started, then stopped. "Thank you. I needed that."

He narrowed his eyes, letting them roam over her naked body. "I'm not done with you yet, lass."

TEN

WILL LOOMED OVER HER, his hands braced on either side of her head.

"Not done with me?" Cybil allowed her eyes to grow wide, no longer the panicked eyes of Effie, but of a more confident, exacting lover—an imperious queen to Will's uncivilized brute. "What on earth can you mean?" She lifted her knee as she spoke and gently rubbed his cock. He gave a feral growl, then leaned down and kissed her—a long, greedy, open-mouthed kiss.

He pulled back and speared her with his eyes. "Don't. Move."

"You *dare* to command me?" She met his gaze defiantly.

He snarled and pinned her arms over her head, sending a jolt of lust straight to Cybil's core. Her breath grew ragged as he leaned in, eyes flashing, until his face was only inches from hers. The day-old stubble shadowed his face, and she wanted him to kiss her, to rub his rough cheek on her soft one, to mark her. "Don't tease me, wench." He pushed her into the mattress, then released her. The motion reverberated through the bed as he stalked to the door of the outer room, closed it, then turned to peel off his wet shirt.

Cybil watched hungrily as each inch of flesh was revealed. She loved Will's body. He was so strong, so vital. Even before she'd known its origins, the scar on his shoulder had intrigued her. He'd lived, and suffered, and survived.

He sat to pull off his boots, then stood again to shuck off his trousers. As soon as it was loose from its confines, his cock, as hard as she'd ever seen it, sprang up to his belly. He kicked the trousers aside and stroked himself, a look of pure animal lust on his face.

"Open your legs."

Cybil was past arguing. She scooted back so her head was on the pillow, then she allowed her knees to fall open, revealing herself to her lover. She was wet, she knew, from the bath and from desire, and as the cool air collided with his scorching gaze on her lush, glistening folds, she couldn't help but reach down to touch herself. She groaned, spearing one finger, then two, into her channel, then she raised her eyes to meet Will's.

Come. Devour me.

He launched himself onto the bed and groaned as he brought his head between her thighs. He licked the length of her seam, once, twice, tasting her. Then he found her opening with his tongue, rapaciously fucking her with it, while at the same time his fingers found her back opening and he gently circled it, just a bit of pressure, not too much . . . He moved his mouth to her nub, and Cybil allowed her head to fall back as she submitted herself to the sublime delight of Will's touch, the torrent of sensation that eddied and swirled, rose and swept her away . . .

She came again, dancing, for what seemed an eternity, on the very edge of joy. She vaguely registered the rush of moisture that came with her climax and the look of desirous victory it elicited on Will's visage. This only ever happened with Will, and at first, it had embarrassed her, but he seemed to relish it, like it was some kind of badge of his abilities.

The bed was already wet from her body. A little more moisture hardly mattered.

When her shudders had finally stilled, Will lifted his head to peer up at her, and that look—pure, unadulterated desire. Raw emotion, on the face of a man made of stone—it undid her.

She grasped for him, whimpering but unable to find the words, and at last, he crawled to her, positioned himself over her, then fused their bodies into one.

The joining was—odd. Surprisingly gentle. It wasn't that he held anything back, exactly, but the way he fucked her, slowly, deliberately, almost tenderly. His eyes never closed or left her face, and those eyes . . . that emotion she'd glimpsed before, it wasn't just lust. It was—*more*. They were Will's eyes, nor

Ruthven's, nor any of the other parts he usually played, and they held some meaning, some purpose that—it was unnerving. Cybil closed her eyes to block him out so she could, once again, lose herself to sensation.

He held himself still inside her. "Look at me, Cybil." *Cybil*, not Effie. Again, unease pushed back against desire. She didn't open her eyes.

He didn't ask again, and as he resumed thrusting, gradually increasing his tempo, her doubt faded. Her hips rose and fell to match his. This. This was the pure, carnal passion that lived between them, just as it always had—but then Will was coming inside her without hesitation, shouting indecipherably as he shot his seed into her body.

And Cybil didn't. For the first time since they'd been lovers, she didn't find release along with him.

Afterward, they lay side by side on the bed, bodies barely touching, staring at the ceiling, at the chandelier reflecting the cold, dim light of the end of day. The grey shadows of the plaster rose it hung from.

Cybil was cold. Her body was still wet, yet she didn't get up. She could only guess what Will was thinking. Did he know she hadn't climaxed? Did he care? And what had he been about with those tender looks and that slow, careful lovemaking? She and Will shared pleasure for pleasure's sake. That was their arrangement. They were lovers, but they could never love. They'd not said as much, but they both knew it.

Didn't they?

She should never have let this happen. She'd been determined not to, but then he'd arrived, and she was in the bath, and the look on his face—

"I take it you're feeling better than you were?" Will's voice broke the silence.

"Yes. This last week . . . I've barely felt ill at all."

"Ann always said the first bit was the worst."

"Jane said the same."

"How is she?"

"Jane?"

"Aye."

Cybil sighed. "The birth was hard. Frightening, to be honest. I'm glad I was there. But the babies are beautiful." She smiled to herself, remembering. Then her throat tightened as the memory turned to Jane when she'd left her—exhausted, overwhelmed, her body still weak and battered from her labor.

"A girl and a boy?"

"Yes. Arthur and Eve."

There was a long silence. The chill began to seep into Cybil's body.

"Have you been out today?" Will asked.

"No. I stayed in bed all morning, reading." She motioned toward the pile of novels beside the bed. "Then I ordered a bath." She moved her head to look at him. "Then *you* came. I've been quite lazy, really." She attempted a smile.

"Good." Will turned onto his side and propped his head on his arm. He reached toward her with the other, laying his hand on her cheek. "You need rest. 'Tis good for the child." Cybil watched his hand move to her stomach. He pressed his palm against it—his warm, work-roughened touch. "There's no sign of it yet . . ." he murmured. "But there will be." His eyes flicked from her stomach to her face. "Cybil, we'll need to speak of the child's future—"

"No, we don't." She rose, ignoring his grunt of surprise as his hand dropped down to the counterpane. "I've told you. It's my decision. I'll make it when I'm ready."

He didn't speak, but she could feel his eyes on her as she found her dressing gown and tied it securely, warding away all thoughts of the child.

A fire had been laid in the hearth. She found the tinder box on the mantle and bent to light it, but Will sprang up.

"Let me." He crouched beside her, pushing her gently out of the way. Reluctantly, she handed him the box, then sat on the plush rug and watched as he struck the flint and lit a match. He touched it to the tinder, and it flared, then almost as suddenly the flame died. He blew it back to life, carefully aiming his breath for the underbelly of the fire.

"It was hard to leave," she murmured, watching the revived flame dance over the tinder. "But 'twas a relief as well."

The guilt of abandoning her friend still ate at her, but Jane's babies had been delivered safely and Cybil was free of Grislow Park—free of the fear she'd be discovered. She'd slept better last night than she had since she'd first realized her pregnancy.

Will didn't respond. He stared into the fire, lost in his own thoughts.

Cybil's stomach growled. She hadn't eaten anything since the breakfast that'd been brought up to her that morning. He started at the sound. "I almost forgot. I ordered food." He rose, then knelt to pick up his discarded trousers. "Are you hungry?"

She nodded. She *was* hungry. Hungrier than she'd been in a month.

She'd survived what was said to be the most difficult stage of pregnancy, and she'd successfully escaped her family. Tomorrow, Will would see her safely hidden away where no one could find her, with people he trusted.

The worst was over.

<hr>

The ride from Edinburgh to Strathaven in Will's gig was only five hours, but it seemed to Cybil as if she were crossing an unfathomable abyss. Each turn of the wheels drew her further and further away from her known world, the world she'd inhabited her entire life. Even the interlude in Edinburgh seemed far away now, almost as distant as Grislow Park.

Will had insisted she sleep in then soak in another bath before leaving the hotel. It was the last such luxury she'd have for a long while, he'd said, so she should enjoy it, and she'd tried . . . but, in truth, his attentions disquieted her. She was used to Will's mask of wicked devilry, his rough manner of bed-sport and his collusive grin. She was not used to, nor did she quite understand, this serious, tender man he seemed to be becoming.

They finally left Edinburgh just before eleven. Cybil had traveled the turn-pike from Edinburgh to Glasgow more than once, but they didn't take that road. This road was smaller, with no tolls, though still well kept. The villages and inns were spread farther apart, insulated from one another by mile after mile of fields and pasture.

For the first few hours, Will sat, silent and still, grasping the reins lightly and staring straight ahead. He seemed content in his own thoughts, and Cybil didn't attempt conversation. There was nothing to say, or to be precise, there was *one* thing that they mayhap should speak of, but Cybil was content to leave it for now—grateful, in fact, that Will didn't try to bring it up again. She had another six months to determine what would become of the child, and anyway, it was her decision, not his. He seemed to have formed some kind of attachment to the unborn babe already. He'd only try to force his own way if they spoke of it now.

"Tell me about your husband," Will asked abruptly.

"Ernie?"

"Aye." There was a pause. He seemed to be waiting for her to say something.

"You're afraid he'll discover me?" she asked finally.

"No. Not really . . ." His voice trailed off. "I just—I find myself wonderin' what he—"

"What he did to me?" she finished for him. "Why I left him?"

"Aye. That."

Cybil drew a long breath. "He's a great friend of Sidmouth's, you know, or—he *was*."

"I know."

Of course he knew. Will read the papers as much as, or probably more than, Percy did.

But she hadn't answered the question. Will drove on, silent, waiting.

"I left because he was cruel, and I couldn't take it any longer," she finally said.

"He hit you?" Will's gaze stayed straight ahead.

"Yes."

He glanced at her sharply, then back to the road. "Once? More than once?"

"Only once." Cybil crossed her arms, hugging herself to keep in the warmth. "But he did other things . . . he wasn't a nice man—*isn't* a nice man," she corrected herself. It had been so long since she'd seen her husband. It sometimes seemed that he only existed in the past, that he wasn't still in London, going to the House, to his club, hosting parties for influential Tories and their wives. But she knew he was. One need only glance at a London paper to know that.

"What kind of things?"

Cybil looked at Will, hoping to show with her expression that she didn't want to talk of Ernie. Didn't want to talk at all. But his gaze remained steadfastly fixed on the road ahead.

She sighed. He'd told her his secrets, hadn't he? "I was nineteen when I married. Fifteen years ago. I'd known him less than a year. I hardly knew him at all, as it turned out."

"Where'd you meet him?"

"At the Assembly Hall in Newcastle, at a dance. His family estate is in Leeds, but he was visiting some cousins . . . I was with Mother and a friend from school." Cybil paused, remembering that night—the heat of the crowded room, the rose silk gown she'd worn. How young she'd been, newly graduated from Miss Pugel's Academy, and certain she knew everything there was to know of the world. "Mother sought him out as soon as she learned he had a title. We were introduced, and he asked me to dance."

"And?" Will prompted.

"And that was it." It had been nothing really, just ten, maybe fifteen minutes of polite conversation. "He called on me the next day and several times after that. And sent flowers. He asked Father for my hand the following week. Father said yes."

"He wanted your money."

"Yes."

"But—did he ask *you*? Or just your father?"

Cybil looked at Will reproachfully. "How would we have become engaged if he hadn't asked me?"

Will shrugged. "I dinna ken how you upper-class folk do these things. When I proposed to Ann, her da had nothin' to do with it."

She snorted. "He asked me. He got down on one knee . . . the whole bit." She paused. "Everyone said I was the luckiest girl in Northumberland."

"Did you love him?"

"Tuh!" Cybil chortled. "I honestly . . . I don't know what I thought of him. The man, I mean. I was flattered. I liked the idea of being a baroness, as did my parents. But I never loved him, or liked him even. Before we were engaged, he was . . . *nothing*." She thought for a moment. "He told me he intended to spend most of his time in London, to go into politics, and that appealed to me. My school was in Yorkshire, but I'd never been south of that and I was excited to think of living in the city, and meeting publishers, and other other writers."

She stopped. If only the story could end there.

"So, what happened after—after you became engaged, I mean?" Will prompted.

Cybil stared into the mass of dirty clouds overhead. "He went home to Leeds, then to London to set up a house. I wrote to him, of course. I probably should have been more demure in my letters, but . . . you know me."

Will chuckled at this.

"I told him how much I looked forward to coming to London, and how I hoped to continue my writing and how I wanted to meet Charlotte Dacre, and—"

"Who?" Will interrupted.

"Dacre. She wrote *Zofloya*." Will gave her a blank look. "*The Libertine*?" she tried. "She was, at the time, my favorite author. She's quite famous."

Will shrugged.

"Doesn't matter." Cybil massaged the bridge of her nose. Her head was beginning to ache. "Ernie wrote back informing me that no wife of his would debase herself with such nonsense, and he could never permit me to associate with the likes of Dacre or—or the other writers I admired." She paused. "I should have broken it off then, when I had the chance, but I thought I could change his mind." She'd been sure she could, certain she was clever enough to bend her new husband to her will, just like Victoria in *Zofloya*.

"But it didn't work out as you planned," Will observed, shooting her a glance.

"It did not. After we married and I went to London with him . . . 'twas miserable. I wasn't permitted to leave the house without him or write anything other than letters. He had the servants watch me, and he shouted whenever I said something he didn't like, like I was his dog. It was even worse after it came clear I wasn't going to conceive a child. I was worthless to him. Less than worthless."

"How long?"

"How long was I there?"

Will nodded.

"Four years, but by that last . . . I couldn't take it. I was so lonely. I'd started writing when Ernie was out, or late at night, and I—" She broke off, realizing too late that she'd said too much. This was the part of the story she told no one. Her immediate family knew, of course. Ernie had seen to that, but no one else—

"What?" Will turned to look at her.

Cybil's head ached in earnest now. She stared at Will, unwilling to continue.

"What? Did he find you writing and beat you?"

"No. Not exactly." She drew a breath. She'd come this far. Perhaps the damning truth would quash whatever tender feelings Will seemed to be developing. "I sneaked out of the house to visit a publisher, to attempt to get my work published, and I—"

"That's my lass." There was a smile in his voice.

"But that's not all."

Will's brows rose questioningly.

Cybil inhaled slowly, steeling herself. "I began an affair with a man at the publishing house. A married man."

She held her breath, waiting for Will's reproach. Of course, she and Will had conducted an affair in the last years, but this was different. She'd been living under Ernie's roof when she'd started her affair with Peter, and Peter had been married, not a widower like Will. It had been wrong of her—of *them*.

But the reproach never came. Will didn't say anything, just held the reins and stared straight ahead, his face carefully blank.

"I was just so lonely, and Peter, that was his name, he was kind, and . . . he understood. Or he *said* he did." Her lower lip quivered. She bit it, blinking rapidly into the cold air.

"Then what happened?" One of Will's hands left the reins and found hers. He pulled it toward him, forcing her to uncross her arms.

She glanced at him, but his countenance was unreadable. A man made of stone. "It was predictable, I suppose. Ernie discovered I'd been sneaking out. He followed me and found Peter and I in a state of . . ." She trailed off.

"Indiscretion?" Was that a smirk on his face?

"Yes. Indiscretion." She returned his look. "Don't worry." She rolled her eyes. "It was never as good as it is with you."

"I dinna suppose it could be," he shot back. Yes, it was definitely a smirk.

An odd, unwanted relief settled in Cybil's limbs. She'd told Will her deepest, most shameful secret, and it had made no difference to him. He was still the same playful, understanding friend she'd always known him to be.

But she hadn't succeeded in pushing him away, had she?

"Peter lied." She forced herself to finish the story. "He denied knowing I was married, though he knew quite well, and he—he apologized to Ernie and blamed everything on me. Then when we got home, Ernie was so angry. He wanted to make something of himself, you see, and he couldn't with a . . . with a wife like me."

"He beat you."

Cybil couldn't answer. She closed her eyes and swallowed, feeling the blunt pain of his fist hitting her eye. The terror as she cowered in a corner, making herself as small as possible as he struck her again, and again.

"And you ran away, back home."

"I didn't know what else to do. I sneaked out the back door in the middle of the night."

"Did he come after you?"

"Of course. I wasn't hard to find, but Father protected me. He and Ernie made an—a business arrangement that allowed us to live separately."

"A *business* arrangement? You mean your father paid him off?"

"Yes, and he, or Percy, continues to. It's quite fortunate Ernie thinks me barren, otherwise he would never have let me go."

"How much does Sommerbell pay him?"

"A thousand a year."

Will inhaled sharply, and well he might. A woman's freedom in trade for a thousand pounds a year. Cybil should have been grateful to Father, now Percy, but instead she felt caged and, in truth, guilty. The whole thing—with Peter, and even marrying Ernie—she should have known better.

"You said he'd threatened to lock you up. When was that?"

"It was that same night. The night I left. I told him I'd leave him, and he said he'd lock me up." She could still remember Ernie's ugly sneer, blurred and hazy through her bloodied, swelling eye.

Try it, I'll lock you up like the baggage you are. You'll never see the light of day.

He *had* locked her in her bedchamber that night, or he'd tried to, but the locks in that house were easily picked. Cybil had tripped it with one of her hair pins, then escaped into the night with only the clothes on her back and a small traveling case. Three days later, she'd arrived at Grislow Park, with Ernie fast on her heels.

"What do you suppose he'd do if he knew?" Will asked quietly.

"About—"

"Aye."

"I don't know. But he wouldn't like it. The arrangement he made with Father stipulates that I stay at Grislow Park, remain chaste, and not make any scandal for him or his family."

"Chaste." Will sighed. "I see."

"I should have told you." She dropped his hand and wrapped her arms around herself again. "He could sue you."

"Aye, you should have." Will snaked an arm behind her. "But what's done is done." He pulled her closer on the wooden seat. "And, anyhow, he's never going to know."

"No. He's not." Cybil didn't remove Will's arm, but she didn't lean into him either.

ELEVEN

THEY STOPPED FOR SUPPER at a tavern in Carluke, just an hour or so from Strathaven, then continued on, arriving at Emily's just after nightfall.

By sheer luck, Emily's house was on the far northeast side of the village, where Will could easily slip in without traveling through the main part of town. Pipperow Street ran along the base of a steep grassy hill, with houses on only the level side. The cottages all had large back gardens and were spaced well apart, giving little chance of being observed by neighbors. Davey's great-granddad had built the house, and it was as if he'd set it up knowing there would be a particular need for privacy at some point in the family's future.

A small light shone from one of Emily's front windows, a sign that she was expecting them and had seen no danger. It was a signal they'd concocted in the early days, during and after Davey's trial when the house had been routinely watched, and though it'd been two years since Emily had seen anything suspicious—and it was probably unnecessary now—the light was an assurance.

Will glanced at Cybil, trying to imagine what this place looked like from her view. To him, the domestic scene—the tidy cottage lit from within, the faint smell of wood smoke, the distant bleating of a goat—was a comfort. There was no hint of poverty, or neglect. But Cybil was used to luxury, a banger of a house on a huge estate, and servants to do all the real work. This was not that. While Davey's da had, at least, managed to put the roof in tiles before he died, the cottage was small. Two stories crowded right up against the road, with just one room per floor and the attached high-ceilinged weavers shop.

But it was too dark to read Cybil's face and there was no time to stop and gawk at the house. Will brought the gig around back. There wasn't a stable or a real barn. Emily only kept a few chickens and a she-goat for milking, but there was a shed where he could shelter his horse for the night. He didn't want to keep Cybil waiting now, so he tied the rig to a post, then turned to help her down. He'd get her settled, then come back for her trunk and attend to the horse.

She sat, staring down at him. He still couldn't see her face, but he could sense her nerves as he reached up to take her gloved hand. "Mrs. *Smith*?" He attempted a smile.

They'd talked through what they would and would not tell Emily. Will trusted his friend with his life and had insisted she know the child was his. But Cybil had decided to keep her identity a secret. He would introduce her as Mrs. Cybil Smith in honor of her imaginary friend from Sunderland.

Cybil drew a long, slow breath, then she took his hand and allowed him to help her down.

"'Tis only till spring," he murmured. "You're a brave lass. You'll make it through." He bent to kiss her, as it was the only way he could think to bring her comfort. She accepted the affection but didn't return it. She simply stood, stiff and unmoving, as his lips grazed hers.

Will straightened up and cupped her cheek. "I'll stay as long as you need—" She shrugged him off, then began walking toward the house.

Will sighed. Ever since the hotel, since they'd made love, she'd been—*distant*. He didn't know why, exactly, but . . . 'twas a fact. Didn't matter anyway. Not really.

He followed her up the slate path to Emily's back door, but there was no need to knock. There was a flutter of curtains in the window, then the door swung open and Emily's younger son, Ewan, appeared on the threshold. The five-year-old reminded Will so much of his father. He had Davey's blue-grey eyes and tousled blonde hair, his crooked smile. But Ewan had no memory of Davey—he'd been but a wee infant when his da was arrested and just shy of his first birthday when the judge passed the sentence that sent his father away forever.

Ewan grinned and opened his mouth to greet Will, but then he caught sight of Cybil and his eyes grew wide. He backed away, colliding with the front of his mother's skirts as Emily came to the threshold to greet them.

"Will." Emily held her hands out as her son disappeared behind her skirts. Her smile was as warm as the soft tartan her husband used to weave, but there was a sadness to it since Davey had gone. A sadness that never quite went away.

"Good evening, Emily." Will took her hands and squeezed them, then he turned back to Cybil, who was standing solitary in the shadows behind him, eyeing the scene. He reached for her arm and drew her into the light.

"This is Cybil—Smith." He stumbled over the words. "Cybil, meet Emily, my dear friend."

Emily turned her smile on Cybil, though it lost some of its genuine warmth to politeness. All Cybil could manage was a tight nod and a nervous curve of her lip. She was trying, Will could tell, but she was uncomfortable. He threaded his fingers through hers.

"I'm very pleased to meet you, Mrs. Smith." Emily's tone was polite and formal.

The women eyed each other, and Will was glad he was staying the night. He was sure they would get on, but it might take some time. The situation was odd, to say the least.

"Please, come in." Emily turned and ushered them in, then closed the door behind them.

The room was dimly lit. An oil lamp stood on the table, and a candle shone from one of the front windows—the one they'd seen as they approached. It was a big room, but as it served as kitchen, dining, and sitting room, there wasn't much space to spare. There was a large, open hearth with an array of pots and kettles and a small oven to one side. Before it was a wooden table with four chairs and an oaken sideboard lined with dishes. Emily's rocking chair and sewing basket sat in front of one of the two front windows, and her box bed—the one that used to be hers and Davey's—was tucked like a cave into the far wall. Eight-year-old Luke sat at a small desk near the other front window, with a book lying open before him. He'd turned to gape at the newcomers.

This house always reminded Will of home. It was different, to be sure, from the Highland farmhouse of his youth, but it smelled the same—of tallow and woodsmoke, with the hint of whatever had last been cooked on the hearth.

"Won't you sit down?" Emily gestured to the table. Her motions seemed wooden, as if she weren't quite sure what to do with her hands.

Cybil was just as awkward. She smiled politely, then began removing her gloves. Will went behind her to help her out of her pelisse. He hung it and her bonnet on one of the hooks by the door before leading her to the table.

"Back to your lessons, love. 'Twill be bedtime soon." As she spoke, Emily walked to the candle in the window and moved it onto the desk so Luke would have a better view of his book. She patted her oldest son's head, then reached behind her to peel the younger one from his refuge in her skirts. "Ewan." Her voice was stern. "The tea."

It was obvious she'd rehearsed this with Ewan—how to make tea for their guests. The lad seemed to suddenly remember the importance of the task. Head down, he shot to the sideboard to collect the teapot. He carefully carried it to the table. Then, with both hands wrapped in a cotton towel, he unhooked the heavy iron kettle from its chain above the fire and poured the hot water in.

Cybil sat stiffly, her eyes darting around the room, taking in the unfamiliar scene. Emily settled across from them but seemed at a loss as well. Will was no good at idle conversation, but as there was no one else to do it, he would need to step in.

"The weather's not bad, for so late in the season," he observed.

"Aye. I got all the mattress ticks changed out this week. It's been so dry." Emily found a use for her hands, pouring tea. She offered a cup to Cybil. "Do you take milk or sugar, Mrs. Smith?"

"Just the tea's fine." Cybil accepted her cup. She inhaled the steam, then seemed, finally, to settle into the room. "Please. Call me Cybil." She met Emily's gaze. "And thank you, for having me, Mrs. Flemming. I'm—I'm most grateful."

"Emily." Emily smiled, and Will felt himself relax. She handed him a cup, then poured one for herself, adding a generous splash of milk. "'Tis no trouble at all. Will's like family to us, and now you are too."

She paused to look at little Ewan, who was gently pawing her shoulder, clearly wanting to sit on his mother's lap. Emily opened her arms, allowing the lad to climb up and nestle close.

"What's your name?" Cybil asked Ewan, though Will had already told her both lads' names on the journey here.

Ewan hesitated, clearly still shy of the stranger.

"Is it—*Alfonzo*?" Cybil's eyes widened, a smile tugging on her lips.

Ewan crinkled his nose and shook his head.

"What about *Ulfred*?"

A slow smile spread over Ewan's face. "No."

"Oh, how silly of me. Of course, it's Golgotha, isn't it?"

Forgetting his fear, the lad let out a peal of delighted laughter. "That's not a real name."

"Oh, yes it is," Cybil insisted, grinning. "It means *skull*, in Hebrew."

Ewan's eyes widened, then he seemed to remember himself and buried his head under Emily's arm.

"He's Ewan," Luke piped up from across the room, apparently forgetting his studies. "Does it really mean *skull*?"

"It does," Cybil replied. "And what's your name?"

"Luke. But—do you know any other—"

"Back to your lessons, lad." Emily's strict directive cut Luke off, and reluctantly, he complied. Emily turned her attention back to Cybil. "Will says it's been three months or so since you . . ." She looked from Cybil to Will, then to Ewan, obviously not wanting to finish the sentence in his hearing.

"Yes." Cybil chewed on her bottom lip. "Two since I realized . . . my condition."

"And how are you feelin'?"

"Better than I was."

Emily smiled encouragingly. "The beginning was hard then?"

Cybil nodded.

"Well, you're in good hands now." Emily smoothed her son's hair absently. "My dear friend's mother, in Auchinearn, is a midwife. They've agreed to come for a visit in a week or so to see how you're farin'." She looked to Will. "That's Margaret and her ma. I told them you might bring them here at Halloween time?"

Will nodded. Margaret was another of the small group of women who'd lost their men to the rebellion of 1820, except instead of transportation, Margaret's sweetheart, Andrew, had been one of the three who were hanged. Davey and Andrew Hardie had shared a cell in Stirling for a time, and Margaret and Emily, visiting as often as they could, had become fast friends.

Ewan tugged on his mother's sleeve, attempting to get her attention. Emily shushed him, then turned back to Cybil. "Agnes and Margaret will come back when your time nears, so they can attend the birth," she explained. "I've had two of my own, but I'll feel better with a more experienced hand."

"Is there no midwife in the village?" Cybil asked.

Emily hesitated. "Since my husband was sent away, things have been . . . difficult here at times. Not everyone understands . . ." Her eyes darted to Luke, and she wrapped her arms protectively around Ewan, pulling him close. "And given *your* situation . . ." She shook her head. "'Tis better to have Agnes."

Ewan tugged on Emily's arm again, more urgently this time. She looked at him expectantly, but the lad didn't speak. He eyed Cybil, then gestured again to his mother. He had something to say but was apparently too shy to say it in front of the stranger. Emily sighed, then bent her head so the lad could whisper in her ear, though it was hardly a whisper. Will could hear every word.

"*Ask Will about Halloween.*"

Emily straightened up. "Ask 'im yourself if you want to know so badly."

Ewan looked at her pleadingly, but Emily only shook her head. Reluctantly, he turned to Will.

Will smiled. "Are you wonderin' if I'll stay for Halloween night, after I bring the ladies?"

Ewan nodded, eyes wide. "Ma says we can have a bonfire and I can stay up."

"I wouldna miss it," he assured the boy. "I'll bring some apples for dookin'"

The lad's face broke into a grin.

"I've never been to a Halloween bonfire, but I've read of one," Cybil spoke slowly. "A Burns poem, I think . . ." She looked at Ewan. "Is it true that ghosts and goblins come out on that night?"

Ewan opened his mouth to answer, then suddenly remembered his shyness and once again buried his face against his mother's breast.

"Aye, they do." Once again, Luke answered for his younger brother. "There's plenty of 'em in the ruined castle, and they roam about on Halloween night."

Cybil was intrigued. "There's a castle here?"

"Aye," Luke replied solemnly. "Just down the hill."

"I do love castles. Will you take me there sometime?"

Luke looked to his mother, and Emily nodded. "You may take Mrs. Smith, when she's settled. As long as you behave."

"I want to go too!" Ewan protested.

Emily studied him dubiously. "We shall see. 'Tis a dangerous place for a wee lad."

"I'm not that wee." The boy pouted.

"Yes, ye are!" Luke spoke up.

Ewan's mouth opened to argue the point, but Emily cut him off.

"That's enough." Her firm tone put an end to the bickering.

"Well, whoever goes, I shall look forward to it." Cybil smiled. "And I *do* hope we'll see some ghosts . . . I so enjoy a bit of a scare." She eyed Ewan, who was peeking out at her again. "Do you like ghost stories, Ewan, or do they frighten you?"

"I'm n-not afraid."

"Good." Cybil raised her brows. "Then I shall save some especially scary ones for Halloween night." She and Ewan grinned at each other.

Emily kissed her youngest son on the cheek. "Time for bed, the both of you." She stood, displacing Ewan from her lap.

"I'll see to the horse." Will rose.

"I've made up a bed in the weaver's room for you," Emily told Cybil. "It just sits there empty now . . ." She trailed off, as if remembering, then jerked back to the present. "'Tis good to make some use of it." She looked to Will. "There's room there for you, too, if you'd like, or you may have my bed and I'll—"

"No." Will cut her off. "Keep your bed. I'll be fine."

"Very well." Emily nodded, and Will felt a rush of gratitude for his friend. From the first moment he'd told her of Cybil's situation, Emily hadn't shown one glimpse of judgement. But even still, he hadn't been at all sure she'd approve of them sleeping in the same bed under her roof.

She turned to her sons. "Lads, get yourselves dressed for bed. I'll show Mrs. Smith"—she caught herself—"*Cybil*, to her room, then I'll come up an' tuck you in."

Emily and her boys had already broken their fast, and Luke was gone to school by the time Will and Cybil emerged into the main room the following morning.

They hadn't made love the night before. Cybil hadn't seemed inclined. She'd warmed to Ewan, Luke and Emily, but not, it seemed, to Will. Once the candle was blown out and they were alone in the dark, though, she'd allowed him to draw her into his arms. They'd slept tight together in the small bed Emily had made up in a corner of the weaver's shop, the smell of fresh oat straw lingering between them. It was a comfort, to feel the movement of her breath, to know the child in her womb was safe, and he'd drifted off quickly, not waking till he opened his eyes to the morning light. 'Twas odd to wake up to the sight of Davey's old loom—the same enormous loom the men of his family had worked for generations, now unused and neglected, covered with a thick layer of dust.

It was a sad room. Filled with ghosts.

But it was perfect for Cybil's use. Private from the rest of the house. It even had doors that opened onto the road, and the back garden and privy.

Emily sent Ewan out to collect eggs, then she sat down to a cup of tea as Will and Cybil ate their breakfast of eggs and toasted bread. By the time they'd finished, the two women were deep in conversation about childbearing and how different one experience could be from the next. They'd almost seemed to forget Will was there.

He pushed back his plate and cleared his throat. "I'll be off then, if it's alright with you both?"

In truth, he was itching to get home. There was much to do, and it would be a relief to see his own bairns again.

Emily looked at Cybil, and Cybil looked at Will. She took a breath and nodded.

"Walk me out?" He rose, hoisting the bag he'd brought with him, then he offered Cybil his arm.

Once outside, she stood and watched as he readied the gig and hitched the mare.

"I like it here," she finally said.

Will smiled. "I knew you would . . . though there was a minute last night I doubted myself."

Cybil shook her head ruefully. "I thought—it seemed Emily might not like me at first, but—I rather think she thought the same of me." She chuckled. "Do you remember when *we* met?"

He lifted his head from where he was cinching the breeching strap, and their eyes connected, both remembering that afternoon in the great hall of Darnalay Castle . . . the next day in the gardens.

Cybil looked away, then was silent again. She took a few steps toward the house, then gazed downward, running her toes over the smooth paving stones.

Will had been avoiding speaking of the child. Of course, it'd been on his mind, but the way she'd been acting made it clear she didn't want to talk of it. But avoidance—well, it wouldn't be possible forever, would it? Now was as good a time as ever.

"About the bairn. I have an idea that—"

"Will you need food for your journey?" She looked up quickly. "I could go ask Emily if she has any cheese or bread to—"

"I'll be fine." Will tightened the last strap. "But Cybil, we must talk of it. We'll need to—"

"No." Cybil's expression was hard. "Not now."

Will sighed. She might not want to speak of it, but he would, at least, start putting together a plan of his own.

He crossed in front of the mare to stand before her. He had a mind to draw her into an embrace, but the way she stood there, stiff, arms crossed . . .

"I'll see you in a fortnight." He planted a kiss on her forehead. "Be sure to send a note if you need anything. The post takes only a day to Glasgow."

She nodded, her lips pressed tightly together, arms still crossed.

Then he climbed up to his seat, snapped the reins, and was off.

A sense of relief came to him as he directed his mare onto the road. Relief at leaving Cybil and her foul mood behind. Relief at the idea of going home, and of life—quiet, normal life—taking hold. But as he drove up the hill, a sense of prickling unease intruded.

Someone was watching.

He chanced a glance behind the gig, to each side, but nothing seemed out of place. Just the empty road with houses on one side, the sloping pasture to the other.

He shook off the nervy sensation. It had been two years since he'd felt this way, and it had been his imagination then, just as it was now. He was on edge because he was leaving Cybil at Emily's. That was all. Still, he was glad when he'd left the town behind and turned onto the turnpike toward home.

TWELVE

A mournful cry wails over the desolate heath. It is a lonely sound, like the despondent keening of a child who has lost his mother to the night and given up every last hope of finding her again. But, in truth, it is only the wind gusting through the barren branches of the gnarled oak outside my window. I can see them now, illuminated by the dim light of my candle, clawing at the glass like skeletal fingers.

For many nights, sleep has forsaken my pillow. Indeed, I think I shall never dream again. Why, Louisa? You ask. Why do you not slumber—not dream? I tell you I cannot! From the very moment I realized my dire circumstance—the worst that can befall a woman—the sweet escape of sleep has ever eluded my anguished mind. And so, I write. I confess my sins to this paper. Yet I do not seek forgiveness, only understanding. For I am a woman—

CYBIL PAUSED, QUILL RAISED an inch above the foolscap, considering what should come next. The first paragraph and the beginning of the second had flowed smoothly. The best kind of writing, where the words seemed to appear of their own accord, strong and true.

"For I am a woman—" she read aloud. Stared at it. Squinted. It was something about a despotic husband. Something about the lonely desperation of it all, the yearning for human connection . . . But for the life of her, she couldn't think of the words.

It had been months since she'd written anything. Her publisher in London had sent an inquiry a few weeks prior, asking when her next work might be complete, but Cybil hadn't even answered him. She'd been too overcome and distracted to pick up her quill, and though her nerves had improved in the week since she'd come to Strathaven, weariness had taken anxiety's place. Emily had no household servants, so Cybil—despite her inexperience and her host's protestations—had felt it her duty to help with the housework. Her days had been full of washing dishes, mending, sweeping, playing nursery games with Ewan and helping Luke with his lessons. She'd even learned to milk the goat, though Ewan was infinitely faster at it than she was. At the end of each day, she'd fallen into bed, too tired to think of anything but sleep.

But tonight, she'd lain awake, kept from slumber by the burning pain in her chest that Emily told her was a symptom of her pregnancy. She'd been listening to the wind moaning around the house, feeling the heavy stillness of the weaver's shop, when inspiration had struck. A novel, written from the perspective of a woman named Louisa, who found herself pregnant with a child not her husband's. The details were still forming. The work would draw heavily on Wollstonecraft's *Maria*—sometimes Cybil felt as if her own life was but a retelling of that novel—but the heroine would be stronger than Maria, more like Gabrielle in Dacre's *The Libertine*, and it would be written in the first person, like Shelley's *Frankenstein*. Louisa's husband would be the villain, and his name would be Mordred, Lord Castiff. The identity of the father of Louisa's child, the man who had tempted her away from her marriage bed, eluded Cybil. Perhaps he would be some kind of supernatural being. A ghost? . . . And he would leave her heartbroken in the end, or kill her even. She'd figure that out when she got there.

Certainly, it was the kind of book critics would hate—unfit for refined tastes. But Cybil didn't care. She needed to write, to get this story out of herself and onto paper.

There was neither a desk nor a table in the weaver's room, but Cybil had brought her lap-desk from Grislow Park, and she sat on the narrow bed, a pillow propped behind her and the rosewood box with its brass fittings resting on her lap. She'd moved her single candle to the very edge of the bedside table, and it gave her just enough light to write by.

She read the lines aloud one more time. Slowly.

"I do not seek forgiveness. Only understanding. For I am a woman—" At last, the words came. *Bastilled for life in a marriage of unfathomable cruelty.* Her quill flew across the paper. *What I have done, I have done for necessity. For does not a person need love as much as she needs food, or drink? Is it not love which separates us from the savage beasts?*

She dipped the quill in the ink, reading that last line back. That was good. *Bastilled* as a verb was a word Wollstonecraft had coined, and it would draw the connection for any reader familiar with her work. But it wasn't so obvious that those who did not know Wollstonecraft, or only knew her through her sordid reputation, would castigate Cybil for the reference.

She chuckled to herself. Perhaps she *did* care a bit what the critics thought.

Three hours later, she'd filled twenty pages and satisfactorily described the decrepit manor house where Louisa resided and the great suffering she'd endured in her marriage. Castiff had married her only for her dowry, then he'd beaten her and forced her to retire to his crumbling country estate where she was forbidden to keep friends or pursue any hobbies that might lessen the bleakness of her days. The only time he'd recalled her from exile was when he'd run short of funds and had attempted to remedy his problem by prostituting her to an acquaintance of his—another trope borrowed from Wollstonecraft. Louisa, of course, refused to cooperate, making her husband hate her all the more.

She had now come to the part where she'd need to introduce the father of Louisa's child, but Cybil was tired and out of ideas.

Yawning, she corked the little bottle of ink, tucked it and the quill away, and closed the desk. Stiffly, she rose and placed it into her trunk, then stumbled outside to use the privy before falling back into bed. Once there, her body spread out under the blanket, heavy and relaxed. It had been so long since her mind had achieved the deep calm that came after a satisfying night of writing. It was akin to the warm contentment she felt after making love . . . after she and Will had wrung each other dry of all thought. All care . . .

The next thing Cybil knew, she was opening her eyes to the yellow light of morning. It was late. The sun had already risen well above the east-facing window. She lay still for a moment, listening. Nothing but silence.

Luke would be gone to school by now. Emily and Ewan had to be outside.

Cybil dressed, then passed into the kitchen. It was empty, so she went to the window and looked out over the back garden. A cauldron had been hung over a fire, and steam was rising, ghostly white in the morning sun.

Ah, yes. It was laundry day. Emily had put all the family's shirts, linens and shifts into that cauldron to soak the night before.

She now came into view, balancing a wooden yoke with two pails of water on her shoulders. Her pace was slow and plodding, her mouth set in the tight, drawn line that Cybil had come to recognize—her back was hurting her. Ewan came behind, lugging two smaller pails that hung from a slender stick across his shoulders. He splashed the contents into a large wooden washtub, spilling half in the process. Emily didn't scold him; it looked to Cybil as if she were in too much pain to speak. She just carefully poured one bucket into the tub, then the next, then hoisted the yoke back onto her shoulders and stoically turned back in the direction of the well.

Cybil hurried to open the door and poked her head out. The chill air bit at her face—surprising for how bright the day was.

"Good morning," she called.

Emily stopped. She forced a pinched smile. "You slept well."

"Yes, I was up late."

"I'll just take one more trip, then get your breakfast." Emily began to trudge back in the direction of the street.

"Wait!" Cybil called. She ducked into the house and grabbed an apron from the peg by the door. Emily looked on blankly as Cybil strode toward her, tying the apron over her muslin. "I'll go to the well, and eat when I return. Then I can help."

Emily stared at her dubiously. She knew nothing of Cybil's life and had made no attempt to press for information. But Cybil's manner, her fine clothes and inexperience with housework no doubt betrayed her privileged upbringing. "Have you ever washed laundry before?"

"No. But you can teach me. Surely, it's not that difficult."

"I'll teach you!" Ewan's small voice piped up from behind his mother. "'Tis easy."

"Perhaps you could accompany me to fetch water as well, Master Ewan?" Cybil reached for the yoke and settled it on her shoulders. Emily visibly relaxed once she was free of the weight. Her face softened, and Cybil understood why. The apparatus was heavy, even with empty buckets. The wooden bar dug into her flesh. It would be unbearable once they were full.

Ewan grinned at her. The boy had lost all his shyness in the last week, and he now seemed to view her as an interesting, if somewhat puzzling, plaything—a grown woman who had no idea how to milk a goat or do laundry. He talked constantly, and Cybil knew Emily was glad to have someone else to listen to him—someone to offer her a few moments of peace now and again.

"Lead the way." She nodded Ewan forward, then followed him around the house.

They turned left onto the dirt lane and headed up the steep hill toward the crossroads and the village well.

There was a notch cut in the wood of the yoke, meant to hold it in place against one's neck, but it slipped as Cybil walked and the whole thing fell out of balance.

"Wait," she called ahead to Ewan, then stopped to adjust it. When she had it just right, she grasped the ropes that held the buckets on either side. That was better. Awkward, but better. As she straightened up, a flicker of movement caught her eye. A man, standing in the shadow beside a house just ahead. She only caught a fleeting glimpse of his face—fair hair, sharp nose, deep-set eyes—before he turned and moved farther into the shadow. She blinked, staring at the space where he had been. He held an eerie resemblance to Townend, the steward at Ernie's Leeds estate . . . But, of course, it wasn't. It was only the neighbor.

Apparently, Cybil's nerves weren't as settled as she'd supposed.

"Are ye ready?" Cybil blinked up to find Ewan eyeing her impatiently.

She nodded, and they continued their walk up the hill.

The rest of the day was a blur of fetching water, boiling water, scrubbing cloth, rinsing cloth, wringing it out, wrinkled fingers, sore back, shivering in her wet dress, skin red and chaffing from the caustic lye soap. Cybil spent a full hour removing buttons and lace from her gowns. Tomorrow she'd spend another hour sewing them back on. How the maids at Grislow Park did this every week and kept smiles on their faces, she would never know.

At least the work allowed ample opportunity for conversation. There was something about having one's hands occupied that made the mind sociable. She'd noticed this in the last few days working side by side with Emily. As they knelt together scrubbing the linens, Emily told her of the time her husband was in prison and how she'd visited him as often as she could, the boys in tow.

"He was sent to Liverpool to be transported," she recounted. "But they transferred him at night, and didna say beforehand." Cybil's friend sat back on her heels and wiped her eyes with the inside of her elbow, the only part of her that wasn't wet with lye water. "I never even got to kiss him goodbye." She blinked several times, then turned determinedly back to her work.

Cybil watched her for a moment, struggling to find words. "You must miss him dreadfully," she finally managed. To have such love, then lose it . . . it would be worse than not having it at all.

Emily didn't look up. "What's done is done. No use cryin' now."

Cybil followed her friend's lead and bent back over the washtub. After a few minutes of silence, she asked a question that had been bothering her for some time. "Why did they stop?"

Emily shot her a questioning look.

"The radicals, I mean. They didn't get what they wanted—the vote, or reform—and they were obviously dedicated to their cause. I understand Will's reasons, but there were others, surely, who weren't transported or hung. Why did they not keep fighting?"

Emily glanced at her, then back to the shift she was scrubbing. "There are plenty of folks left. I've no doubt they'll rise again in time, but . . ." She set the shift aside and picked up a shirt. "I suppose what happened to Andrew and Purlie—it scared people. Proved the Six Acts would be enforced."

"The Six Acts?"

Emily looked up, surprised. "You've not heard of 'em?"

Cybil shook her head.

Her friend gave her a strange look, as if she were shocked at Cybil's ignorance. "'Tis a set of laws passed just after Peterloo." She turned back to the wash, scrubbing hard as she spoke. "Sidmouth's doing. They make it a crime to go to meetings and take up arms. The newspapers, too. They make it harder for the smaller ones to keep goin'."

"I see." Sidmouth. Everything seemed to come back to Sidmouth. Probably Ernie had something to do with the passing of those Six Acts.

Cybil sighed and scrubbed the shirt she held with renewed vigor.

They finished just before the sun set. Emily sent Ewan to fetch the goat from her pasture across the street, then to collect the dry linens while the two women went inside for a quick cup of tea before getting supper.

The fire had burned low, though the house was warm with late afternoon sun streaming through the front windows. Cybil started to lift the teapot, but Emily waved her away. "Sit," she commanded. "You've been working all day. Will would never forgive me if he knew."

"What's Will got to do with it?" Cybil plopped down into a chair, glad to rest her aching feet, but not glad to be reminded of Will, or his dictates. She'd been trying not to think of him all week.

"You know men." Emily rolled her eyes, then knelt to stoke the fire. "As soon as a woman's with child, they think she's fragile. He made me promise you wouldna exert yourself."

"I'm not fragile."

Emily seemed not to hear. "Will's not just any man, though," she mused, feeding the fire one small stick, then another. Her gaze darted quickly to Cybil, then away. They hadn't spoken of how Cybil had found herself with child. Emily was curious, surely—who wouldn't be?—but, thankfully, she seemed content to leave the matter alone.

There was a long pause, then Emily rose. As she did, she winced and put a hand to her lower back.

"Has it always pained you?" Cybil asked, glad to change the subject.

"Only since Ewan was born." Emily heaved a breath. "I dinna know what changed, but it's hurt me ever since, especially after a day like today." She hung the kettle over the flames that were now leaping and crackling in the hearth, then she moved to the sideboard and spooned tea into the pot. "It's not so bad really. Plenty of women die in childbed. I've noth—" She stopped suddenly, realizing what she'd just said. "Oh. I'm sorry. I didna mean—"

"Don't be." Cybil put a hand up. "I'm well aware of the danger." She smiled, hopefully more bravely than she felt. The possibility of death was real, of course, but it was too much to think about. She couldn't dwell on it. "I'm made of sturdy stock. I'll come through."

"I'm sure you will." Emily shot her an encouraging look, then walked to the front window. She moved the curtain aside and peered out. The western sky was ablaze in crimson and gold.

"Shouldn't Luke be home by now?" Cybil asked.

"Aye. I'd think he would be . . ."

A banging sounded, then Ewan appeared at the back door. He'd had to kick it open since his small arms were heaped full of clean white shifts, sheets and shirts. A chill wind gusted through the house as he deposited the load on Emily's bed, then he turned and went out to get more. He left the door open, and neither woman moved to close it since he'd be coming in with full hands in just another minute.

"What kept you up last night?" Emily crossed to the fire again, but Cybil rose quickly and beat her to the now steaming kettle.

"Sit. I'll pour." She grasped the iron kettle with a towel, then poured hot water onto the tea leaves Emily had measured out. "I was writing," she confided.

"A letter?"

"No. A book." Cybil paused as she returned the kettle to its hook, considering the wisdom of what she was about to say. "I write stories. Novels."

"*Novels*." A wondering smile spread across Emily's face. "Are they published?"

Cybil felt her cheeks warm. "Yes, some of them. I use a pseudonym. Rosemary Grey—"

"Ma." She was cut off by a voice coming from the open door. Luke stood on the threshold. His nose was bloodied. One of his eyes had a cut above it and the beginnings of a bruise.

Emily was to her son in an instant. "What happened?" She led him to a chair and sat him down.

"I—" Luke began, then stopped. He stared at the floor. "Some boys at school," he muttered. "They dinna like me much."

Emily put her palms on his cheeks, tilting his face and examining his wounds. "Is it only your face?" She felt up and down his arms. "Is there more?"

"Na." Luke gazed at his hands, curled in his lap.

"Look at me." Emily gripped the boy, staring at him intently.

Luke rolled his shoulders to shake her off, but his eyes rose to meet his mother's. "I'm fine, Ma."

"You are *not* fine." Emily's lips pressed together as she poured hot water from the kettle into a small bowl. She dipped in a towel and began to clean her son's wounds. Luke winced but held himself steady. "It was 'cause of your da, wasna it?"

Luke was silent.

"Answer me." Emily's tone was as stern as Cybil had ever heard it. "Why did they hit you?" She drew back and took Luke's chin in her hand. "Was it because of your da? Did they speak of him?"

Luke looked at his mother for a long moment, then silently, he nodded assent. The boy's face crumpled, and wordlessly, Emily pulled him into her arms. She didn't see to notice the smudge of blood that stained her dress as she held him and he cried.

Thirteen

"Must you go, Da?" Rose was on the floor by the hearth, cuddling her newest acquisition, a retired bulldog that had somehow avoided death in a bull-baiting ring. The pitiful thing had a torn ear, was missing most of its teeth and walked with a limp. It shied away from everyone in the house except ten-year-old Rose, who had decided all it needed was kindness to bring out its true nature.

Will had put off telling his bairns about his upcoming trip, but it could be avoided no longer. He would leave early the next morning to get Margaret and Agnes in Auchinearn, then bring them to Strathaven in time for the planned Halloween celebration.

"You only got back from Edinburgh a week ago," Rose complained.

"*Two* weeks," Will corrected. "And I told you, this business is proving stickier than I thought. This likely won't be the last time." The lie was bitter in his mouth. "'Tis only one night. I'll be back, quick as a bee." He forced a playful smile.

Rose's bottom lip protruded into a sad pout. "I don't like it when you're away." She blinked up at him, as if warding away tears. "I worry."

Her agonized look cut straight to Will's heart. Why shouldn't she worry? He'd left her once, promising to be back by nightfall, only to return after midnight with a bullet hole in his shoulder.

"Ach, Rosie. Rosie." He squatted down and reached out to smooth her hair. "You mustna worry. 'Tis only Edinburgh and meetings with solicitors. The biggest danger is I'll be bored stiff."

The bully startled at Will's nearness. He tried to move out of Rose's lap, but she shushed him, then kissed the top of his head as he settled in again.

She stroked the dog's back with her scarred hand, looking at it instead of Will as she spoke. "Did you tell Nat?"

"Not yet, but I will."

"How many more times?" She still didn't look at him.

"I dinna ken exactly. At least a couple, through the winter." He could barely speak through the tightness in his throat. "I'm sorry, lass."

Rose looked up at him and nodded, granting her reluctant approval. "Just be safe. And come home as quick as you can."

Not trusting his face to remain steady, Will drew his daughter into an embrace. This time the bully did scramble up and away, allowing him to squeeze her tighter, to relish the comfort of knowing his child was safe in his arms. It struck him suddenly, how similar they were. Rosie and him. She worried when he was away, and he, though he did his best to ignore it, always had a worry for her—and for her brother—in the back of his mind whenever they weren't under the same roof.

Rose squeaked at his force, then giggled and pulled away.

He sat with her a bit more, chatting about her dogs and the best way to care for them, then he left her and went to his study, sighing as he settled behind the desk and wrapped his spectacles around his ears. He'd been at the new factory most of the day and hadn't been able to catch up. There was a shipment of cotton to be ordered, a grievance against one of the managers to be considered, last month's ledgers to be approved, and on top of it all, the school for the workers' children had lost a teacher. He'd need to advertise for a new one. Usually, as overseer of the school, Jane Sommerbell handled those matters, but with the new babes, Will wouldn't think of bothering her.

He'd be up late, but it'd be worth it. He'd see Cybil tomorrow.

He hadn't heard from her since he'd left her in Strathaven, and he was itching to know how she fared. Was her belly grown? Would she be pleased to see him? He hoped so, but her moods had been . . . complicated. Confusing.

It was all so bloody complicated.

He moved the candle and started sorting the documents. At least tonight's tasks were sure and simple. Black and white words and numbers on paper—

"You wanted to see me?" Nat was at the door with his usual serious, stolid look.

"Aye. Come in." Will shook himself. He'd forgotten he asked the maid to send Nat to the study. *How had he forgotten?*

Nat crossed toward the desk, his expression unchanged.

"I need to go back to Edinburgh tomorrow," Will said. "I'll be gone overnight." Why did his words sound so terse? That was not how he meant them.

Nat nodded. "I'll watch Rosie then. Is there aught else you need done?"

"No, but it likely won't be the last time, so you know." Nat's expression still didn't change. He didn't ask any questions, just nodded again before turning to go. But Will couldn't let him. "I'm—I'm sorry to leave, son." He spoke to Nat's back. "It's been a lot of late. I hope it doesn't—inconvenience you."

Inconvenience?

Nat pivoted and eyed him. "'Tisn't a problem. I'll look after things."

But it *was* a problem. Will's thirteen-year-old son was much too comfortable shouldering the responsibilities of an adult. He'd been doing it since he was four.

But there was not a damn thing Will could do about it. Not now. "Thank you, Nat." He smiled, a false smile that he could only hope covered the guilt. "Perhaps we can go riding, when I return." Nat loved horses, and they'd recently started riding out of the city together when Will had the time. It seemed a good way to spend time together, though they seldom talked.

Nat stopped short, and his eyes lit up. "Can I ride the gelding?"

Will's riding horse was a spirited young gelding, not fit for a beginning rider. "No, lad, not yet. The mare's a fine mount."

Nat said nothing, but his expression fell, returning to the same dull look he'd had when he came in. He nodded once more, then left the room.

Will was up before the sun to begin his journey to Auchinearn. The day was windy, though not too cold, and a thin layer of clouds were just lighting up pink and orange as he drove north out of Glasgow. He spent much of the time mulling over the mournful, anxious look on Rose's face as she had bid him goodbye . . . and the stoic, serious one on Nat's.

Will had grown up with the Halloween tradition. The glens of Strathfarrar had always burned bright with bonfires on that night, and he and the other children would dress up and race between them, wreaking all kinds of havoc. He so badly wanted the same for his own bairns, that kind of unrestrained, joyous childhood. Yet here he was, traveling to spend the holiday with another family, leaving his own behind. Even if he *could* bring them, Rosie would be afraid, and Nat would probably think himself too old for the fun. Childhood was lost to them.

Will used to get angry at these thoughts. He used to rage at the system that put them where they were, but now . . . now that rage had all burned through him, leaving only the ashes. The system was at fault, surely, but so was he. He'd done the best he knew how, but it just hadn't been good enough.

What would Ann have thought?

She'd been gone so long, his Ann, the love of his youth, the mother of his children. Funny, he never felt her censure when he was with Cybil. His and Ann's marriage bed had been different from what he shared with Cybil, no doubt, but it had been a great joy to them both. Ann understood him. She never would have begrudged him his pleasure. But the children . . . that was a different matter. Ann had been such a devoted mother, a happy, carefree soul, always laughing and singing. She would have been so disappointed to see what had become of the family she left behind.

And now there was another child to think of. *Christ.* Will was already a piss-poor father. 'Twas too much, but it didn't matter. The babe was his family too, his responsibility. To have its care foisted on others was unthinkable. He'd mulled it over every which way, and there just weren't any other options. He'd have to bring Cybil's child into his household.

But how? It wasn't as if he could claim it as his own.

The question rolled in his mind as he left the city and came into the more sparsely populated suburbs. The sun was fully up now, and a light mist was rising over the fields. It would be a warm day for the season.

He could leave the infant on his own doorstep, as if some desperate mother had abandoned it there, then adopt it. But why would someone leave a child on Will's doorstep? It would seem suspicious, especially if it looked like him. No, the bairn needed a story, a reputable one.

What if—his mind flickered back to the notice he'd written seeking a new teacher. What if he hired someone, a housekeeper perhaps, and paid her to pretend to be the babe's mother? That held possibility . . . no one would question it. But it would mean trusting a stranger with his secret, and to ask someone to become a child's mother—even if it were only an act—it would be too much.

Maybe there was someone already in his household who might help? He didn't employ many servants, just a maid, a footman and a cook, plus the char-woman who came in to help with the laundry. Were any of them trustworthy enough?

He wished he could talk it through with Cybil, but every time he'd tried to bring it up, she'd brushed him off, insisting the child be sent to France. Surely, knew, deep down, that their bairn deserved more—deserved to be close to its parents, to know them, to have them looking after it—even if it didn't call them Ma or Da. Cybil didn't know what it was to be a mother yet. With time, he was sure, as she started to feel the child move inside her and it became more real, she'd understand.

And if, by then, he'd set something up that was undeniably good for all involved, she'd have to see the wisdom in it. Wouldn't she?

He'd think on the possibility of confiding in one of the servants. Perhaps they could say their sister died, leaving them ward of a child . . . or . . . something.

He arrived in Auchinearn at midday and ate a quick bite with Margaret and Agnes before climbing back into the gig and turning south toward Strathaven. The women's chatter helped take his mind off things, and gradually, he felt the weight slip from his shoulders as his anticipation of seeing Cybil grew. It was a wonder, the pull that woman had on him. Despite everything—the guilt, the lies and the secrets he had to keep—he still wanted her, and her being with child only increased his lustiness. Her soft curves, ripe and swelling with his bairn. Her sweet playful smile that could so quickly turn wanton. Ye gods, his prick was growing hard at the thought.

He could only hope she'd be happy to see him.

It was almost sunset when they drove into Emily's yard. Earlier than Will usually arrived, but there was no one lurking. There hadn't been in years, and he was too anxious to see Cybil to wait any longer. She was outside with Ewan and Luke, moving armfuls of firewood from the woodshed to the small circle of stones that would house the bonfire. She was bareheaded, wearing a red dress with a full skirt that blew about her. A tartan shawl was draped around her shoulders, and a large apron tied about her waist.

What was she doing? She was with child and not used to such labor. 'Twas dangerous for the bairn. He opened his mouth to say as much, but then she looked up at him, still laughing at something Ewan had said, and the words caught in his throat. Her cheeks were pink with exertion, her dark eyes sparkling. She was in fine fettle—happier than he'd seen her in a long time.

And she was glad to see him.

His pulse sped up. He could feel it pounding in his chest, his belly, his prick.

Hurriedly, he saw to the horse as Emily was making introductions, then he crossed the garden to join the women. They grew silent as he approached. He could feel their eyes on him.

"Ladies." Will tipped his hat to the four of them—Emily, Cybil, Agnes and Margaret. As one, they grinned back.

Will cleared his throat, then turned to Cybil. "You're looking fine today, Mrs. Smith."

Cybil nodded, an amused quirk on her lips. "Thank you, Mr. Chisolm."

"I wondered if you'd care to come for a walk with me." He allowed his eyes to move up and down her body, telling her without words what he really wanted. Then he raised a brow and allowed a small grin to slip through, asking her if she wanted it too.

Cybil's brows rose in response. "A walk?" she mused. "But it's nearly dark."
"A short walk."

"Supper'll be a while yet," Emily piped up. "I'm just about to put the bannock in." She grinned at them. "It'll be ready when you return." Then she turned to Margaret and Agnes. "Callie's set to come with Johnnie at half eight. We'll light the fire then."

Callie was Purlie Wilson's daughter—Purlie being another one of the men who'd lost his life to the gallows four years before. Callie and her son John lived in Strathaven and were some of the only friends Emily still had in the village.

Will playfully winged his arm at Cybil. "Shall we then, m'lady?"

Cybil rolled her eyes, but she'd already relented. She snaked her arms behind her to untie her apron, deposited it in Emily's waiting hands, then threaded her arm through his.

"You and your brother better not eat all that shortbread," she called over her shoulder to Ewan as Will led her out of the yard and onto the street.

When they got there, Will hesitated, not sure which way to turn. Cybil looked left and up the hill, her eyes tracking a figure who was walking away from them. Then she turned right, pulling Will along with her.

It was a warm day for late October, but windy, with wisps of clouds shrouding the pale blue of the sky. Dry leaves danced around them and crackled underfoot as they walked down the dirt lane.

"You're getting on, then?" Will glanced over just in time to meet Cybil's eyes.

"I like it here." She smiled. "It's simple."

They walked in silence for a while, listening to the rattling of the wind through the dry leaves. Finally, Cybil looked at him again, her eyes twinkling mischief. "So . . . what exactly did you have in mind for this . . . *walk*?"

Will feigned innocence. He shrugged. "I just thought to stretch my legs after the drive. 'Tis been a long day." He faked a yawn.

"Let's go to the cemetery." Cybil's eyes tracked to a small staircase cut into the stone wall that bordered the street. Another, taller stone wall lay beyond, and he could just make out the pointed tops of gravestones. "I've wanted to, ever since I realized it was there."

"A cemetery on Halloween," Will mused. "How fitting."

It took them a few minutes to find the iron gate that provided entrance to the burial ground. It creaked as Will pushed it open, then it shut behind them with a clang. Long rows of weathered gravestones, green with moss, stretched out before them, some tall, others lying flat on the ground.

Cybil walked to the nearest one, then squinted to read the inscription.

"Here lies the corpses of William Paterson and John Barrie who were"—she bent down to get a closer look—"*shot* to death for . . . *adhering* to the word of God and our Covenants." She looked up at Will, a gleam in her eye. "In 1685, that was. There's a story there." She narrowed her gaze. "What was the *real* reason they were shot, do you suppose?"

But Will didn't want to speak of death, or shootings. Not now. He had other things on his mind, and instead of answering, he advanced on her.

Her eyes widened at his approach. She backed up one slow stride. Two. Then, without warning, she wheeled around and ran deeper into the cemetery.

"*Cybil.*" He ran to keep up. "You canna exert yourself."

She just laughed at him, luring him on.

He sprinted after her, past the rows of weathered stone, paying no mind when his hat was blown off his head. When he was near enough, he reached out to grasp her arm. She let out a peal of laughter, feigned struggle for a moment, then gave up and let herself be drawn under the spreading branches of an ancient yew tree. It was quiet there, and dark, the air heavy with the smell of decaying yew needles. The bark of the tree was rough, with deep crevices furrowing its surface. Even if he and Cybil had joined hands, they wouldn't have been able to circle the wide trunk.

"Naughty wench." He pushed her against the tree and leaned over her, bracing his hands on either side of her head. She gazed up at him, her dazed, heavy-lidded eyes tracking his mouth as he lowered it to hers.

There was something about the way Cybil kissed—yielding and soft, yet demanding and strong at the same time, luring him deeper, ensnaring him. Just like the woman herself. Ye gods, he could kiss her forever, just like this, sheltered from the wind and the world under the towering tree. He left her lips and bent to kiss her neck, her collarbone, the tops of her breasts. She leaned back, opening herself as his arms came around her, ran down her back, grasped her arse. Then he lifted her and rubbed her mound against his cockstand.

She groaned.

"You want this, dinna ye, lass?" He growled in her ear as he mashed her cunny against him. She gasped, and he nipped her neck with his teeth. "Say it. Tell me what you want."

She hesitated, so he bit her again. "*Say* it."

"I—I want you—to fuck me. Now." Her voice trembled, and all thought was washed away by the desire flooding Will's mind, drowning out reason.

She shrieked as he lifted her higher and turned her 'round so she was facing the rough bark of the tree. Her feet balanced on a protruding root and elevated her to the perfect height. Straddling the root, Will bent down and grabbed the hem of her skirt, then pulled it up to expose the pale backs of her legs and the soft pillowy flesh of her arse. The cold air caused the gooseflesh to rise on her skin, and she shuddered as he slid a hand between her legs. Testing.

Christ. She was so wet. So smooth. So ready.

With one hand he held up her skirt, while with the other he fumbled open the buttons on his trousers, freeing his aching prick. The wind blew cold against the hot and he must be inside her. Now. He bent and growled in her ear—not a word, just a raw, bestial command that only Cybil would understand. Obediently, she took hold of the hem of her skirt, then braced her hands against the tree and arched her back, pushing her arse toward him.

Both hands free now, he reached down and opened her wide, exposing the rich pink folds, the puckered flesh of her back entrance. He sucked in a breath at the sight, then he dipped a finger into her, two fingers. She was slick, hot and lush. She shuddered at his touch, head listing backward limply as she ground into his hand, taking him deeper. She turned her head slightly, and in the profile, he saw she was biting her lip to keep from crying out, her teeth digging into the moist pink of her flesh.

He moved one hand to grasp her hip as he guided himself in, burying his cock inside the perfect wet heat of her quim.

Cybil's lip escaped her teeth, and she let out a low, earthy moan as slowly, he withdrew, then impaled her again, harder this time, shoving her into the tree. Each thrust was more than the last. Pushing harder. Delving deeper. Growling and snarling like a wild beast. The contrast of the cool air on his prick, then the heat of her closing around him . . .

She matched his rhythm, pushing into him with equal measure. Urging him on with her body, her words. "Harder. God. Please. Yes."

Until, all too soon, his balls tightened, and he was hurdling over the edge, spilling his seed deep inside. Her muscles contracted around him as she found her own pleasure, squeezing the spend out of him. Accepting every bit.

He wrapped his arms around her, holding her as the tremors of their joining echoed through them both.

When they'd caught their breaths, he gave her one last squeeze, then gently slipped himself out of her, letting her skirt fall into place.

She accepted his outstretched hand, then stepped down from the root. "I thought—I feared we'd never do that again," she murmured. "But we are—we did—I'm glad."

"Aye," Will agreed, biting back a grin. He loved her like this, the woman who knew every word in the dictionary, at a loss for words.

She bent to gather the shawl she'd let drop, and when she straightened, he noticed—*her shape was changed.* Her belly had a new curve to it. Without thinking, he brought his hand there, feeling the firmness under the softness of her flesh. The flesh that held, and nourished, his child.

He looked to her face, the emotion thick in his throat. She was watching him with an inscrutable expression. Their play had been short, but she appeared satisfied—her cheeks were flushed, her hair had fallen out of its pins on one side, and her lower lip was marked red from where she'd bit it. A light scratch ran down one cheek, likely from the tree bark.

Will raised his hand from her stomach to trace the mark on her cheek. "You're hurt. We must take more care, now that—"

"I'm not made of porcelain." Batting him away, she turned and ducked under the branches, then disappeared from sight. Cursing, Will followed. He emerged to see her already twenty feet away, walking back toward the entrance of the cemetery. It was now nearly dark, with a full moon rising yellow and huge in the east.

He'd have a devil of a time finding his hat.

But she'd already found it. She bent to pick it up, then looked back at him impatiently. Even like this, she was beautiful. Cast in moonlight, the wind whipping her hair in every direction, leaves swirling around her skirt.

An aching sort of sadness fell over him. For the first time since he and Cybil had started this affair, there was something missing, or—something between them. Holding them apart.

What he wouldn't give to go back in time, to be the happy, lusty people they'd once been. No barriers. No distance. Perhaps once the child was accounted for, once he'd solved that puzzle and put their minds at ease, they could be.

FOURTEEN

CYBIL WATCHED WILL MAKE his way past the rows of gleaming white grave-stones. The rising moon was just over his head, shrouded in gossamer wisps of clouds, but still bright enough to bounce pure alabaster light off his dark curls and cast his eyes in forbidding shadow.

Oh, he was handsome, with his broad shoulders and his rugged, planed features. She still felt a pang of desire when she remembered the scrape of his day-old beard against her skin, the way he'd roughly entered her from behind and pounded her against that tree . . . But why did he have to go and muck up such a perfect encounter with his irksome new habit of treating her like some sort of beloved, breakable object?

It had been quite obvious what he wanted from the moment he'd stepped down from his gig and raked her body up and down with those golden hazel eyes. Even Emily had seen it, and probably the two women he'd brought with him from Auchinearn. Cybil had been resolved to keep him at a distance, but the pull of those eyes . . . it was irresistible. She'd wanted it just as badly as he did. And it had been glorious—fast and intense and raw and just what she'd needed. But then he'd touched her protruding stomach and given her a look of tender care that left her feeling like a caged animal.

This child was not his. *She* was not his. Even if she wanted to be, it was an impossibility. Why couldn't he understand that?

He finally arrived to where she stood waiting. Silently, she held out his hat, and he took it, giving her a look that was some cross of pity and confusion and only left her feeling more frustrated. She turned and began walking back toward the iron gate.

"Wait." His voice followed her.

She didn't wait, but he caught up with her anyway, just as she passed through the gate. He followed her down the narrow stone stairway, then they fell into step on the road.

"I dinna ken what I've done, exactly, but I'm sorry," he panted, sounding weary. When she didn't reply, he continued, "Cybil, what's wrong—"

"I've started writing again." She couldn't let him keep talking.

Will sighed in resignation, or frustration, but he let it pass. "Really? A story?" He sounded vaguely interested.

"A novel."

"What's it about?"

She gave him a brief description of what she'd written so far. Louisa and her unborn child. The evil husband.

"But you havena come up with the father of her bairn yet?" He was interested now.

"No." Cybil had spent the last week trying to work that out, to no avail. "I'd like him to be not quite human, but—not a monster either. And not a ghost. Something in between. A fairy maybe? Or a selkie? Do you know much about those?"

Will considered. He was something of an expert on Scottish folklore from his childhood in the Highlands. It wasn't the first time she'd prodded him for ideas. "Do you know the ballad of Tam Lin?" he asked. "I wonder if there's not somethin' you could use there."

"Tam Lin . . . no. It's Scottish?"

He nodded. "I was just thinkin' of it. 'Tis a Halloween tale, but not so scary as some of the others. I thought Ewan might like it if he doesna ken it yet."

"Tell me."

He turned toward her, a teasing grin playing on his lips and his dimple on full display. "I'll warn ye. It has a happy ending."

Cybil raised a brow. "Endings can be changed."

He chuckled, then cleared his throat and began. "There was a fair lass, the daughter of a laird. Janet was her name, and she was bonny. Yellow hair that fell down to her knee. Eyes as blue as—"

"She was beautiful. I understand," Cybil interrupted dryly. Will laughed. He knew her distaste for the typical fair-haired heroine.

"I dinna actually ken what color her eyes were," he confessed. "But her hair *was* yellow. I remember that. 'Twas probably matted, though, and dull." They'd been walking side by side, and without warning, he grasped her hand, holding it as he continued the tale. "One day, this Janet was off by herself in the wood, and she met a fairy knight named Tam Lin. Now, *he* must have been a handsome cove, and convincing too, because not long after she found herself with child."

With child? Cybil studied Will's face, only a darkened profile in the gathering night, but he didn't notice her looking. He was gazing straight ahead, lost in the telling.

"Janet's da and brother were none too happy, and not long after, she found herself back in those woods. But this time, she was lookin' for certain plants, herbs that would . . . rid her of her problem."

He glanced at Cybil. She quickly looked away.

There was a moment's silence, then he continued. "Weel, lo and behold, Tam Lin appeared, and when he saw what Janet was doin', he begged her not to do it. Turns out he was a mortal lad, a noble's son who'd been havin' a nap in the forest and'd been caught by the fairy queen. Enchanted. He implored Janet to keep her bairn, said he'd be a father to it, but she'd have to free him from the fairy curse first."

"Free him," Cybil repeated.

"Aye, on Halloween night, the fairy queen leads all her knights out into the human world, somethin' about meeting with the devil." A gig came into view up the hill, and Will dropped Cybil's hand, instead threading his arm through hers. "Tam told Janet to find him that night," he continued, "at a certain crossroad, and to pull him down from his horse. She'd know him because he'd be on a milk white steed, and he'd be wearin' only one glove. Then she was to hold tight to him no matter what, until she could bear it no more. Then she must let go, and the queen's curse would be broken."

"Only one glove? That's rather odd."

Will nodded at the gig driver as it passed. "'Tis how the story goes. Anyway, she did as he said. She pulled him down from that horse. But the fairy queen was a crafty ol' cat. She turned Tam into a snake with the sharpest of fangs, then a fox, then a stag. But Janet didna let go. The queen turned him to a red-hot coal. It burned Janet's hand, and she threw it down a well. She thought she'd lost 'im . . . but then," he paused dramatically, "Tam appeared before her, whole, and naked as the day he was born."

"Naked?"

"Aye. The queen was right mad, but there was nothin' she could do. The curse was broken. Janet took Tam home, and that was that." Will chuckled. "I always wondered what her da thought of her comin' home with a naked man, but that was never part of the tale. They were married, had their bairn and lived happy together till the end of their days."

"What a strange story." But Cybil's mind was already whirring with the possibilities. An enchanted knight. That was good, especially if he were kind and handsome and offered escape from Louisa's troubles in his arms—

"Cybil?" Will's expectant voice broke into her thoughts. She started, realizing that they were back at Emily's house. She'd nearly walked right by.

———◇———

As promised, Callie and her son Johnnie arrived at half eight. Cybil had met Callie once before when she'd come for tea the previous week. She was a widow who lived outside Strathaven, the only daughter of another one of the men who'd been executed as part of the upheaval four years ago. Johnnie was close in age to Luke, and the two boys appointed themselves firekeepers, adding logs when needed and making torches from thick tree limbs to wave about. Much to their mothers' dismay, they marked their faces black with the ash and made a racket, moaning and shrieking like ghouls.

Will had brought apples and nuts, which were apparently the foods one ate on Halloween, though Ewan was the only one who wanted to try dookin. Emily questioned him, hinting that it wasn't perhaps as delightful or easy as he supposed. But he insisted, so she obligingly floated three apples in a small tub of water. Will demonstrated how it was done, slowly lowering his face into the tub, then coming up with an apple in his teeth and only the front bit of his hair wet. He then stood back with the other adults and watched as the small boy tried it out. After only three attempts, Ewan's face, hair and shirt were thoroughly soaked, and he was sobbing at the disappointment of it.

"We can try again next year," Emily crooned as she ushered him inside to put on dry clothes. Ten minutes later, they reemerged and Will told the story of Tam Lin, though he omitted the part about Janet being with child and told it as a simple story of a woman in love with an enchanted knight. By the time he was finished, Ewan was asleep on Emily's lap and the two older boys had calmed. They sat together, poking sticks into the fire.

The women—Emily with the sleeping Ewan, Callie, Agnes and Margaret—were settled on one side of the dying fire, chatting about their lives since their last reunion. They seemed a close group of friends indeed. Will and Cybil sat on a large log on the other side, their bodies pressed together.

Thankfully, Will had said no more of the child she carried or her supposed weakened state. And it was pleasant, with his arm around her and the warmth of the hot coals soaking into her body. Cybil studied the women opposite them, their faces reflecting the glowing light. They looked like any group of friends—laughing, reminiscing, giving each other bits of gossip—but of course they were not. They were the most extraordinary group Cybil could imagine. Young Margaret, rosy-cheeked and fair-haired, had lost her sweetheart to the gallows. And as if that weren't enough, the poor boy's body had been beheaded in front of the crowd. Emily had told Cybil that despite her friends' and her mother's advice, Margaret had attended the execution so her beloved would know to the very end just how much he was loved. Callie's father, Purlie, had shared the same fate. The night after he'd been killed, Callie and her niece had sneaked to the unmarked grave he'd been put in, in Glasgow, dug up the coffin and moved his body back to Strathaven where they'd buried him in the backyard of their home. And Emily's husband, Davey, well, he wasn't dead, but he might as well have been.

And according to Will, all of it was because of government men, disguised as radicals, who worked for Viscount Sidmouth.

It still seemed so strange, that connection. Ernie had been such an admirer the Viscount, and Cybil had hosted him plenty of times. He'd been out of power when Cybil was in London, but he'd been hungry to return and had, apparently, been successful. According to the papers, he'd been appointed Home Secretary the year after she'd left. Perhaps Will's loathing of the man colored her memory, but even still, there had been something menacing about him, his eyes in particular . . . they were cold and biting.

She couldn't have written a better villain if she'd tried.

"Did you ever meet the man who betrayed Margaret's beau?" Cybil kept her voice low, not wanting to interrupt the women's conversation.

"Oliver?" Will said bitterly. "Not *met* exactly, but I saw him once at a tavern meeting."

"Could you tell he was . . ." Cybil hesitated, unsure what to label the man.

"A damned spy?" Will turned to her, and the contempt in his eyes stole her breath.

She nodded, not knowing what to say.

Will turned back to stare into the fire, then spoke more quietly, almost under his breath. "No, I couldna. Same as I couldna tell Wilcox was a bloody blackleg neither."

"Wilcox. That's the man who suggested you blow up the bridge?"

"*Suggested*." Will snorted. "'Twas his plan. We just went along." He paused, then muttered, "Idiots that we were."

"No sense in dwelling on it now," Cybil soothed. She was sorry she'd brought it up. She'd not meant to send Will into a black mood. She snuggled closer, breathing in the clean woolen scent of his coat. "I'm glad you're here."

"Mmmh . . ." His arms tightened around her.

"You'll leave in the morning?"

"Aye. I'll come back in three days to bring Margo and Agnes home."

"It must be difficult to leave home so often."

Will gazed into the fire. His lack of denial was a clear sign that it was, indeed, difficult.

A sudden wave of warmth crested in Cybil's chest. It wasn't Will's fault that she was in this situation. She'd led him to believe she was barren, that their couplings could have no consequence. Yet, he'd been nothing but kind. He'd even seemed to give up on the notion that it was his duty to find a place for the child. She'd told him she didn't wish to speak of it, that it was her decision and she would make it on her own time, and he'd listened. It was true that she found his instinct to protect her aggravating, but would she really have wanted the alternative, for him to leave her entirely to her own devices?

Poor Will. She'd put him in an impossible position, hadn't she?

And he was such a good man.

Cybil snuggled closer to her lover. Emily had given her bed to Agnes for the duration of her stay, and she and Margaret were planning to sleep in the weaver's room with Cybil. Will had been assigned a pallet upstairs, with the boys. But that didn't mean Cybil couldn't show Will just how much she appreciated him.

She craned her neck to whisper in his ear. "Shall we go on another walk before we retire?" She nibbled at his earlobe.

Will chuckled. "Canna get enough, can ye, lass?" He made a show of stretching his limbs, then rose and extended a hand. "I do believe I'll get some air before I turn in," he said loudly. "Would you care to join me, Mrs. Smith?"

She grinned and took his hand. "That sounds lovely. It *is* rather warm by the fire."

Will pulled her to her feet, and they made their way into the chill night air, followed by the giggles of the four women who remained.

FIFTEEN

WILL LEFT EARLY THE next morning, with a promise to return in three days for Margaret and her mother. His visit left Cybil inspired, and all day long she wanted nothing more than to write, to flesh out the Tam Lin story. But the added activity in the house with the visitors made it impossible.

It was market day, and after breakfast, Emily and Margaret took Ewan into town, leaving Agnes and Cybil alone. The midwife ushered her into the weaver's room, then bombarded her with questions about her pregnancy—when she'd last had her courses, how she felt now, how she'd felt in all the weeks since she'd conceived, what she knew of her mother's and grandmothers' experiences of childbearing. After Cybil had answered everything, she was submitted to an examination that included her abdomen being thoroughly poked and prodded, then an inspection of the color and aroma of her urine—after which Agnes declared the baby was most likely a boy. Thankfully, the midwife did not feel it necessary to view Cybil's female anatomy. Will was the only one who ever looked at that part of her, and though of course it would be on display when her labors began, she was happy to avoid the embarrassment for now.

In fact, the examination proved much more comfortable than Cybil had expected. Agnes was of a similar age to Mother, but she had none of Mother's judgemental air, nor the self-serving melancholy. The midwife dressed plainly, as befitting her station as a farmer's widow. Wisps of white hair escaped her white cotton mobcap, which was tied under her chin with a thick black ribbon. A rust-colored woolen shawl was wrapped around her shoulders. Her grey eyes, the same eyes as her daughter's, were kind yet sharp at the same time, as if she noticed things that others did not. There was something nourishing about her presence that Cybil couldn't quite explain.

Cybil reclined on the bed during the examination. When it was finished, Agnes helped her rise to a seated position.

"You're gettin' along just fine, lassie." Agnes smoothed her apron over her skirt. "I'd expect your wee one'll come the middle o' April." She studied Cybil, tilting her head to one side. "Have you thought of what you'll do when he's born?"

Cybil froze. She'd not expected *this* question. A midwife's only worry was getting the child out safely, was it not? What did she care what became of it after? Yet, the woman had asked, and Cybil found herself unable, or unwilling, to betray the kindness in her eyes.

"I plan to find someone—a family—to take it." She tried but couldn't bring herself to meet Agnes's gaze. "If you know anyone . . ." She let her voice trail off.

"And what does William think?" Agnes was the only person Cybil knew who called Will by his full name.

"He thinks—I don't know what he thinks, exactly. We haven't spoken of it."

Agnes's brow furrowed. "He hasna proposed marriage to ye?"

"No," Cybil said quickly. "I can't—or—" She closed her eyes, as if that could stop the woman's judgement. "I can't marry."

"Ahhh." Understanding colored the midwife's voice, then she patted the top of Cybil's hand. Cybil opened her eyes and gazed down at the old woman's fingers, knobby and work-roughened, yet incredibly gentle.

"It willna be easy then," Agnes murmured. "Best to start talkin' of it now."

Cybil forced herself to meet the woman's dove-grey eyes, then without warning, her own welled with tears. They overflowed, tracking warmth, then chill down her cheeks. She wiped her face with the back of her hand.

"Ach, lassie." Agnes drew Cybil into an embrace. "William's a fine man, and you're stronger than ye think. Ye'll find a way."

———— •✦• ————

In those long, dreary months of my imprisonment, I would often steal away from my husband's house and wander, solitary, through the barren heath. In truth, I found no comfort in that bleak expanse. The windswept landscape was too open, too exposed, the vault of the sky too vast. It eroded my spirit, carving away what little felicity remained. But the alternative—to dwell forever locked inside the cramped confines of my chamber—was more unbearable still. So, I roamed farther and farther afield, until one day, I came upon a wood in the far reaches of the estate.

It was a lush, tangled grove, thick with gnarled oak and shimmering birch. Rose brambles grew rank upon the ground, their sharp thorns protecting the beauty within. It called to me in seductive whispers, luring me into its dark embrace. The verdant green, the deepening shadows, the lambent sunlight beaming down like slanting veils of gold . . . it seemed a balm, meant to sooth my agonized soul. I approached, and as if by magic, the roses gave way and a path appeared, leading into the silent, enchanted forest.

I did not hesitate. I entered the wood. And there, I met Tam Lin.

Cybil set the pen in its holder and sat back to read what she'd just written, blowing gently on the wet ink. The more she'd pondered the tale of Tam Lin, the more perfect it seemed. It wouldn't be an exact retelling, of course. Unlike Will's Janet, Cybil's heroine was married, and she wouldn't have yellow hair. Louisa's hair was black as night, and she was strong, claiming the comfort she needed from Tam Lin then wresting him loose from the spell of the all-powerful fairy queen. Louisa's fate would be tragic, but she would never cry. Would never doubt herself, or give in to despair. She would take her pleasure, then accept her punishment without flinching.

Cybil arched her back, stretching out the kinks. She used one hand to massage the tender spot between her thumb and index finger. Emily and Margaret's whispered late-night conversations in the weaver's room had made it impossible to work in there, so she'd brought her pen and ink into the main room where she'd sat hunched over the table for the last hour. Agnes's snores sounded softly from the bed.

She read the last sentence aloud, though quietly, so as not to wake the old woman. *I did not hesitate. I entered the wood. And there I met Tam Lin.* Then she picked up her pen again, held it just above the paper—but the only words that came were the midwife's from earlier in the day. *You're stronger than ye think. Ye'll find a way.*

But Cybil wasn't strong, was she? She couldn't even bring herself to think, much less talk, of her child's future. As if not thinking of it would make it any less real, or easier to bear.

Her eyes closed, and her hand dropped to the table. *A boy.* He would be a boy. A breathing, smiling, laughing baby boy, with Will's eyes, his curly hair and his dimple. Cybil's mouth. Her nose.

Her hands went to her stomach. It was growing—*he* was growing.

Little man, I am so sorry.

She blinked away the tears. Clenched her jaw, and took a stealing breath. He would come from her, but he was not hers. Would never be hers. She had to accept that. She had to be strong.

She stared at the page, dipped the quill in the ink and gently tapped it against the well, then lowered it, once again, to the paper. It hovered there, but again, nothing came, or—nothing worth writing. A drop of ink, blue-black and shimmering, formed at the end of the quill, and Cybil watched as it stretched and then fell onto the blank sheet.

Sighing, she began to put her writing things away.

Louisa would have to meet Tam Lin another night.

———⚬———

The women spent Margaret and Agnes' last afternoon in Strathaven making apple jam from the nearly two bushels of apples Will had brought with him from Glasgow. He would arrive for supper, then bring them home in the morning.

Agnes oversaw the making. She measured out sugar and spice as Emily and Margaret deftly peeled the fruit, removed the cores and pared the apples into thin slices. Ewan sat across, studying a book of letters Emily had put before him. Cybil had no skill with a knife, so Agnes set her to stir the pot over the fire.

Cybil's arm was aching, but not intolerably. Her seat by the hearth was warm and pleasant, with the sweet aroma of apples and cinnamon wafting up in a cloud of steam.

And all she could think about was Jane.

She so wanted to tell these women of her friend who grew the most exquisite apples, who'd heroically saved Cybil's own brother from a dungeon, who was Cybil's best friend just as Margaret was Emily's, and was the new mother to twins.

Perhaps it was the familiar smell, or the memories, or the companionship of other women, but without warning, the homesickness hit her like a blow to the stomach, and for a few seconds, Cybil struggled to draw breath. She would have given anything, in this moment, to have Jane with her, and Henri. To be able to confide in them—

"You have a long face," Emily observed as she dumped a bowlful of apples into the pot. Cybil stirred, watching the crisp white fruit disappear into the mushy yellow mass of cooked apples.

Not knowing what else to do, she smiled, a weary, enduring smile, one intended to communicate to her friend that she was sad but could not talk of why.

"Will'll be along soon, dinna you worry." Emily's tone was reassuring.

Cybil kept the same stoic smile plastered on her face. Better to have Emily think she knew the cause of her melancholy. It would stop her asking more questions.

"Cybil," Agnes called abruptly as Emily resumed her seat, "has William ever told you of his heroics in the Highlands?" The old woman was sitting beside Ewan with her legs stretched in front of her, absently massaging one work-roughened hand with the other. Her eyes were twinkling at Cybil—clearly, she'd misinterpreted her expression just as Emily had.

Cybil looked down at the steaming mass of fruit, avoiding, for a moment, Agnes's inquisitive stare. Rose Chisolm had once told her a tale—something about Will rushing into a burning house and rescuing an old woman, but as Rose hadn't been born at the time, and the girl was prone to exaggeration, Cybil had passed it off as fiction. And she hadn't asked Will about it because—well, because they never spoke of their past, or of their lives outside the world they'd created for themselves.

Agnes must have grown tired of waiting for Cybil to respond. "Of course, William's too humble to tell the story himself, but Davey told us. Said he got it out of Will one night when they'd fuddled themselves with drink." Agnes paused, and Cybil looked up to see that Ewan had abandoned his letters and had climbed onto her lap. "'Twas early one mornin', when the laird's factor came to the glen where William lived." The old woman's voice turned soft and lilting, as if she were reciting a ballad. "They only had the one bairn then, of course, his boy Nathanial. Wee Rose hadna come yet."

"How old are Will's bairns now?" Ewan piped up.

"Have you not met them?" Cybil asked, surprised. Surely—but no. Of course not. Why would Will bring his children here and risk them keeping his secret?

Ewan shook his head. "I think I did when I was wee, before . . ." His voice trailed off. "I dinna remember."

Agnes hugged the boy tighter. "Well now, let me see." She considered for a moment. "I havena seen those bairns these last years either, but wee Rose would be . . ."

"Ten, almost eleven," Cybil supplied. "And Nat is thirteen."

Agnes nodded, then turned back to the story. "Anyway, that factor was a cruel man, as so many such men are. He had red coats with him, too, ten of 'em, all on horses and carryin' rifles. They banged on the doors of the farmhouses, tellin' all the people to get out. Then they set fire to the thatch and watched 'em burn."

"That happened to *Will's* house?" Ewan's eyes were wide.

"Aye, lad, it did," Agnes replied. "Through no fault of his own. His family'd been farmin' that land for hundreds o' years, but the laird decided to put it over to sheep instead. He evicted William's family, and all his neighbors too."

"But, *why*?" The look on Ewan's face was heartbreaking.

"Greed. Pure and simple."

Emily's voice cut in. "Ewan, why don't you go out and play. You can watch for Will."

"But I wanna hear the story," Ewan argued. "Dinna worry, Ma." He cocked his head, speaking in a reassuring tone that only betrayed his innocence. "I know nothin' like that'll ever happen to us."

Emily stared at her son. The Clearance, as Agnes described it, was only happening in the North, but certainly Emily and her boys could lose their home. They would be destitute without Will's support. Finally, she nodded to Ewan, then glanced at Agnes with a look that clearly warned the older woman to keep the story light for her son's ears.

"Weell. Will and his family got out just fine. They even had a wagon already packed with all the things they'd need in Glasgow. But their neighbor, she was an old woman—"

"As old as you?" Ewan asked.

Agnes chuckled. "Older, if ye can believe it. And ill. She was too weak to get out of her bed."

"So then . . ." Ewan's eyes were wide.

Agnes nodded. "Aye. You have it. When the soldiers came a knockin', she didna get up. She couldna. But they burned her house even still."

"On *purpose*?" Ewan turned in Agnes's lap so he could look at her face.

Agnes eyed Emily over Ewan's blonde hair. Emily shook her head. Firmly.

"Well. No one can say, can then?" Agnes said. "But what we *do* know is that the goodwife would have been burned up, surely, had it not been for our William. His family was drivin' by on their wagon, leavin' their own home behind, when he came upon them red coats just touchin' their torches to the old woman's thatch. He jumped down from that wagon, fast as can be, and asked the soldiers if an old lady had come out. They said nae, no one had come out of that house when they knocked."

"They thought she wasn't home." Ewan seemed very sure of the idea, and Agnes didn't contradict him.

"William knew better. He knew that old goodwife was stuck in her bed. But by the time he was done talkin' to the soldiers, the flames were leapin' high into the air." Agnes's voice rose as she described the scene. "'Twas mornin' still, but the sky was black as night from all the fires burnin' in that glen.'"

Cybil shivered. Imagining Will, his wife and child, the burning houses.

"William didna think of the danger. He ran into that house, thick with smoke though it was, and sure enough, there she was lying on her bed, half dead from fright."

"But she wasna burned up yet?"

"Nae. He got to her in time. He picked her up and ran out. No sooner had he got through the front door than the whole roof fell in, burnin' ever last inch of what was inside.

There was a long pause.

"Will saved her life." Ewan's small voice was full of wonder.

"Aye. That he did, an' he brought the old woman to her daughter's family before he left for Glasgow."

"Did her daughter's family lose their house too?"

"I suppose they did."

"What happened to them?"

"I'm sure they're fine," Emily answered before Agnes could.

Cybil knew enough about the Clearance to know that the chances of them being fine were quite slim. Probably either they'd been moved to a croft on the coast and were hungry, or they'd booked passage to America. And the odds of an old, sickly woman surviving the passage were poor indeed.

"Ewan." Emily's tone broached no argument. "Go on out and play now. Your brother will be along shortly." Luke hadn't been waylaid by the bullies again, but Emily had confided her worry for her older son in Cybil. He seemed quieter than usual, she'd said, since the attack. Sullen.

Wordlessly, Ewan slipped off Agnes's lap. He donned his coat and went out the back door.

As soon as they were alone, Emily fixed Agnes with an accusing stare.

Agnes shrugged. "He's got to know the way of the world some time. Why, his own father is—"

"Hush, Mama." Margaret was usually so quiet that Cybil sometimes forgot she was there, but when she *did* speak, both her mother and Emily tended to listen.

Agnes said nothing. She rose and came back to the pot, peering down into it. "Keep stirrin', lassie." She bent to add a log to the fire. "We'll let it boil full out for a bit, then I'll check if it's set."

With each circle of the wooden spoon, more apples disintegrated into the hot, formless mass. Bubbles started to appear on the surface. Tiny at first, then larger, more insistent. It was mesmerizing, and Cybil found herself thinking of the witches' song from MacBeth.

Double, double toil and trouble
Fire burn and caldron bubble

One large bubble broke, flinging hot applesauce onto Cybil's forearm. She flinched but didn't stop stirring. The women had put so much work in, that it would be unthinkable to let the jam scald due to one tiny burn.

One tiny burn. What injuries had Will sustained when he went into that burning house? Surely, he could have lost his life in the effort . . . and yet, he'd gone. Like the most selfless of heroes, he'd done what needed to be done.

Just as he had for Cybil. And for Emily. And his children.

Cybil had imagined she'd never feel passion or warmth toward him—or any man—again. But she'd proven that idea false, hadn't she? Maybe there would be a way to keep on, with what they'd had, after—

The door opened, and Ewan burst in with a rush of cold air, followed by Luke. "Will's here!" the younger boy cried. "He's just comin' down the hill!"

SIXTEEN

CYBIL WAS STANDING BY the back door when Will drove into Emily's yard. She'd put on her pelisse to ward away the cold, but beneath it, she wore a plain work dress covered by an apron. Her hair was pulled into a loose bun, and a bright smile lit her face as she watched him climb down from the gig.

He could get used to this—a beautiful woman welcoming him home. A pity he'd have to leave her again so soon. He'd promised Nat he'd be home before dark tomorrow night, so they'd have time for a quick ride in the Green. And that meant he'd need to be gone with Margo and Agnes at first light.

"You look pleased to see me." He took both her hands and squeezed them. He'd have liked to kiss her, but he could see Ewan's curious face in the window.

"I *am* pleased to see you." A gust of wind whipped around them, and she shivered. Her shoulders tightened. "It's frigid out here, though. Come in. We made apple jam." She grinned and tugged him toward the door.

Apple jam. Christ, he *could* get used to this. Will released her hands and turned to the horse. "As soon I'm done here."

The night flew by—too quickly. It was a miserable evening for a walk, cloudy with a cold, biting wind, but they took one anyway after supper, just to be alone. Cybil told him of her novel and her ideas for Tam Lin. He told her of the work being done on the new factories and his idea to add a nursery to the workers' school—a place where mothers could safely leave their infants while at work. They did not, however, speak of their own bairn. Of course, Cybil didn't mention it, and Will hadn't had the time to develop his ideas yet. Better to wait.

When they returned, Will could sense neither of them wanted the night to be finished, so on a whim, he pulled Cybil into the goat shed. There was barely room for the two of them, and no windows, but it was warm and protected from the wind. They made do.

Afterward, they settled on the earthen floor, Cybil nestled between his legs, her head leaning against his chest. Will sat with his back to the bare board wall, his chin resting on the top of her head and his arms looped securely around her.

They were silent for a long while, the only sounds the wailing of the wind, the rustling of the livestock and the small, contented murmurs of Will and his lover. He could feel her heartbeat under his hands. His seemed to beat in time.

"Can you not stay a bit, in the morning?" she finally asked. "I could read what I have of the Tam Lin story to you. I'd love to hear your thoughts."

Will waited a few breaths before answering. It had been an enchanted night, and he was reluctant to break the spell, but of course it had to come to an end. "I canna. I must be home tomorrow in good time. I've promised Nat—"

"Never mind. I shouldn't have asked." She reached up and rubbed her eyes. Her voice was dull.

Will squeezed her tighter, but it did no good. She was slipping away.

These two lives would tear him apart.

"When will you return?" she asked wearily.

"Not for a while. Three weeks or more, I'd expect. After these two visits, I've—it's hard to leave them, Cybil."

"Your children?"

"Aye."

There was a long pause.

"I understand. Truly." She paused. "You're a good father."

"I'm tryin' to be."

———◇———

In the lambent light of the forest, in the shelter of the trees, the shackles of my miserable existence seemed to fall away. I was beholden to none, my heart winged to gentle ecstasy by the sweet breeze that ruffled the birch leaves, the sun tinctured air. In that fleeting, perfect moment, my mind was freed.

And then, I beheld a man.

He was shrouded in the shade of a towering boulder, a silhouette in the dark. But I could feel his eyes upon me, his unwavering adamantine gaze.

My heart leapt in my breast, and I stopped short, not knowing him for friend or foe. Was he an inimical wretch, a depraved bandit or murderer encroached on my husband's lands? Would he kidnap me for ransom, or kill me, my fair form never to be found?

He did not move, nay, he seemed not to breathe, but to be a statue—a man made of stone. And for many long, fraught moments, we stared at each other as I awaited my fate.

But then, as I gazed upon his dark visage, something strange happened. I did not lose my fear, yet I was drawn to him. There was something in his eyes, some enchantment, some allurement, a promise of tender joy.

I took a step forward. Then another.

"I mean you no harm." His voice was deep and melodious as a cataract falling over myriad stones. Slowly, he moved from shadow into light.

Her pen stopped.

How to describe Tam Lin's appearance. That was a puzzle.

The usual hero was beautiful, benign and unthreatening. Brave perhaps, but more a boy than a man. Cybil wanted Tam to be different, complex and dark. Like the typical villain perhaps, passionate and mysterious, but with a heart of gold.

Like Will.

The paper blurred, and she cast the quill aside, then allowed her hands to cover her face. Her fingertips pressed against her closed eyes, pushing away the tears.

She'd tried not to show him how disappointed she'd been last night, when he told her he couldn't stay, that he wouldn't be back for three weeks. It had been such a wonderful night, the happiest time they'd spent together since

Cameron's wedding. And she'd thought with a bit more time, perhaps she'd even be able to gather her courage and broach the subject of their child's fate.

But now she'd have to wait three weeks. Perhaps more. He'd been gone only a day, and already, she ached for him.

What *was* this? Cybil rubbed her eyes, but still, the tears threatened. She'd always enjoyed her time with Will, but she'd never pined for him, not like this. What had changed?

Everything. Everything had changed.

A sudden energy infused her limbs, and heat spread across her chest. Of their own volition, her fists drove down and pounded the mattress, jostling the lap desk and nearly upsetting the inkpot.

Why couldn't she have love? It was so close, she could feel it, see it. It was like an image, a mirage appeared before her then yanked away.

She closed her eyes and forced a long, slow breath. She'd made her choices—headstrong, and foolish as they'd been—and she'd known, when she'd began her affair with Will, what would happen. She'd known it would only lead to misery.

She'd known, yet she'd done it anyway. And now, she must bear the consequences.

Will would never be her hero.

There would never be love between them. There *could* never be love between them.

There were no happy endings.

She had to accept that.

She wiped the tears away, then furiously shook her hands out, grasped the quill and began to write.

He was the most beautiful man I'd ever beheld, his yellow curls gleaming in the golden light, his brow smooth as alabaster, his eyes innocent and as azure as the sparkling South Seas. His form was slight and lithe, his silver-toned voice like a soothing—

No. She couldn't do it. She hated that man, that beautiful, innocent blonde boy with no secrets, and no flaws, who was modest, and amiable, and could never bring himself to tell a lie, who lived in the light, tiptoeing about harmlessly.

Louisa could never love such a man, and he would never understand, nor love her—not truly.

Cybil snatched up the paper and crumpled it, then threw it across the room. She wanted darkness. She wanted brooding, heavy brows and old, mysterious scars. An overwhelming passion that left her breathless with desire one moment and gasping with laughter the next. She wanted a hero with secrets. A hero who told lies and thoughtlessly sacrificed himself for those he loved. A hero who understood and accepted her—*all* of her. Who loved her, and was loved in return.

This was fiction, not real life, and what did it matter if the critics hated it? Blast it, she would write the hero that Louisa deserved.

She put a blank sheet before her and, once again, began to write.

SEVENTEEN

THE NEXT THREE WEEKS went by in a blur. Will spent as much time with his bairns as he could, trying to make up for his absences. Nat was still sulking about having to ride the mare, and Rose was still her fearful, timid self, but in all, they seemed content, or, as content as they normally were.

Then there were the factories. The new ones were getting close to production, and workers had to be hired. There seemed an endless stream of people needing employment in Glasgow, and it was a trying process deciding who to take on and who to turn away. It wore on him.

Will also took some time to ponder the question of the babe, and after much thought, he called his cook into his study and told her the bare bones of the story. Mrs. Goode seemed surprised, but not scandalized. Certainly, he wasn't the first man to find himself in a position like this, and Mrs. Goode approved of the fact that he planned to take responsibility for his child. For an increase in her wages, she agreed to take the babe into her care and claim it as her niece, or nephew, recently orphaned.

He couldn't wait to tell Cybil, and even leaving the bairns for a night didn't smart as it had when he finally climbed into the gig and turned on the road toward Strathaven.

The weather turned cold as he drove, and big downy flakes began to fall just before he reached Emily's, disappearing to nothing as they hit the ground. It reminded Will of the cotton that floated in the air at the spinning factories, only colder and wetter.

His heart skipped a beat when he thought he saw Wilcox walking on the road just outside the village. But whomever it was turned off in another direction. Will shook himself. Emily hadn't seen anything of worry in years, and Wilcox himself hadn't been seen or heard of since the canal—and with good reason. Glasgow, or even Strathaven, was a dangerous place for a scoundrel like Wilcox. Not everyone sympathized with the cause, but there were enough of them left that he'd be wise to think twice before showing his face.

But all such thoughts faded when he turned into Emily's yard and saw Cybil smiling in the window. And they disappeared completely when he came into the house and beheld the sweet curve of the belly, unmistakable, under her dress. It didn't seem possible, but she'd grown even more beautiful since he'd seen her last.

Not bothering to take off his greatcoat, Will asked her for a walk. He was half afraid she might balk at venturing out into the snow, but Cybil didn't hesitate. She only grinned and shrugged into her pelisse, then tied on her bonnet. Emily gave her mittens, and they were on their way.

Cybil walked out ahead of him onto the empty street. There was no sign of traffic from any direction. The falling snow muffled all sound, making it feel as if they were in an enclosed space meant only for them.

She turned a few circles, face upturned and arms outstretched to catch the snow. "Oh. This is sublime," she breathed. "I feel like a snow queen."

"You look it." Will stood back, drinking in the sight of her in her red wool pelisse trimmed with brown fur—sable perhaps, or mink. She'd pushed her bonnet down her back so she could feel the snow. There was still a bit of daylight filtering through the clouds, but it was dark enough that the white flakes were lit up by the faint light coming from Emily's window. They clung to Cybil's pelisse but melted every place else, wetting the little bits of hair that had escaped and turning them into thin black tendrils that clung to her face. Her lips and cheeks were stained pink against the white of her skin, and her eyes sparkled . . . She wore an expression of pure joy.

She stopped whirling and raised her brow haughtily as she came to him and grasped both his hands. "And you shall be my most favored knight, Sir Chisolm." She inclined her head ever so slightly, acknowledging her subject.

"I'll be more than that, lass," Will growled. He advanced on her like a wild animal, and Cybil giggled as he picked her up and twirled her around. *Ye gods,* but she felt good in his arms.

He set her down and bent to kiss her. After a long, slow greeting of lips and tongues and teeth, he gave into temptation and buried his face in the soft fur around her collar. She inhaled sharply, then squirmed as his lips found the warm skin beneath. The silky brush of fur against his cheek, the earthy smell of clean wool combined with Cybil's own spicy ginger and honey scent, the smooth heat of her skin against his mouth . . . for a moment, he felt thoroughly buffed, as if he'd had a dram too much whisky.

Oh, but Cybil was better than whisky. Better by far.

Reluctantly, he straightened up. They blinked at one another, then simultaneously, their faces broke into grins, then laughter.

He bowed low and offered his arm. She took it.

They turned left, walking uphill and away from the village. The wind was to their backs, and the snow fell thick and silent around them. It was beginning to stick to the ground in some places, Will noted, like where the dead leaves had blown into piles beside the road.

"I have news." He couldn't wait another moment.

"News?" Cybil's mood seemed to shift. She looked worried. "Jane's babies? Or is my dog—"

"No, no, nothin' like that. 'Tis *good* news."

"Cameron and Letty are expecting," she guessed.

He shook his head. "Not that I've been told. They're in London, I think. They plan to travel to the Bay of Honduras after the New Year."

"What is it then?"

"I've found someone—" Will was so keen to get it out that he stumbled over the words. "My cook has agreed to act as the babe's foster mother. She'll say it's her sister's child, orphaned at birth." Cybil's steps slowed. "It'll be raised in my house, part of my family." He paused, but Cybil still didn't respond. He stole a glance at her face. Her expression was blank, or perhaps—considering. "She's a widow, and well educated for her station. She's from a family of farmers just north of the city. She's perfect, kind and trustworthy. All she's asked is a small increase in her wages. 'Tis easily done." Cybil still said nothing. "It's perfect," he repeated, not knowing what else to say.

"Part of. Your family." Cybil's tone was oddly flat.

A small spot of worry clouded Will's excitement. "Of course you'll see the bairn too," he assured her. "I'll slip away with it and meet you, like we used to. I've got an idea that—"

But Cybil continued talking, as if she hadn't heard him "You're paying someone. To be my child's mother." Her voice was rising.

"No." Will shook his head, though she wasn't looking at him. She was staring straight ahead. "She'll *act* as its aunt. Its foster mother. Not its *real* mother. Of course—"

Cybil stopped, dropped his arm and whirled around to face him.

"A woman to raise *my* child but live in *your* house." She glared at him, lips pressed in a trembling, tense line. Her jaw muscles worked. Then she spoke, slowly and deliberately. "Will you *fuck* her too?"

"*Cybil!*" His voice sounded just like when he chided one of his bairns, but he didn't care. Didn't matter anyway. She was gone.

They'd reached the point where the road ended at the village well, and they'd either need to turn right and continue out of town or left and angle back toward the village. Cybil set off to the right, the red of her pelisse rapidly disappearing in the gloom, leaving Will standing alone in the driving snow.

Christ.

He jogged to catch up, then grabbed her by the elbow, pulling her around to face him. The color on her cheeks was no longer rosy and pink, but an angry, burning red. She'd been walking quickly, and her breath came in short pants as she looked up at him with the most hostile expression he'd ever seen her wear. 'Twas a wonder the snow hitting her face didn't come off as steam.

"Of course, I'm not going to fuck her," he said. She rolled her eyes and tried to pull away, but he held tight, forcing her to look at him. "You should be *pleased*. The child can still be in your life. *Our* lives. It'll be taken good care of. Mrs. Goode is the most—"

"The child is not an *it*, Will. He's a boy."

"Oh—" Will stammered. "You didna ever tell me—"

Cybil's eyes narrowed. "All this time, you've been planning. And you didn't bother asking me."

"Well, I'm askin' you now. If you dinna—"

"No, Will. You are not asking. You're *telling*. You've already made an agreement with this woman."

"Aye, but—"

"After I specifically told you the child's future would be my decision."

"You have to see that it's the best—"

"I don't *have* to see anything. What I see. What I do, is up to me—"

"*Damn your eyes,* Cybil," Will exploded, unable finally to stop the words he'd been biting back for the last month and a half. "You dinna even have a plan."

"I was planning to—"

"When? How?" She opened her mouth to answer, but he didn't let her. "You willna even *talk* about it." Once again, she tried to pull away, but he held her where she was, forcing her to face him. "I canna stand back and allow you to ruin my child's future all because of some misplaced, selfish sense of—of *pride*."

"He. Is. Not. Your. Child." She barely got the words out through gritted teeth.

"What the *hell* does that mean? Am I the father or not?"

She flinched at the accusation. "Of course you are. But you *can't* be. Just as I can't be its mother." She closed her eyes and took a long breath. "The child is growing in *my* body. *I* will be the one to decide what happens to it."

Will shook his head. "Aye. And if you ever get around to it, you'll send him off somewhere all by himself. A family who cares nothin' for him. You dinna have bairns, Cybil. You dinna understand. I canna allow it. I *willna*. Not my child." Suddenly, inexplicably, a hard lump formed in his throat. He swallowed it.

Cybil opened her mouth to answer, then closed it again. She stared at him for a long moment, then wrenched herself free of his grasp. This time, he let her go.

She turned back the way they'd come, and Will stood, rooted in place as her retreating form blurred in the snow, then was swallowed up by the dark.

His pulse pounded in his temples, hot and insistent. He wanted to go after her, to shout at her, to hold her down till he broke her to his will. But he knew better. Cybil would never break. Not really. She pretended to sometimes, when they made love, but she was really just bending. Bending and bending, but never breaking—like the strong pond reeds his ma used to weave her baskets from.

It was one of the things that drew him to her.

It was so quiet now. So dark. They hadn't seen one person or vehicle since they'd left Emily's. Everyone in Strathaven was sheltering from the storm.

Will took off his hat, tipped his head up and closed his eyes, allowing the snow to fall on his heated face. A flake landed like a soft kiss on his cheek, his eyelid, his chin.

When he opened his eyes, it felt as if he'd just woken from a dream. *Had that really happened? Had they really quarreled?*

Sighing, he set his hat back on his head, turned and began to walk toward town.

He'd been so damn sure of himself. What a fool. He should have seen this coming. It was true. She'd made it clear she wanted a say in what happened to the bairn—no, not a say. She'd wanted to *decide*. But just how would she do that? She knew no one, had no connections. Like it or not, she needed his help.

Confounded woman and her pride.

But that didn't excuse him from the blame, did it? He should have told her sooner. Eased her into the idea, or at least taken the time to view it from her side. And now he'd mucked it all up.

He passed the well and turned onto Emily's street. The wind gusted up the hill with surprising force, and suddenly, the world turned bitterly cold.

He put up the collar of his greatcoat, then pulled his hat down over his face and lowered his head into the gale as he set off down the hill.

What was he to do now? She could say what she liked, but it *was* his child and he'd be damned if he'd let his own bairn call another man Father. Just the thought of it brought an ache to his heart. Cybil was mad as a wet hen right now, but she'd calm. Even when she did—the image of her enraged face loomed large. Could he bring her around? Was it even possible? He could *force* the idea, simply take the child after it was born. But she'd never forgive him—and she'd be right not to.

How had this seemed a pleasant, gentle snowfall? The flakes weren't soft. They were pelting shards of ice hitting him hard in the face, like tiny knives. The wind howled in his ears, and there was pain everywhere he looked. The pain of giving up the new bairn—a lad—to strangers. The pain of losing Cybil. And if he had to choose . . . Christ, he couldn't lose her. She was the only one who knew him. The only one who saw him as he truly was. Without her—he'd lose himself.

He had to make it up to her. Had to make it right.

The snow had started to pile up everywhere now, a thin layer overtop the road's surface. He peered ahead, searching for any sign of a light. Surely, Emily would have left the candle in the window.

There it was, just ahead. A single point of glowing yellow in the roaring blur of white.

EIGHTEEN

How soon the transitory delights of the fairy knight's embrace were overcome by a violent tempest of misery. In but a month's time the truth came clear. The offspring of shame and guilt, the legacy of my afternoon with Tam Lin—a time I had once thought enchanted, but now knew to be cursed—was growing within me.

Oh, despair! Oh, bitter regret!

I dared not tell a soul, for fear the news would reach the ears of my husband. For if he should learn of it, who would deny his right to reprimand the poor wretch, his unfaithful wife, in as cruel a fashion as he could devise? I feared for my life, and so I hid my shame. I concealed it. Yet the anguish ate away at my person. My form faded. My cheeks lost their bloom. I did not eat, nor sleep.

There was but one cure for the infection of my gloom, one way to escape the torture of my days. And so, I piled sin on top of sin. I began to plot the destruction, the annihilation of an innocent life.

CYBIL LIFTED THE PEN, scowling at the paper. How stupid that one couldn't just use the word pregnant. *I was pregnant* would be so much more impactful than *the offspring of shame and guilt was growing within me*. But, of course, she couldn't—not if she wanted anyone to read this work. Wollstonecraft had used that exact phrase—*I was pregnant*—in her novel *Maria*, and look where that had gotten her. Her work had been condemned as vulgar, then forgotten. It was only by chance that Cybil had unearthed Aunt Cynthia's

dog-eared copy when she'd been visiting Glasgow after Percy's wedding four
years ago. If only she'd read it before she agreed to marry Ernie.

It was difficult to see in the dim light. At home, she used three candles to
write by. Here, she only dared ask Emily for one, and even then, she felt guilty
for burning it half the night. But she could make out the writing well enough
to notice the ink had flooded badly on this last page, each word bleeding out
into the next. She'd need to sharpen the quill. She reached into the recesses of
the desk and found her pen knife, then began the tedious work of cutting and
trimming the tip.

Pregnant. She herself had dared to utter the word aloud only once, on that
dreadful afternoon in Dunbar when she'd told Will. She'd been so tired, so
thoroughly depressed that she hadn't the energy to dance around the word with
pretty dissimulations.

Oh, Will. For what seemed the millionth time since he'd left that morning,
the tears prickled her eyes. She wiped them away, then dipped the quill in the
ink, carefully scraping the excess away before lowering the pen to a blank page
to test the cut. She wrote a large, looping P, then r-e-g-n-a-n-t. Better, but the
letters still weren't crisp enough. She took the knife up again, cutting away at
the quill.

She'd been cruel, probably, and unreasonable. Not just when they'd argued,
but afterward. She could tell he'd wanted to talk to her this morning before he
left, to smooth things over, but she'd resisted his every attempt to get her alone.
She'd been too angry, too hurt by his betrayal.

Even now, a full day later, it stung. He'd ignored her wishes completely.
Dismissed her as he would a child. The fact that she'd been so excited to see him,
that she'd finally gathered the courage to speak to him of the child, made it even
worse. She'd been expecting the hero she'd written for Louisa, the seductive,
understanding Tam Lin, and instead he'd acted the dismissive, despotic father.
Or husband.

She shivered. That wasn't fair to Will. He might have betrayed her trust, but
that was only a flickering shadow compared to the looming darkness of Ernie's
cruelty.

The fact was, like Louisa, like Wollstonecraft's Maria, *Cybil was pregnant.* She'd avoided making a plan for her child, just as she'd avoided speaking the word. And he—well, fatherhood was everything to Will. He'd done what he thought was right.

She tried the quill again. Wrote the same word, larger this time. *Pregnant.* The ink flowed just as it should, crisp and sharp on the page.

She owed him an apology, or at least a conversation. He'd promised to come back in two weeks' time—she'd make it up to him then.

The next day was Saturday. Luke had been late coming home from school the previous day, waylaid by the same bullies he said, though, thankfully, not hurt. He'd seemed shaken, though, and thinking to make his day happier, Emily let him sleep in as long as he liked, then the four of them—Luke, Emily, Ewan and Cybil—sat down to a later-than-normal breakfast.

"I thought . . ." Luke looked at Cybil over the table. "I thought I could show you the castle today." He eyed her expectantly, then quickly averted his eyes.

"What a wonderful idea." Emily smiled at her son. "'Tis the perfect day for it." She was clearly pleased. It was hard for Cybil to judge, since she'd only met the boy recently, but Emily worried that Luke had been withdrawn ever since that first attack. Suggesting an outing was clearly a positive development.

"That would be lovely." Cybil grinned at the lad.

It *was* the perfect day. The cold, overcast weather that had been lingering for the last week had finally broken. What little snow was left had melted, and sun streamed in the eastern windows. It caught the steam rising from Cybil's tea, illuminating it into a billowing white mass of light. It was the kind of day that would be wasted by staying indoors.

Luke's eyes darted to her. He gave her half a smile and a nod, then shifted his focus back to his food.

"Can I go too?" Ewan's shrill voice piped up from his place to Luke's right.

"No," Luke answered quickly, then he looked to his mother for confirmation.

Emily considered. "I think it's best if it's just Luke and Mrs. Smith this time." Ewan opened his mouth to protest, but she cut him off, a twinkle in her eye. "Besides, I need someone to help me make the Petticoat Tails."

The protest died in Ewan's throat, and he broke into a grin. "We're makin' Petticoat Tails?" The lad lived for shortbread. "Can I mix the dough?"

"Aye." Emily laughed. "And you can test it too."

<hr />

Emily packed them a picnic lunch, all the while showering Luke with instructions. "Watch for falling stones and uneven ground. Mind your manners when you eat and be sure to help Mrs. Smith up the hill. She mustna overexert herself."

"Yes, Ma," Luke answered dutifully.

They stepped out the front door, and as they always did, Cybil's eyes darted up the hill. There was a woman coming toward them, carrying water, but otherwise the street was empty. She shook herself. She'd only seen the man who reminded her of Townend the one time. Obviously, it was nothing. There was no reason to keep looking for him.

"This way." Luke started off down the hill, the picnic basket in one arm and his other hand stuffed in his pocket. His eyes remained trained on the ground in front of him.

Cybil followed, hastening her steps to catch up. "Do you ever go there?" She pointed ahead to the cemetery—the one she and Will had visited on Halloween.

"No."

"Really?" She was surprised. He lived so close, and surely an ancient cemetery held some appeal to an eight-year-old boy.

Luke glanced at her. "Ma doesna allow it," he muttered. Then his eyes darted back to the road.

"Would you like to?" Cybil grinned at him, though he still wasn't looking at her. "I could take you sometime if you'd like."

"Na." Luke shook his head, as if brushing her off. Odd. She'd expected him to be excited for this outing, but instead it seemed a chore. Perhaps Emily did have reason to be worried for the boy.

They walked on in silence, until finally the castle wall came into view. That was all that was left of the ancient fortress—a three-story stone wall connected to a looming tower. From this angle, the tower appeared whole, but it must not have been. Cybil could see daylight filtering through the arrow slits and small windows that ran its length. The other side must have fallen away.

Luke was ahead of her again, leaving Cybil to puzzle out the structure by herself.

The castle was built above the street on what she supposed was a man-made hill. The road they walked on terminated at a modern stone wall as tall as Cybil, and above that rose a steep, overgrown expanse of grass and trees, then the castle itself. When they reached the wall, they could either turn right and go over a bridge and into the village, or left, to follow a road that ran below the castle and then passed what looked to be a flour mill.

Luke was now in the shadow of the high stone wall at the base of the hill. He stopped and looked back, ensuring she was still behind him.

"How will we get up there?" Cybil, finally caught up, gestured to what remained of Strathaven Castle, looming above them.

"This way. There's steps—" Luke started off to the left, but Cybil caught his arm.

"Wait a moment." She needed to catch her breath, but more than that, she wanted to experience the castle from this angle before getting closer. She craned her neck, peering up at the towering stone structure. The wall itself was in a beautiful state of ruination. The mortar had long since worn away, leaving an expanse of pitted, uneven stone. The ancient rocks were sharp and jagged, but their colors—greys and browns—were warmed by the slanting November sun and softened by the green-grey of the moss that covered them. The barren tree branches seemed to be reaching toward the crumbling structure, as if to complete the work that time had begun . . .

A shiver went down her spine. "Are there ghosts?" she asked Luke. Surely, the prospect of the supernatural would intrigue any young boy.

But he just shrugged. "I dunno." Then he started off to the left.

Cybil sighed. Why had he brought her here if he had no interest in the place? And hadn't he specifically told her there *were* ghosts here, the night she arrived?

Her eyes wandered back to the castle wall. Perhaps she'd bring Will here, when he came next, after they'd made up from their quarrel. *He* would understand the appeal of this place, and its weathered, ghostly feel. Indeed, she and Will had made good use of ruined castle walls before—

"Lady Falstone."

Not Luke's voice, but a man's. Familiar. Just up ahead. He'd called her—

He stepped out of the stone wall as if by magic. No, not magic. There was an alcove.

Her eyes settled on his face. The shadows had to be—

"Luke!" *Townend,* Ernie's man, was striding toward her.

Surely, the boy was just up ahead, but she couldn't see—*where was he?*

Cold panic stabbed through her, and she opened her mouth to scream, but it was too late. Townend wrapped one arm behind her neck and covered her mouth with his hand. His other hand gripped her upper arm, tight and painful. He smelled of stale sweat and tobacco.

She couldn't turn her head, couldn't scream, but her eyes searched desperately for Luke, for anyone who might come to her aid.

There was no one.

She tried to elbow her captor in the gut, to wrench her body out of his grasp.

"None o' that, m'lady," he snarled, his grip like iron. "'Specially not in your delicate state."

He knew.

He pushed her forward, toward a side road that must have led to the mill she'd seen. A coach stood waiting—*Ernie's traveling carriage.*

Cybil planted her feet on the pavement, locked her knees and angled her body back against the man.

"Go." He tightened his grasp, pulling her arm back painfully.

She lifted her chin and pushed her face into the hand that covered her mouth, then she bared her teeth, straining to find flesh.

There. She bit down. Hard. The taste of blood.

"Rot you, woman." He jerked his hand away, waving it in pain. Mouth now free, Cybil screamed, but only for a split second.

"Quiet!" His rough, fleshy hand clamped back down over her face, then he pushed her toward the coach, harder this time. Inch by inch, her feet gave way as she slid forward.

No. *This couldn't be—*

Her feet came up against a stone, and the forward movement stopped. She struggled against his grip, twisting her body in an attempt to get free.

Then, suddenly, she *was* free. She'd done it.

She screamed for all she was worth, a long, piercing cry for help as she darted forward, away from him.

But his hands were on her again, spinning her round, then hoisting her up and slinging her over his shoulder like he might carry a sack of flour.

She could see behind him now, and finally she caught sight of Luke standing above them, halfway up a crumbling stone stairway. It must have been the stairs he'd been taking her to. But he wasn't moving. He was just standing there, watching, his eyes wide.

"Luke!" she screamed. "Help me!"

He didn't move. *What was wrong with the boy?*

Townend was running toward the coach, jouncing her hard against his shoulder as he did, but she kept screaming. Kicking. Struggling.

"Tell Will . . ." She only hoped Luke could understand her panicked shouts. ". . . Ernie found me."

Then Townend opened the coach door. The world tumbled, and she was slumped on the leather seat. Without a second thought, Cybil launched herself toward the opposite door and grabbed for the handle.

The door behind her slammed shut, but she wasn't alone. She could hear his ragged breathing. Smell his rancid smell.

She had the handle. She pushed the door open—

But his hands were on her again, pulling her backward. The door handle slipped from her grasp . . .

She pounded his chest with her fists, kicked her feet, but it was no use. He had her pinned, and for a long moment, they sat there, staring at each other. Both breathing hard.

Then Townend reached into his coat pocket and came away with a piece of rope. He forced her wrists together, then looped the cord around them. He had to slide down on the floor to tie the knot properly, and Cybil took advantage by kicking up hard. Her feet connected with his stomach.

"S'blood, woman. Be still, would you?" he barked.

In response, Cybil kicked again with all her might, but he was ready this time. He shifted to the right, and her toes found only air.

Satisfied with his work, Townend rose and sat beside her. He threaded one arm behind, and clamped his hand on her shoulder, holding her down. With the other hand, he reached into his waistcoat pocket and fished out a small, clear bottle filled with reddish liquid. *Laudanum.* Cybil clamped her lips together as he bit out the cork, then put the cold glass to her mouth. "Sorry about this, m'lady. Just followin' orders is all," he muttered as he moved his hand from her shoulder and pinched her nose closed. "Drink up now. It'll make everything easier."

Cybil pressed her teeth together, refusing the liquid. But she couldn't breathe. She stared at Townend, eyes wide, imploring. His expression was grim and hard. He didn't let go. Her lungs burned. Her pulse pounded. Stars of black light appeared in her vision . . . she couldn't—her mouth opened, she gulped in air, coughing and spluttering as the bitter liquid flowed down her throat.

When he was satisfied she'd choked down enough of the morphine, Townend rifled in his pocket again, this time bringing out a thin strip of cotton and more rope. He went to work securing the cloth around her mouth, cinching it tightly so the fabric bit into her flesh—dry and rough against her tongue.

She cried out, but the sound was muffled. Her heart beat impossibly fast.

He began binding her ankles. She kicked. Screamed. Tried to roll away.

It did nothing. He tightened the knot, and the rope burned into her skin, just above her half boots.

"That'll do," he muttered. He looked up at her. "Be good and go to sleep, would you? We've a journey ahead."

He reached over to secure the coach door she'd tried to open, then he backed out of the carriage and closed the door behind him.

Cybil was alone in the dark, breath coming in great heaves, mind racing.

The curtains were all pulled closed, blocking any view of the outside world. Was Luke still out there? There was no way to know. Perhaps he'd come to his senses and would try to rescue her before Townend got the carriage moving.

But he was only a boy. What could he possibly hope to do?

And already, she could feel the laudanum at work. Dulling her senses. Lessening the weight . . .

The coach dipped slightly. That would be Townend ascending to the driver's perch.

"You've done well, boy." Townend's voice. "Now run along home. And remember what I told you."

Then another voice. Luke's. "You're not going to hurt her, are—"

"That's none of your concern," Townend barked. The harsh sound of it splashed and rippled through Cybil's mind. There was a short pause, then the voice came again. "Come 'ere." Another, longer pause, and the darkness seemed to stretch and pull . . . then Townend spoke again, his voice oily and flowing like grease over water. "So help me, boy. If you tell a soul, I will find you, and you will pay. Understand?" If Luke responded, it wasn't with words, or Cybil didn't hear them. "Now get." *Now get. Now get. Now get.*

She shouldn't give up. She should fight. But . . . she was tired. Slipping into . . .

"Giddyap." The coach began to move as Cybil lagged against the cushions, her body weightless, her mind tumbling and echoing and crumbling, and falling into a deep sleep.

Nineteen

"WHAT DO YOU MEAN she just *wasna there*?" It was taking all Will's self-control not to reach out and shake the boy.

"She—she just—she was there, then—she wasna." Luke, clad in only his nightshirt and still bleary with sleep, cowered in the seat of Davey's old desk. It was late, and Emily had had to wake him when Will arrived a few minutes ago. The boy's eyes refused to meet Will's. Instead, he focused on the space just over Will's left shoulder.

"Look at me, lad."

Luke dragged his gaze to Will's face, then blinked away again.

Will squatted down so he was on Luke's level. He put a hand on the lad's shoulder and spoke slowly, forcing himself to calm. "Tell me what you remember. Every detail."

Luke stared over Will's shoulder. "Starting when?"

"From the minute you left this house."

The lad drew a long breath. Blinked twice. "We walked down the hill." His voice shook a little, as if he were about to cry. "Then we got to the castle."

"Did she say anything, as you were walking?"

Luke thought a moment. "She asked about the cemetery. If I ever go there. I said no, Ma doesna let me. And then—Mrs. Smith said she might take me sometime."

Will waited for more. Nothing. "Anything else?" he prompted.

"No."

"Did she carry anything with her? A valise?"

"No. I—I had the picnic basket." Luke's eyes darted to his mother for affirmation. "But Mrs. Smith didna have anything."

"That's true," Emily confirmed. She was standing just behind them, her arms crossed. "Her things are all still here."

"You got to the castle. Then what?"

"Then . . ." Luke's voice trailed off as if he were searching his memory. "I went up the steps to the ruin." His eyes finally met Will's, and for the first time, he sounded sure of himself. "I thought she was behind me, but when I got to the top and I turned around, she was gone."

"Did you look for her?" Will ground out through clenched teeth.

"Aye." Luke nodded vigorously. "I went as far as the mill, then into the village a way, but she was just . . . gone."

Will grunted and pushed up from his squatting position. This was going nowhere.

He paced to the far window, then stared out at the night. His jaw and fists were tight, and his thoughts seized with unspent rage. It seemed an impossible task, yet he forced the breath in and out. In and out.

Cybil had been gone a full day and a half. Six-and-thirty bloody hours. Emily had sent a courier posthaste to fetch Will, and he'd gotten here as quick as he could, missing an outing he'd promised Rose—once and for all breaking his daughter's heart. But what use was it? Cybil could be far, far away by now, and all Will had to guide him was this infuriatingly vague story from Emily's boy, and the equally infuriating sympathy on the lad's mother's face. Emily knew he and Cybil had quarreled. She would have had to be blind not to notice Cybil's haughty avoidance of him after they'd returned in the snow that night. The way Emily had been looking at him since he arrived, it was obvious she thought Cybil had left because of it.

But why wouldn't she have taken her belongings? Certainly, she had the money to buy herself new clothes and whatever else she needed, but it wasn't as if Emily would have prevented her from leaving if she'd chosen to. Surely, Cybil knew that.

But if Emily had known Cybil was leaving . . . she would have alerted Will. And he would have followed her. *Of course.* The truth hit him like a punch to the gut. Cybil had sneaked off when no one expected so she could be rid of him, for good. That was what she'd wanted from the start, wasn't it? To make her own decisions, and to see an end to their affair. She'd been reluctant to come here at all, and after what he'd done—

He pushed his fist into his palm till his arms shook, but no matter how hard he pressed, no matter how much he regretted his actions, nothing changed.

He'd lost her. The one person he'd never wanted to lose. Through his own foolish bullheadedness, he'd lost her.

"Luke." Emily's voice sounded from across the room, soft, but with an edge. "You promised you would help Mrs. Smith up those stairs."

There was no response. Slowly, Will turned away from the window.

Emily was holding the boy in her stern gaze. "Why did you not help her?"

Luke stared at his mother. "That's why I turned around." An odd sort of smirk crossed the lad's face, not a smile exactly, but a grimace, almost as if he were in pain. "To help her. But then, she was just, gone."

"But, I dinna understand." Emily paced toward Luke, peering intently at her son's face. "Why would you go up the steps at all, without her?"

"I—I forgot." Luke blinked twice, then that odd grimace again.

"Luke." Emily's voice was still calm, but with iron underneath. "Are you lying to me?"

Luke flinched. "No. I—"

Will crossed the room in two strides. "If there's somethin' you arena tellin' us. Anything. You need to say it. Right. Now."

Luke looked from his mother to Will. His lower lip began to quiver.

"Did Mrs. Smith ask you to keep a secret for her?" Emily coaxed. "Is that why you're—"

"No."

"Then what—"

"I canna . . ." Luke shook his head, his eyes wide in panic.

"*What*? What canna you?" Will grasped the boy's shoulders.

"I can-na tell." Luke choked out.

"Why not?" Will thundered. His grip tightened.

Emily came between them. "Will, stop, you'll—"

"*Because he'll come back,*" Luke blurted out. Then, as if a plug had been pulled, the words drained out of him in a rush. "He'll hurt Ewan and Ma and me, and he'll *take* you. Just like they took Da." His voice cracked. "You willna be able to help us anymore, and we'll starve like—like *dogs.*"

Will and Emily glanced at each other. She was clearly as confused as Will was.

Will took his hands off the boy and backed up a step. The lad was clearly frightened out of his wits, and it wouldn't help to scare him more. Gentling his voice, he spoke. "I'm not goin' to let anyone hurt you, lad. But whatever this has to do with Cybil—Mrs. Smith, you must tell us."

"But—he's got the law on his side. Just like with Da. He said—"

"Who?" Emily knelt beside her son. "Who said this?"

"The—the man. He waits for me by the castle after school." Luke sniffed. "It wasna the boys who hit me." He looked past his mother as he made the confession, unable to meet her eyes. "'Twas *him*. He wanted to know all about her—Mrs. Smith." The lad swallowed, then looked to Will with red-rimmed eyes. "'Twas him. He took her."

Will's mouth went dry. "Took . . . *her*? Took Cybil, you mean?"

Luke nodded, then the tears started to fall.

"But—" Will's legs were weak, threatening to buckle under him. "Tell us, Luke. Everything. I swear to you, no harm will come." He could only pray he was right.

"I was to bring her to the castle, or else he'd—he'd hurt Ewan, and Ma and me. And he'd see you taken away."

"So that's what you did."

"Aye." He shook his head vigorously. "But I didna know he would take her. He said he wanted to talk to her was all, but he didna. He tried to make her go into the carriage, but she wouldna go, so he picked her up and put her in it. She was kickin' and screamin', and she didna want to go . . . but he didna care."

"Who was this man?" Will's entire world had narrowed to a single point—the answer to this question.

"He—he didna tell me his name."

"What did he look like?"

Luke stared at him. "I—I canna remember."

"What color was his hair?" Emily prodded. Thanks to God she was here. Will couldn't think straight.

"Yellow. Longer than most gentlemen's hair is." Luke paused. "His nose was crooked, and . . . kind of . . . pointy. He smoked sometimes when I saw him."

"Cigars, or a pipe?" Will asked.

"C-Cigars."

"What kind of coach?"

"A big one. 'Twas blue, with shiny gold wheels."

Blonde hair, beak of a nose that'd been broken. A smoking habit. If it weren't for the carriage, Luke could have been describing Wilcox. But that was impossible. Wilcox knew nothing of Cybil, and even if he'd been snooping around and learned of her, why would he take her and not Will?

"Will?" Luke's soft voice cut through his thoughts.

Will forced himself to focus on the boy. "Aye?"

"She shouted to me—Mrs. Smith did. As he was carryin' her off. She said to tell you . . . to tell you *Ernie* found her."

Will winced, then closed his eyes. When he opened them again, it was with certainty. He knew what had to be done.

He paced to the table where he'd laid his traveling bag. "Pack your things," he told Emily. "You and the boys will go to my house in Glasgow first thing."

"But—" Emily straightened up and followed him.

"I'll not see you hurt on my account. And if this man comes back—"

"But your children—Will, who's Ernie?"

He ignored the question and began rifling through his bag, looking for paper. "I'll send a note with you for the bairns." He had no idea what Rosie and Nat would think. All his hazily explained absences, then this . . . What would they make of a strange family arriving on their doorstep with only a note from him?

But it didn't matter. What mattered was that Emily and her bairns would be safe. No one knew to look for them in Glasgow, even this man who had to be a servant of the Baron's couldn't have made that connection.

He'd also need to write to his man of business, and his managers, to inform them of his extended absence. And the architect working on the new mill. He was scheduled to meet with the man tomorrow afternoon—

"Will. *Will.*"

Emily's voice filtered to him. Given her tone, he suspected it wasn't the first time she'd tried getting his attention.

He looked up. "Aye?"

"Where are *you* going?"

"Leeds. I ride at daybreak."

"Leeds? What's—"

"Cybil's husband. Ernie."

"Oh." Realization dawned on Emily's face. He'd never said as much, but of course she must have supposed Cybil was married—else why wouldn't Will have married her himself?

"But if he's her husband . . . wouldna he be the father of her bairn too?" Luke's confused voice piped up. Will had forgotten the lad was there.

"Enough of that. Off to bed," Emily commanded. She and Will watched as Luke slowly walked toward the stairs.

The lad hesitated at the foot of the steps. He turned back. "I'm sorry," he choked out. "I didna meant to—"

"It's alright, lad. 'Tisn't your fault." Will couldn't bear to look at the boy's face for another second. It *wasn't* his fault, truly. He'd been coerced, *beaten*. But that didn't stop the anger from welling in Will's chest every time he looked at the boy.

But if it wasn't Luke's fault, whose was it? How the devil had the Baron tracked Cybil to Strathaven? How had he known to threaten the law on Will?

Luke turned and trudged up the stairs, leaving Will and Emily alone.

"Be careful." Emily gazed at the darkness where her son had just been.

"Of course," Will replied, but in his head, he'd realized one more thing he had to do. A letter to Sommerbell, confessing everything. It was only a matter of time before Cybil's husband informed her brother of the situation. Will had to get to him first.

TWENTY

MRS. BROWN'S BOMBAZINE SKIRT made a faint swishing sound as she climbed the stairs. Cybil could feel the heat of Townend's eyes on her back, but she didn't care. She was mesmerized by the subtly shifting texture of the housekeeper's dress, the reflection of candlelight on cloth. How would she describe it? *The lambent light flickered over the fabric, engendering a dull luster. Silk and wool. Black and grey. Shadow and shadow.*

The effects of her last dose of opium were fading, but the echoes of the potion still wound their way through her mind, soothing her, connecting the words and thoughts with a thin, fine filament. Like a spider's web, or smoke.

She was in Leeds, at Netherby House—Ernie's house. It was night, and it was real, but it didn't matter. None of it mattered.

They reached the top landing, and instead of entering the familiar chambers Cybil had always occupied when she and Ernie stayed here in the past, the housekeeper turned right, toward the guestrooms. Cybil hesitated, confused, but Townend grunted, pushing her along, and she didn't resist. She followed Mrs. Brown down the corridor, except her feet didn't touch the ground. She was floating in the darkness, following the candle's flame . . . A door opened, and they were in a room.

It was small, but well appointed. A soft carpet covered the floor, and a bed hung with thick velvet drapes occupied one corner. There was a small escritoire placed in front of one of the two windows, and a comfortable-looking chaise stretched in front of the hearth where a bright fire was burning. A slight damp smell permeated the air, sticking in Cybil's throat, as if the chamber hadn't been used in some time.

Mrs. Brown turned to Cybil, inspecting her with pursed lips. The housekeeper had aged. Her skin was lined with more wrinkles than Cybil remembered, like parchment that had been crumpled then smoothed back out. Her eyes were rimmed with red. Wisps of grey hair escaped her crisp white mobcap.

"Still drowsy, is she?" The housekeeper's sharp gaze remained on Cybil, but she directed her question at Townend.

"Aye. She'll come out of it soon, no doubt."

They were talking about her as if she weren't there, but Cybil didn't have the strength to protest, or . . . or perhaps she *wasn't* there. Perhaps this was all a dream.

"Is there any luggage?"

"No. She'll need clothes."

Mrs. Brown nodded once, then released Cybil from her attention and moved to the windows to draw the drapes. "I'll have Cook send up a tray," she told Townend over her shoulder. "His Lordship is expected within the hour."

His Lordship. *Ernie.* A thin needle of fear pierced Cybil's languor.

She watched, unable to speak or move as Mrs. Brown bustled past and out of the room. Townend followed, shutting the door behind him. There was a thud of wood, or metal, then silence.

She crossed to the door, lifted the latch, and pushed. Nothing happened, as if she were pushing on a wall.

The prickling sense of fear returned. But . . . she was tired. Floating and languid. The fire was warm. Its radiant heat pulled her away from the door, away from the cold, and the dark and the fear.

The breath exhaled from her lungs, and she sank onto the chaise. No longer light, but impossibly heavy. Impossibly weary. Her wrists and ankles were red and raw from the rope that Townend had only just untied, but she couldn't feel them.

Couldn't feel anything.

Her eyes were closed. Her body numb. She slipped away.

Cybil had no idea how long she slept, only that when she'd first entered the room, the log in the hearth had been whole and firm, and her mind had been addled by laudanum. Now the log was glowing red, with black, jagged lines webbed throughout, threatening to fall into coals. Her mind was clear, but her body ached. A tray of food sat on the table before her, and rain splattered the window.

She felt as if she were awaiting execution.

Well, perhaps that was a bit dramatic. *But was it?* She was fairly certain Ernie wouldn't kill her when he arrived, but whatever he did, it wouldn't be pleasant.

She stretched her limbs, feeling the ache in every muscle, and the burning of her wrists and ankles. How many days had she been in that carriage? Three, probably. The time it would take to travel to Leeds. But she remembered none of it, or—*almost* none of it. Just the dark. The jouncing of the coach. The smell of Townend. The bitter taste of laudanum.

The log collapsed with a sigh, breaking into a hundred red hot coals and sending up sparks.

How had he found her?

It was a confounding question. Luke had betrayed her, but how? And why? Had Emily discovered who Cybil was and gone to Ernie? Or had Luke? That seemed out of the question, but . . . how else?

Did it really matter? However it had come about, Ernie had found her. He knew of her condition. What he would do *now*, that was the real question. Her eyes darted to the windows shrouded in thick green velvet. Could she find a way out—?

Voices sounded outside.

Ernie, and Townend.

Cybil's stomach hollowed. Her heart pounded. But she pressed her lips together, forced her face into a neutral expression, took a breath. She must not show fear. Ernie relished her fear.

She stared into the fire as the door opened, then closed. Slow, heavy footsteps came toward her, but she didn't turn to see who approached.

"Cybil." Ernie's scraping, resonant voice. He stepped between the fire and the chaise, forcing her to look at him, but she wouldn't give him the satisfaction. She kept her eyes focused straight ahead—at his pantaloon clad knees. "I apologize for coming so late. I only got home."

Cybil gritted her teeth.

"Not feeling well this evening?" Ernie's legs disappeared from view, then the chaise dipped a little as he sat at her feet, so close she could feel the heat rolling off his body. He smelled the same—that expensive cologne he favored. Bergamot and rosemary. The memory of it—she recoiled, pulling herself away and tucking her legs under her.

"Really, my dear. Is this any way to greet your husband?" He leaned over and grasped her chin, forcing her to look at him. His fingers were soft and cold. They dug into her, and oh, how she wished for more laudanum, for that peaceful delirium she'd been living in the last few days.

Like Mrs. Brown, and like Cybil herself, Ernie had aged. His bushy brows had the odd wiry grey hair sticking out. His eyes, which had always had a sleepy look to them, were now positively droopy. His bulbous nose and prominent chin remained unchanged, as did his arrogant lips, the corners of which were turned up in an almost indecipherable smirk.

He shrugged. "Looking a bit worse for wear, I'd say." Then he released her.

She lifted her chin in a sign of defiance and moved her gaze back to the fire. "What are you going to do to me, Ernie?"

"*Me? Do to you?*" He rose and once again came between her and the fire. "I believe the doing is already done, my dear. And not by me." The last bit had an edge to it. A blunt one. One that promised pain. "It's what *you* will do now that I've come to speak of." He paused. "My *wife*."

"What does that mean?"

Ernie paced to the fire, holding his hands out as if to warm them. "As I see it, we have two options."

"Options." Cybil felt the heat rise in her cheeks. He was toying with her. "*I have no options, Ernie. You—*"

"Don't. Interrupt." He turned toward her, voice rising. "The first option is to show the world that we have reconciled. Return to the happy times we had *before . . .*" He trailed off, leaving Cybil to fill in the blanks. London. No writing. No life. His lips curved in a cruel smile as he once again sat beside her. He cupped her chin and ran a thumb over her cheek. "I've come up in the world, Cybil. I hold great influence, and power. You could be a part of that. We could have our happy ending at long last."

Bile rose in her throat. She swallowed it down, turning her head to rid herself of his touch. "And the second option?"

"Well, there's two more actually. Either you stay *here*, without me. Or if that's not amenable, I'll find you other suitable accommodations."

The subtext could not be more clear. If she stayed in Leeds and tried to run away again, or caused any kind of trouble, he would have her locked up.

"Would I be allowed to write?"

"Heavens, no. We're precariously close to scandal as it is."

"And what of the child?"

"Ah, yes. The child. I must say, I was surprised about that." Cybil's chest tightened. Instinctively, her hands went to her growing womb. Ernie's eyes followed the movement. "It will live in London with me. I've need of an heir."

She'd been expecting this. But even so, a wave of nausea rolled through her. "But the child—he's not yours." She stumbled over the words. "He's—"

"Of course, it would have been preferable to preserve the Bythesea bloodline." He shrugged. "But needs must when the devil drives, as they say."

"It could be a girl," she snapped.

"True . . ." He let his voice trail off as his hand once again moved to touch her. This time, he swept an icy finger down her cheek, her neck. "I did so enjoy bedding you, Cybil . . ."

She pulled away in revulsion. "What are you getting at?"

Ernie's eyes shifted away, then back to her. "I must face the facts. I cannot sire a child." He was silent for a few beats, staring at her with those watery blue eyes.

Then his hand crept toward her and he brushed his knuckles over her growing womb, sending cold chills through her entire being. "But *you* can." He pulled his hand back, and she waited for him to finish, but he didn't. He just looked at her, brows raised as if expecting something . . . *Oh.*

"*Who?* Who would you—" She couldn't finish the sentence. She didn't want to know the answer.

Ernie's gaze turned pensive. He shrugged. "I haven't quite decided. Townend perhaps, or some other servant. One that looks like me preferably, but it's more important that it be someone I trust." Another wave of nausea, worse than the last. "Let's hope it's a boy and it doesn't come to that, shall we?"

Cybil's stomach heaved. She sprang up and ran for the chamber pot that sat behind a screen in the corner. There was almost nothing in her stomach, yet she wretched again and again until she was wrung out completely.

When she came out from behind the screen, Ernie was gone.

⚬

Cybil woke the next morning to the sound of wind gusting over the house and raindrops hitting the pane. Then came a quiet, scraping sound. A maid cleaning the hearth. She blinked her eyes open, but kept them narrowed against the dim light filtering through the cracks in the bed-curtains.

Her stomach was still unsettled, though she didn't feel ill as she had the night before. It was more a shifting, skittering feeling. Perhaps a lingering effect of the opium? Or hunger? Hopefully, it wouldn't linger.

She lay still and listened as whomever it was built a fire. The dull thud of logs. The clicking strike of flint against steel. The flare of a match. The crackling of sparks. Every so often, a gust of wind rattled the pane, pelting it with hard rain.

She drew the blankets close. They kept out the chill, but they offered no protection from the bone-chilling future that stretched before her.

Options, Ernie had said, as if she had a choice.

There was no way she could go back to London. It would be unbearable to pretend to be a good wife to a man she despised, to entertain his cronies, to watch him turn her child—Will's child—into a copy of himself. Even if she tried, she knew she'd fail. She'd do something rash, then he'd have his excuse to get rid of her for good.

No, it was better to stay here in Yorkshire, where she wouldn't have to watch what Ernie did to the child. Was it really all that different from her exile at Grislow Park? A country house, no visitors, no life of her own . . .

Yes, a small voice said. It *would* be different. Here, there would be no Jane. No small nephew to bring childish joy to her life. No illicit journeys to see Will. No writing.

She would go mad. Or lose herself to laudanum.

Then there was the threat he'd made, or the promise rather, if the child were a girl. The idea of Townend on top of her, inside her . . . or some other of Ernie's men. She couldn't bear it. Couldn't.

A sound came from Cybil's throat, something between an angry growl and a miserable groan. She pounded her fists into the mattress. *She had to get out.* Escape. She tried to sit up, but the movement was too quick. Dizziness overtook her, and she fell back onto the bed. When had she last eaten?

"My lady?" A voice sounded from the other side of the curtains. "Are you alright?"

Blast. She'd forgotten there was a maid in the room.

"I'm fine," she croaked. "I'd like tea, and something to eat."

"Of course. Right away." A pause. "Shall I draw the curtains, m'lady?"

Cybil took a breath, slowly pulled herself up to a seated position and smoothed her hair. "Yes, please." She was still Lady Falstone after all. Surely, she could preserve some dignity in the eyes of the servants.

There was a sudden influx of light. Cybil blinked, and a silhouette came into focus, then features. The maid wasn't one Cybil recognized. She was of middling age—similar, probably to Cybil's own age—plump and red-cheeked. The kind of woman one could imagine breaking into a smile at any moment . . . except, she wasn't smiling. Her small mouth was pulled into a tense line. Her clear brown eyes were fixed on Cybil rather than demurely pointed to the floor as they should have been.

Cybil's heart sank. It was obvious this woman knew of her status in the house. Her demure words were only a ruse.

"Will there be anything else?"

"No."

The maid curtsied, then turned to leave—

"*Yes*," Cybil called after her. "A bath." The servant pivoted, then nodded, and Cybil continued speaking before she could turn away again. "What's your name?"

The woman hesitated. "Phoebe, m'lady."

"Phoebe . . ." Cybil repeated, stalling for time while she tried, and failed, to find a subtle way to ask the question she wanted the answer to. "Am I permitted to leave this room?'

Phoebe's look went from uncomfortable to mildly panicked. "Mr. Townend . . ." Her voice trailed off, and she shook her head no, answering Cybil's question without words.

"Is he guarding the door?"

"No, but—" The maid glanced furtively toward the door, then took a few steps toward Cybil. She spoke in a hushed tone. "They had a man come and fix the door. There's a bar on the outside blockin' it. I'm to secure it when I leave."

"I see." Cybil pressed her lips together. A barred door. How medieval. It was effective, though. She'd have been able to pick a lock. Ernie knew that as well as she did.

An awkward silence ensued as the two women eyed one another. Finally, Phoebe cleared her throat, bobbed a curtsey and left. Then came the sound of the wooden bar falling into place.

Cybil rose, shrugged into the dressing gown the maid had left, then paced to the window. She was on the second floor. Could she climb down somehow? Certainly not today. Phoebe had drawn the drapes, but the gardens below and the moor beyond were invisible, lost to the streaks of water streaming down the pane.

And where would she go? Back to Percy? He couldn't offer protection, not after this. And going to Will was out of the question. She'd only be found again, and who knew what Ernie would do then. A cold draft blew past her skin, and she shivered. Even France seemed too near. Whatever she did, wherever she went, she couldn't afford to fail. If Ernie caught her again, she would be doomed to an asylum. Forever.

Her eyes swept the room. Comfortable. Warm. She could stay here . . . It would be a miserable existence, but it would be safe. And certainly, Ernie would give her all the laudanum she desired. That could dull the pain . . .

She could see herself now. An opium addict, consigned to her fate and fading away in a remote estate, until she died. Unknown. Unloved. Forgotten. A fitting ending.

She swallowed and brought a hand up to rub her eyes. That odd feeling in her stomach was gone, but she was so hungry. Perhaps after a bath and some food, things would be more clear.

———◇———

Bloody rain. It hadn't stopped in two days. The road was nothing but mud.

At the last minute, Will had decided to leave his horse at the inn in Strathaven and take a post-chaise instead. It was an exorbitantly expensive way to travel, and being cramped in the tiny space was far less enjoyable than riding out in the open air, but it meant he could go 'round the clock without the need to rest his horse, or himself. In theory, the string of coaches should have gotten him to Leeds in two days rather than three . . . but then it had started raining, and here he was, two and a half days into the trip and nowhere near Leeds.

The conveyance inched along, slogging through the mud. Without warning, it jerked hard to the left, skidding to the side of the road. Will braced himself, tensing every muscle to keep from falling against the door. Then the coach stopped. One of the postillion barked at the horses, and they started again.

Will exhaled, leaning his head against the seat and closing his eyes. He was weary, but sleep evaded him. All he could see was Cybil. Cybil being forced into a carriage. Cybil struggling, panicked, restrained . . . His bonny, black-haired lass who loved to pretend wanton helplessness but was, in fact, the strongest, most resilient person he'd ever known.

Her husband had not been able to break her the first time. But now . . . who knew what the Baron would do? A man like that. A Tory. A bully. A man who put his own superiority and reputation above all else. A man who was friend to Sidmouth. Will's mouth turned bitter at the thought.

Once he found Cybil and got her out of that man's clutches, she, and the child would have to go far, far away, never to return. And Will? Ach, it hurt like the devil to think of leaving Scotland, his work in the mills, Emily, Cameron, the Sommerbells. To uproot Rose and Nat from their lives. But if the Baron truly knew about his past . . . he'd have no choice.

If only Cybil would agree to come with him. He'd try to convince her, of course, but after their quarrel, he held little hope.

This damn rain. He could only pray she was in Leeds, that the devil hadn't hurt her—

The coach lurched again, and this time, Will was caught unprepared. He knocked his head against the door, then fell to his knees on the dirty straw floor. The vehicle halted, and he took the time to crawl back onto the seat, rubbing his aching crown. He waited, but nothing happened. No movement, just stillness and the steady stream of raindrops on the windows.

What was it now? He drew a breath, then wrenched the door open. Cold rain hit his face. One of the postillions, soaked to the bone, was kneeling beside the carriage, inspecting the front wheels, which were sunk deeply in the mud. The horses, too, were up to the knees in it.

The man looked up. "We're stuck, sir."

Will heaved a breath, then reached for his hat—not that it would do any good—and descended the steps. "I'll help."

TWENTY-ONE

You cannot imagine the tempest of sorrow that raged in my breast as I once again entered that enchanted grove, the depths of my soul's despair as I sought out the glossy leaves which had been described to me. For by some cruel whim of fate, the herbs that would bring an end to the innocent life growing in my womb flourished in that same bower where Tam Lin's ethereal charms first tempted me into sin.

You judge me, dear reader, but it is not possible that you judge me more than I judged myself. Because the truth . . . the truth is that I wanted that child. I wanted to love and to cherish his sweet cherubic form, to feel his infant fingers tightening around my own. I dreamed of suckling him at my warm breast, of beholding his first, angelic smile, of inhaling the milky sweet redolence of his skin. I had so little to live for, you see. This babe. This flesh of my flesh . . . It was everything. And oh, how I wanted it.

A TEAR FELL ONTO THE paper. For a fraction of a second, it held its round, glassy form, reflecting Cybil's face and gemming the soft glow of the candlelight. Then it collapsed, melted into the fibers and turned the letters to nothing but a muddy stain of ink.

Cybil set the pen down and wiped her eyes before more tears could fall. She only had five precious sheets of notepaper that she'd found stuffed in the far reaches of the escritoire, and just a bit of ink. She couldn't waste it. But . . . *Oh—what was the point?* She was only bringing herself more pain, and it wasn't as if she'd be able to finish the novel anyway. Even if she found more paper, all the beginning pages were in Strathaven, tucked away in her lap desk. There was no conceivable way she'd ever get them back.

And if Ernie found her writing—no, she would not think of that. She hadn't seen Ernie since that terrible night anyway, two days ago now. Hadn't seen *anyone* other than Phoebe, the maid. The silence, the loneliness, it was deafening . . . defeating.

Strathaven. Will. Emily. What did they think? What had Luke told them? Townend had threatened the boy if he didn't keep the secret, but . . . *had he*? Did Will think she'd left him of her own accord? They'd just quarreled after all. It seemed so distant now, so foolish.

But perhaps it was better if he thought she'd left of her own free will. That would be painful surely, but the truth was worse.

That odd feeling was back in her stomach, diverting her attention. It had been plaguing her for days now, like tiny bubbles fizzing inside. She hadn't been eating enough to warrant indigestion, and it couldn't be the opium still.

There was one last tremor, more emphatic than the rest, then it stilled. It wasn't like bubbles, exactly, it was more random, with no rhyme nor reason, almost as if a tiny creature were—

Dear God. Her hands flew to her stomach and she leaned back in the chair, staring down at herself.

It was him.

She held her breath and he jumped again, as if he were dancing—joyously bouncing within her. She could imagine his smile, so like his father's. His sweet, childish laugh.

The air was forced from her lungs as grief came crashing down, nearly knocking her from her chair. Cybil choked on the sobs as she cradled her son. Her body leaned forward and in, curling around him, and she held him, gripped him tight, as if she could protect him from the terror what was to come.

But she couldn't. This innocent child who lived within her would grow up to call an evil man Father. He would suffer the same cruelty that Cybil had known, and worse—he would be trained to perpetrate that evil himself. He'd be his father's enemy. His mother's jailor. He'd be taught to bring pain and injustice into future generations . . . He would never hear Will's laughter, or be nourished at Cybil's breast. Would never know their love.

No. She couldn't bear it. She—

He moved again, not a kick, or jump this time, but a long, smooth, flowing motion, as if he were stroking her, attempting to comfort his mother, and assure her of his love. His trust.

"I can't." She spoke aloud, gazing through the tears at her swollen belly. "I can't let him take you. I *will not*."

Her words hung in the still air. Defiant and true. *How had she not seen it sooner?* Whatever Cybil had done, whatever end she may deserve, it didn't matter. What mattered was her child. Will's child. The future. She must get him away from here.

Hands still on her babe, Cybil closed her eyes and drew one, long smoothing breath. Then another.

"You will be safe. I will keep you safe."

Then she snatched up the paper and strode to the fire, throwing it in, quicker than thought.

When it was burned to ash, she crossed to the window and stared into the impenetrable blackness. The rain had stopped, and a thin mist was rising.

Tomorrow, she would devise a way out.

———— ◆ ————

It stopped raining just as Will left the inn at Leeds. He'd chosen to stay on the northern outskirts of the city, which cut the trip down from ten miles to nine, but even still, he was glad to avoid the long walk in the pouring rain.

He quickened his strides, not even slowing to pick his way around the patches of mud that still dotted the road. His boots were already well soiled from the hours he'd spent pushing that coach through the mud. What difference did a bit more dirt make now?

He'd arrived in Leeds at midday, three and a quarter days after leaving Strathaven. By then, between the lack of sleep and the labor of freeing the stuck coach, he'd been so tired he'd had no choice but to sleep a few hours before indulging in a hearty supper. The barroom was full of locals, and Will presented himself as an out-of-work gamekeeper looking for employment with the local gentry. After buying a few pints for a particularly friendly and loose-lipped cove who regularly delivered milk to the Baron's house, he was able to glean some information: Baron Falstone didn't keep any dogs, was in London most of the time and wasn't much of a sportsman. There was a gamekeeper on his estate, and only a skeleton staff besides—the housekeeper, a few maids and footmen, the cook and the steward. The man hadn't seen or heard anything of Lady Falstone. Hadn't heard about her in years, in fact. He thought she might have passed.

Tonight, Will would walk the grounds, determine the lay of the land and, if at all possible, get some idea of what part of the house Cybil might be in. Tomorrow, he'd make a plan to get her out of there, and then—*No*. His mind wanted to go further, but he couldn't let it. He'd see her to safety, that much he knew. But the details of her exile, and his part in it, he'd leave up to her.

It was a black night with almost no light at all coming from the overcast sky. He passed through a village, and in the bit of light that flickered in the windows of houses, he could see a mist had started to rise. There was no wind. The air was heavy, chill and close.

After he'd come clear of the lights, he stopped and lit the lantern he carried. He didn't trust himself to follow the landmarks he'd been given without it, but he'd douse it again before he got too near the Baron's house. The lantern light didn't cut far into the darkness, but he could see where the ground fell off to his left, then a weathered sign for a quarry. Soon, dim lights came into view to his right, which had to be the grange he'd been told of—the last drive before the turn to Netherby House.

He was close.

Suddenly, he was aware of every noise. The dull sound of his footfalls on the muddy road, the slight clinking of metal as the lantern swung on its short chain, the thudding of his heartbeat. His breath fogged the air and soaked up the light, making him feel like a beacon, not that anyone would be out on a night like this.

Much sooner than he'd anticipated, another drive branched off to the right. A faint light glinted in the distance. Netherby House. He peered ahead. The terrain was flat and seemed to be clear of trees. He turned into the drive, then after a few dozen paces came face to face with a tall, wrought-iron gate. He held the lamp up. Imposing stone gate piers flanked the thing, topped by statues of reclining lions that stared down at him.

Ignoring the animals' stony glares, Will left the drive and skirted around the gate. He expected more wrought iron, or a wall of some sort, but no, there was nothing more than a low stone fence blocking entrance to the estate.

He shook his head. Ass-headed, that—a big, fancy iron gate with no fence to back it up.

He doused the lantern, set it at the base of the fence, climbed over and then continued on.

He was now close enough to make out the shape of the house, though not much more. All was still. It must have been past midnight. A dim light showed in one of the large-paned windows of the ground floor, but the second floor was dark, as was the rustic—the lower level where the servants likely slept and worked.

Will paced a wide circle around the structure. It was huge. He counted eleven tall windows spanning the front, and there was a stone ramp made for carriages to ride right up to the door. Two smaller buildings attached to the main house like wings, connected by covered walks. One must be the kitchen, Will supposed. Who knew what the other was for? For whatever rich fucks like the Baron did in their free time.

Another building, large, with a clock tower, loomed nearby, almost invisible in the shadows. The stables.

Ach, he'd never find Cybil in this monstrosity. If she was even in there. She could be in an outbuilding, or an inn somewhere, or London.

Or an asylum.

Will forced a breath. Thoughts like that did no one any good. If she *was* in the house . . . where would the Baron keep her? Not the main floor. It was probably all formal rooms, none of them a good prison. It was possible he'd put her in the basement with the servants, but Will doubted that too. She'd be too easily noticed. And she *was* the Baron's wife. Even if she were his prisoner, Will doubted he'd flaunt propriety by housing her with the servants. No, chances were he'd lock her up on the top floor . . . but which room? All the windows were dark, at least from the front.

How would one get into a house like this? Will scanned the structure. There was no lattice work or ivy growing up it, nothing but bare walls . . . Though it would be a small matter to climb to the roof of one of those covered walks—there were plenty of ledges and footholds in the stone, and it would put him almost level with the windows on the top floor. If one were unlocked, he'd be able to get in without much problem—

Something cold and wet scraped against his cheek. He started. *Hell,* he'd been so intent on the house, he'd run right up against a tree branch. He extricated himself, then continued till he'd rounded to the backside of the house.

There. One window was lit, albeit dimly, as if only one or two candles burned. Will crept closer through what appeared to be a formal garden. Rose brambles snagged his trouser legs, but he didn't stop. All his attention was focused up, on that window, trying to find any clue to the owner of the room.

It could be the Baron's bedchamber . . . but wouldn't that have windows to the front? Faugh, he had no idea.

He stood, looking at the window for a long time. Dare he attempt to throw a pebble against the pane? If he did, and it *wasn't* her, he'd risk getting caught. But he could easily slip into the shadows below the house, then run back to the road . . . and the Baron had no dogs.

He crouched to gather a few small stones from the gravel path, and when he straightened, she was there, at the window.

His breath caught. He wasn't near enough to see the detail of her face, but it was Cybil. She had on a dressing gown, and he could see the swell of her belly underneath. Her hair was pulled back, her face pale, and even at this distance, there was something—her shoulders perhaps, or the way she held her head. She looked . . . defeated, yet proud. Like a tragic heroine in one of her books.

She gazed out for a long moment. Of course, she couldn't see him, but she seemed to be searching for something in the dark. Something far away, just out of reach. Then she pulled the curtains closed, and a few seconds later, the lights in the room went dark.

Will sprang into motion. Without stopping to think, he threw one of the pebbles he held, then another. *Tick . . . Tick.* If she was still in that chamber, she was certain to notice.

He waited a minute, two. She didn't come.

Tick . . . Tick. He threw two more, then stared up at the darkened panes, as if concentrating hard enough would bring her into view. *Please. Cybil. Come to the window.*

TWENTY-TWO

TICK . . . Tick.

What *was* that? Had it started raining again?

Cybil drew the blankets closer. She'd only just climbed into bed, and though she held no illusions of sleep—it likely wouldn't come for hours—she was weary and cold.

Thankfully, the babe seemed to have tired of his flitting about. She pictured him curled up within her, tiny eyes closed in peaceful slumber. She needed rest, too. Tomorrow, they would—

Tick . . . Tick.

A chill ran down her spine. It was too insistent a sound to be rain. *Then what was it?* Tree branches? Perhaps the wind had picked up.

She rolled over so she was faced away from the sound—not that she could see anything through the thick bed-curtains—and forced herself to think of something else. How would she escape? There was no trellis below her window, and no trees, but perhaps if she—

No trees. There were no trees or branches close enough to hit the pane, not even in a strong gale.

Tick . . . Tick . . . Tick.

Her heart began to pound. She rolled over and slipped between the bed-curtains, then padded to the window, shivering in only her night-rail. Of course, it wasn't Will, or anyone else, but it was better to know what it *was* and put her imagination to rest.

Tick . . . Tick. She pulled back the drapes and examined the pane. A leak of some kind? Or a night bird? She peered through the blackness. *Tick.* Something small hit the pane, then bounced off.

A—a stone?

She flung open the sash. "Who's there?" She peered through the dark, straining to see. It might *not* be Will . . . but pebbles didn't just throw themselves.

"Cybil."

There. He was standing on the path in the garden, not ten yards from the house. She could just make out the pale shape of his face looking up at her.

Her breath stopped. *He'd come.* But he was in danger— "You shouldn't be here."

"I'm coming up."

"No. It's—" But his shadow had slipped away.

The next ten minutes were, in fact, an eternity. It was quiet. Too quiet. How would he get in? He wasn't climbing to the window, obviously. There was nothing to climb. He'd just . . . disappeared. Slowly, quietly, Cybil closed the window, then stood motionless beside it, not daring to breathe, waiting for—something. A noise. A crash. A shout.

But there was nothing. Only silence.

Then, at last, came the soft rasp of the bar being lifted. Slowly, the door swung open.

She watched, wide-eyed, as Will soundlessly entered the room, then turned and pulled the door closed behind him.

He was only a silhouette in the blackness, but she could see he was dressed in dark clothes and gloves, a hat pulled over his eyes. Oddly, he wore no boots, only stockings.

"How did you—" she began, but her words were stopped by his arms wrapping around her. His coat was damp against her cheek, and he smelled of the outdoors, of wool and leather. She inhaled, bringing his scent, his very being inside herself. It was almost as if—as if her thoughts had made him appear.

Could this be a dream?

He pulled away and ran his palms down her sides, feeling her, as if he too feared she was an illusion. Then he grasped her cold hands in his gloved ones, bringing them to his lips. "Are you hurt?" His eyes darted to her stomach, then back to her face. "Is the—"

"I'm fine." Her throat caught, and she brought both their hands to her belly. She placed his palms over her womb, then covered his hands with her own. "*We're* fine."

The warmth of him—even with gloves on—poured into her, through her, and somehow, she knew the babe felt it too. The love of his father.

Cybil swallowed and looked up into Will's face. It was dark in the chamber, with only a tiny bit of leaden light coming in through the windows, but his eyes were shining, as if with unshed tears.

She loved him. She'd always loved him. All those times she'd told herself they could never have love . . . they'd had it all along.

Unable to bear the ache in her heart, or the love in his eyes, she fell back into his embrace, and he caught her, his strong arms holding her close.

"I was so afraid—" He exhaled into her hair.

"I know."

He pulled back again, his expression clouded. "I'm sorry, Cybil."

"Sorry? What for?"

"For disregarding you. I deserved your anger." He drew a breath. "I thought you'd left me because of it, and I— I hated myself." He blinked once, twice, and a single tear ran down his cheek, then another. "I was so sure I'd lost you—" he choked out.

Cybil smiled through the dark. "I'd already forgiven you the next day." She reached her hand up and cradled his cheek. It was rough with day-old whiskers and wet with his tears. She wiped them away with her thumb. "You were misguided, true, but you were only doing what you thought best."

Will was silent a moment. He swallowed. "I willna ever ignore your wishes again. I swear." Then he bent down and kissed her—a long, achingly tender kiss that both mended and broke her heart.

Because he *had* lost her, just not in the way he'd supposed.

She swallowed back the tears, then pushed away from him. She had to put distance between them. This tenderness—this *love*—would only bring more pain.

"He knows about the child." She sat on the edge of the bed.

Will seemed to sense her shift in mood. He remained standing. "I'd guessed as much. How did he find out?"

"I don't know. But I do know that Luke—"

"I know. He confessed, poor lad. 'Twas the Baron's man who'd been harassin' him. He threatened to hurt Emily and Ewan if Luke didna lead you to 'im."

"Townend, yes. He's the steward here." Then a sudden thought occurred. "But if Luke told you, then . . ." A chill went down Cybil's spine as she remembered the violence in Townend's voice when he'd sent Luke home that afternoon. *So help me, boy. If you tell a soul, I will find you, and you will pay.*

"They're safe, for now," Will assured her. "I sent them to my house in Glasgow . . . and there's no reason yet for the Baron to know Luke said anything. But—Cybil."

"Yes?"

"He threatened me too." His voice took on a new, dangerous edge. "He told Luke he'd turn me in to the law if Luke didna do what he wanted."

"*You?*" Cybil looked at him sharply, though she couldn't see his expression in the dark. "He knows?"

"Seems that way." Will shrugged. "He told Luke he'd see me shipped off like his da was."

"But, how?"

"That's what I hoped you could tell me."

"I—have no idea. Ernie doesn't know you. He'd have no way to. I don't think he's ever even been to Glasgow."

"Have they said anything, or—"

"They've told me nothing, just took me here. Townend gave me laudanum on the journey. I slept the whole way, and then . . . I've been locked in this room ever since."

Will's hands balled into fists. He was silent for a few breaths, then he stretched out his fingers. "Have you seen him?"

"Ernie?"

"Aye."

"Yes . . ." Cybil hesitated, feeling the weight of that conversation all over again.

"What did he say?"

"He—" Cybil stopped, took a breath and willed her voice to be steady. "He gave me a choice. I can go to London and act as his wife, or I can stay here, alone. Either way, if I make a fuss or begin to write again, or—anything he doesn't like, he'll put me away."

Will had been hovering, but now he sat beside her. "An asylum?"

"Yes," she whispered.

"And the child?

Cybil swallowed. "If he's a boy," she spoke slowly, forcing the words through unwilling lips, "he plans to take him and raise him as his heir."

There was a long silence. Once again, Will's hands were balled into tight fists. "And if it's a lass?"

"Ernie didn't say, but I suspect he'd raise her as his own, try to use her for some political advantage, but—" She stopped, unable to continue.

"But, what?"

Cybil opened her mouth. Closed it again. Stared into the dark. She couldn't—she couldn't say the words.

Will turned to peer at her. He took her hand. "What?"

His eyes—she couldn't deny him. "If it's a girl, he plans to force me to bed someone else, to conceive his heir."

Will's eyes widened, and his hand tightened. "What? Who?"

Cybil shrugged. "Townend, he said. Or . . . I don't know . . ." Her voice broke. "I couldn't bear it, Will. I *couldn't*. I can feel him now, inside me, moving." Her free hand went to her stomach. Will's eyes followed the movement, then he opened his mouth, but she kept talking. "He can't grow up Ernie's son. He *can't*. I must get him away from here. I'd thought to escape—"

"Aye. You're coming with me. Tomorrow." There was a hard resolve in his voice. "I wish to God it could be tonight, but—better to wait and have a solid plan."

"But—" Cybil had planned escape, but not with Will. It was too dangerous.

"I'll bring a ladder, and a carriage. 'Twill be easy."

Cybil sprang up from the bed. "I can't go to Glasgow, Will, or Strathaven. And if Ernie knows about *you* . . . Where would we go?"

Will reached for her hand and drew her back to him. Reluctantly, she sat down. "Where *you* go is up to you." His hand still clasped hers, and his eyes searched her face, as if looking for an answer to an unspoken question. "But it must be very far away. France, or farther." He drew a long breath. "And you canna come back."

His words stung, though they shouldn't have. Where *she* went, of course she'd be going alone. That was her plan from the start, was it not? Will had come to rescue her like the hero he was, perhaps he *did* even love her, but he was right, she couldn't come back, and he couldn't leave his life in Glasgow, his employment, his children.

"I'll support you wherever you are, or—" He hesitated, and in the gloom, she could see his countenance tighten, as if he were bracing for a blow. "If you like, we could go together. After this—I'm not safe in Glasgow either, Cybil. I thought I might go to America, to New York. I could find work there no doubt." Cybil inhaled sharply, and Will blinked in response. "No one knows us there. We could change our names—"

"But what of your children?"

"They'd come too."

"You'd—we'd—*America*?" For the first time in days, a beacon of hope, real hope, shone into the bleakness of Cybil's mind. It was insanity, surely, her life never worked in such a halcyon way. She'd hoped for something better for her child, never for herself, but—*what if it worked?*

Will removed his hand from hers, though his eyes never left her face. "If you'd rather go to France, or somewhere else, alone, I'd understand. I'd support you." He paused, a long, tortured silence. "I love you, Cybil."

He loved her. He loved her enough to set her free.

Cybil drew a long breath. "I don't want to be anywhere, without you, ever again." She grasped his hands. "I love you. I think—I always have."

His smile blossomed in the dark. She could barely see it, so she ran her hands over his face, feeling the dimple, the ridges of his brows, the web of lines by his eyes, the soft curve of his lips.

Even if it all went wrong, if she was captured and he was exiled, their child raised a monster, this was real. Their love was real. And in that was hope.

Hope for the ages, if not for their own lives.

They sat a while longer, planning. Cybil would make the crossing immediately, then Will would follow a week later with the children. He'd already, apparently, sent a letter to Percy and Jane, telling them everything before Ernie had the chance to, but he'd draft another, giving his formal resignation and informing her brother of their whereabouts. That part smarted a bit. Cybil wished she could have told her family herself, or at least had the chance to say goodbye.

"What about Emily?" Cybil wondered. "Will they be safe here alone?"

A shadow crossed Will's face. "I'll help her, of course, but . . ." He shook his head. "It'll have to be up to her, what she does."

"You think she should leave Strathaven."

He shook his head. "I dinna ken, Cybil. I really dinna ken." He rose. "I should be goin'. I'll need my sleep tonight."

But Cybil's mind was whirring. There was so much they didn't know. So much that could go amiss . . .

"Will?"

"Aye?"

"If—if something goes wrong—"

"*Ach*, lass—" He put a hand on her shoulder.

"No, hear me out." She shrugged him off. "If something goes wrong, don't sacrifice yourself for me. You have your children to think about, and—" She stopped, swallowed. "While this child lives in me, Ernie daren't hurt me. I'll find a way to escape and save him, no matter what."

"But, Cybil—"

"Promise me. Promise you won't sacrifice yourself. You have too much to risk, and I—I couldn't bear it if you were transported or—" Her voice broke off. She couldn't bear to finish the sentence.

Will watched her for a few long breaths, then finally, he nodded. "I promise, though I hope to God it doesna come to that."

TWENTY-THREE

WILL SPENT THE NEXT day in a whirlwind of preparation. He would leave nothing to chance. Cybil had to be freed from the Devil's house, then they had to make their escape unnoticed and undetected.

The first problem was, of course, transport. He hadn't brought his own gig to Leeds, so he'd need to secure one. Something fast and light, yet durable for the two-day trip to Liverpool, where he'd put Cybil on the first packet he could find passage on. He settled on an old but well-built gig purchased from a local carriage maker. At only twelve pounds, it was an expense he could spare, and he'd be able to sell it once he returned home. The horse he could borrow from the inn and change along the way.

Next, he'd secured a length of rope and spent a tense hour in his room, constructing a ladder that he hoped Cybil would be able to descend.

As he sat, tying knot after knot, his mind fell to work on the long list of things he'd need to attend to in the coming week.

He'd had a vague idea of going to New York, but it hadn't seemed real without Cybil. Now that he'd secured her assent, it was time to devise a real plan. He'd need to divest himself of his house. He'd need to inform Sommerbell of his resignation and assure him of his sister's safety. His first letter had surely broken any ties of friendship he might have held with the man, or his wife—he'd not even told them that Cybil had been kidnapped, or where she was—so this seemed easier. A formality only. He'd also need to convince Rosie to give up all but one, maybe two, of her bullies. He'd need to secure Emily's finances and determine her future. Perhaps he'd have his man lease his house and funnel the funds to Emily. That way, no matter what happened to Will, she'd be secure.

And he'd need to do it all in secrecy, because once it was clear Cybil had escaped, there was no telling what the Baron might do. Will would need to hide himself, his bairns and Emily's family from both the Baron and the police. They'd go to a hotel perhaps, one as far from his house, and Emily's, as they could get.

It was daunting, but not any worse than what he'd had to do when he left Strathfarrar.

Christ. This would be the second time Will had to restart his life. He could only pray this time had a better ending.

It would have seemed odd to leave the inn in the dead of night, so Will set out with his new gig in the late afternoon, as if he really were going to visit a country squire's estate to inquire about employment as he'd told the innkeep. He paused a mile out of town, pulled the transport off on a cart track and waited, hidden behind a stand of trees.

It was a clear afternoon, warm for the season. Will unhitched the horse, allowing him a bit of grass before their ordeal, then stretched out on the ground and attempted sleep, though of course he couldn't.

Time slowed. He waited.

The sun set.

He waited.

The moon rose, thin and sharp, like the sickle he used to use to cut hay. As he watched it clear the treeline, Will allowed himself to think, for the first time that day, what might happen if his plan went wrong. If he were captured. Certainly, the Baron would give him up to the police, which would mean transportation, or worse. Sommerbell and Jane were godparents to Rosie and Nat, but would they still agree to a guardianship? And what about Cybil? And Emily? Perhaps he should have written to her to appraise of her his plan . . .

He pushed the worries away. There was nothing to do about them now.

He must have checked his fob watch a thousand times, but finally it was half-eleven.

He rose, hitched the horse, and was off.

———◇———

Will arrived at Cybil's door at exactly the time they'd decided, an hour past midnight. He'd had no trouble finding a spot to secure the gig, hidden in a little copse of trees just outside the gates. Just as he'd done the night before, he scaled the wall to the roof of the covered walk between the kitchen and the house, using a window ledge and a few protruding bricks to heave himself up. The broken window he'd discovered the previous night was still broken, allowing easy entrance into a deserted bedroom, then the hall. This time, he kept his boots on after shimmying in through the window. He couldn't leave them behind, and unlike last night, he wasn't worried about muddy footprints left on the Baron's carpet. It would be quite clear in the morning that Cybil was gone and that someone had come for her. But by then, they'd be well on their way to Liverpool.

He stood before her door, running his mind through the next five minutes. The rope ladder was folded and stowed in the bag he carried over his shoulder. A faint light spilled from under the doorway. Cybil was behind it, ready and waiting. All they'd need to do was open the window, secure and unfurl the ladder, climb down, slip away to the gig, then they'd be on their way.

He took a long, steadying breath, then moved to draw the bar from the door.

But it wasn't there.

The door had been barred the previous night. Will was sure of it. And Cybil had told him it was always kept that way.

He froze, staring at the painted wood, mind whirring.

Was someone beside Cybil in the room? A servant? Her husband?

Had the Baron moved her elsewhere?

But there was light. *Someone* was in the room.

He held his breath, listening. The blood pounded in his ears, but all else was deathly silent.

Then he took one last, long breath and pushed the door open.

The door swung open, and Cybil wanted desperately to cry out, to scream, to tell Will to turn around, to run as fast as he could, but the deadly gleam in Townend's eye, the revolver he trained on the door and the piece of rough cloth tied securely around her mouth prevented it.

If she moved or made a sound, Townend would shoot Will. That was what Ernie had ordered him to do, and she had no reason to doubt him.

Ernie and Townend had come into the chamber just a few hours before, though it seemed a lifetime ago. Ernie had settled himself on the chaise, watching lazily as Townend tied her to the straight-backed chair that sat before the escritoire and bound her mouth. Her husband had explained calmly and in great detail how it had come to his attention that there was a Scotsman come to Leeds who was asking about the goings on in his house. The milkman had said as much to the scullery maid, who'd told a footman, who'd told a housemaid, who'd told Mrs. Brown, who had, of course, told Townend.

"Didn't take much figurin' to know what that was about." Townend was obviously pleased with himself. He cinched the rope tighter, and it bit painfully into her wrists.

"Apparently, the man purchased himself a new gig today, then set off this way on *business*," Ernie crooned in that deep, scabbed voice. "I almost can't believe my good fortune." He smirked. "'Twill allow me to settle an old score." Then he met Cybil's eye. "And a new one."

Cybil flinched and looked away. Any old score was with her, not Will. But now Will would pay the price. How had she allowed him to put himself in such danger? He had enough trouble of his own without taking on hers too. She'd known that vision of America was impossible. That was not the kind of life Cybil was meant to lead. She'd known, yet she'd drawn Will right into Ernie's trap.

After that, a dreadful silence had taken over the room. As Cybil and Ernie occupied the only two chairs, Townend stretched himself out on the bed.

Waiting. Then, a half hour ago, at Ernie's command, he'd gotten up and stood by the door, weapon trained at the threshold.

Perhaps Will wouldn't come after all. Perhaps he'd find out, somehow, that their plan had been discovered.

But that chimera evaporated as the heavy door swung open and her lover's shadowy form came into view.

He was bareheaded tonight but once again dressed in dark clothing, and this time, he wore boots. A cloth bag was slung over his shoulder. His brows were drawn together into a dark, shadowy line as he warily took in the scene.

Cybil couldn't help it. She cried out through her gag, emitting nothing more than a whimper.

Will didn't notice Townend in the shadows by the door. His eyes darted from Ernie to Cybil. He dropped the bag he was carrying, then made to cross toward her, but he was stopped abruptly when Townend grabbed his arm and jabbed the iron muzzle between his shoulder blades.

"Welcome, Mr. Chisolm," Ernie said. "Do come in." Will was staring at him, wide eyed, and it was then that Cybil realized what he'd already seen. Ernie had pulled a pocket pistol—a tiny little thing with a mother of pearl handle—from his waistcoat and was pointing it directly at her.

Townend pressed the metal barrel of his much larger flintlock into Will's back. "You heard 'im. In you go."

Will strode forward. His eyes met Cybil's. He wanted to fight, she could tell, but she shook her head, praying he would understand. Being captured was bad enough. She couldn't bear it if he was shot on her account.

Ernie rose, then took Townend's place behind Will, burrowing the muzzle of the small gun into Will's back. "Tie him," he ordered.

Townend crossed in front of Will, pulling a length of rope from his coat pocket. Will's attention diverted to the man in front of him. His eyes widened as if in shock. "*Wilcox.*" He said it as if he were accusing Townend of something.

As if he knew the man.

Cybil could only see the back of Townend's head now, but he seemed to look up and into Will's face. "Richie." His voice held an odd mix of satisfaction, accusation and . . . *regret?* "We meet again."

Wilcox. Wilcox was the man who'd betrayed Will and Davey, all those years ago. The third man, the spy who'd concocted the plan to destroy the bridge, then disappeared.

But that wasn't possible. Townend wasn't a spy. He'd worked for Ernie for years, since before Cybil had married him. He'd never been to Glasgow—

Townend had worked for Ernie.

And Ernie was a close confident of Sidmouth, the Home Secretary, the same man who'd unleashed the government spies in Glasgow four years ago—

"You work for *him?*" Will hadn't yet put the pieces together.

Townend stayed silent. He broke Will's gaze to force his hands behind his back and tie them. Will grunted in pain as the steward drew the knots tight.

"There's so much you never knew, Mr. Chisolm." Ernie tucked his pistol back into his pocket, then crossed in front of Will. "It's such a pleasure to finally know your real name, by the way."

Will growled.

Ernie ignored him. "You think it was a coincidence that the mill where your old friend Wilcox worked was owned by my father-in-law? He was a good man, James Sommerbell. A good Tory. It's a pity my brother-in-law isn't the same."

Cybil's stomach dropped. *Father.* Father had conspired with Ernie to allow a spy into his factory. Another form of payment, perhaps, for her freedom—

Will spun around, causing Townend to stumble, then he kicked hard—one solid boot to the bullocks. The steward yelled, then slumped forward in pain. Ernie sprang up, frantically digging in his pocket for his pistol, but before he could get it, Will kicked again, sending him sprawling and cursing. Will's arms were still tied, but he backed to the door, reaching for the latch with his bound hands.

It all took too long. Townend was standing again, with his revolver in hand. "Come now, Richie, my lad. None o' that." He resumed his place behind Will, cold metal pushing into his captive's back.

Cybil stared at Will. At Townend—Wilcox.

All of this had been her doing. Will being shot. Davey's transportation. It had been a result of the debt owed by her family to her husband. Because of her.

"Ah . . . you see now, don't you, my love?" Ernie had recovered and was watching her in amusement. He turned to Will and Townend. "Get him out of here," he spat.

"Where are you—"

"We're goin' on a little trip, you and me," Townend said, cutting Will off, "for old times' sake."

"Cybil, I—" But Will didn't get to finish. Townend pushed him out, and they were gone.

Ernie closed the door behind them, then took his time unbinding Cybil's wrists, her mouth. His hands were cold as ice.

Just after he'd removed her gag, he bent down and whispered in her ear. "Try anything, and he dies." Then he turned and left the room, barring the door behind him.

TWENTY-FOUR

ANY HOPE WILL MIGHT have had of escape was felled by the two burly footmen waiting in the shadows just down the corridor. He must have walked right past them on his way in. Wilcox—or Townend, or whatever the fucker's name was—grunted at the men as they passed. They fell in beside Will, grasping his elbows while Townend walked behind.

They took him down some steps, then through the front door and into the night. The air was colder than before, or Will was. The stars were out, bright, allowing a view of the drive, the gate with the stone lions, the wee group of trees where the gig waited and the moor beyond.

The men dragged Will down the stone ramp to the drive, then stopped, allowing Townend to take the lead.

"Where are we going?" Will didn't have much hope of an answer, and none came. Townend led them to the left, where the stables loomed, and in through a set of large doors. The smells of horse dung and piss, hay and leather met Will's nose. A boy sat on a low bench, nodding off. Townend barked an order, and the lad darted up and away—it seemed he'd been waiting for them.

Will was pushed onto the bench, and Townend and his two men silently stood guard. A quarter hour later, the boy returned. "'Tis ready, sir."

Will was hauled up and pushed back out into the night.

A large traveling carriage—darkly colored with shiny wheels, just as Luke had described the carriage Cybil was taken in—stood waiting, a driver on the perch. Townend motioned for one of his men to circle round to the other side and protect the far door, then he opened the near one and shoved Will up the steps. Without the use of his hands, Will lurched as he climbed, nearly falling on his face, but he managed to right himself and settle onto one of the benches. Townend followed. He knelt to tie Will's ankles, then he took the seat across. The door closed, and the coach began to move.

For a time, Will stared at the shadow of Townend's face, willing the scoundrel to look at him. To talk to him. The traitor. There were so many insults he'd been waiting years to hurl at this man. Where to even begin?

Townend fished a cigar from his pocket, lit it, then smoked in silence, his gaze trained out the window and his face drawn into an unreadable glower. He ignored Will completely.

The smoke chafed at Will's nose, burned his throat. "Arena you even goin' to gloat, ye fuck?" Will finally spat out. "Ye fooled us good, dinna ye? Just as your master bid ye."

Townend didn't respond.

"Like a wee dog, ye are." Will couldn't stop. "Doin' just as you're told. Spyin'. Kidnapping. *Rape*." He choked on that last word—that awful, unthinkable promise the Baron had given Cybil if their child was a girl.

"Rape?" Townend's head jerked toward Will. "I haven't raped anyone."

"But ye would, wouldna ye, if Cybil's babe is a girl." Will's fists balled, itching to pummel the man. "An' so help me, I'd hunt ye down, and I'd—"

"I know nothing of such things," Townend interrupted, clearly confused. "I'm no rapist." Something in his tone made Will believe him. It seemed even this man had his limits.

"Na, only a kidnapper then, and a bloody spy settin' good men up to—"

"Shut up," Townend barked. "Or I'll make you." He pulled a piece of cloth from his pocket, making the threat real.

Will glared at him. Every muscle in his body was tense, ready to fight.

But what was the point? A voice, a reasonable one, whispered in his head. It would be better to seem harmless now, then strike later when the chance arose.

Will forced a few breaths, stretched his fingers out, then relaxed his shoulders as best he could with his arms tied behind him. Seemingly satisfied, Townend looked back out the window, took another pull on his cigar and fell silent fell once again.

As best Will could tell, they were headed North. Glasgow, most likely. There was still a warrant out for his arrest from four years ago, and the Glasgow Police would be more than happy to take him into custody and bring him to trial. They'd love it, in fact. With the Six Acts in place, and Hardie, Baird and Wilson's death sentences, it'd been years since anyone had dared take up arms. With peace, the populace to begin to forget, and the fear of reform that Sidmouth had so effectively created was waning. There'd even been talk of repealing some of the Acts since they weren't needed anymore. The trial of a wanted, violent radical would be just the thing to frighten the masses and cement the continued need for vigilance—to keep the Acts in place, keep the Tories in power and quash any talk of reform. Hell, a trial dredging up the events of four years ago would play right into the Baron's hand, and all the other Tory fucks in Parliament.

That was exactly what the Baron wanted, wasn't it? Probably why he'd ordered his man to snoop around Emily's in the first place. The police had given up finding Will years ago, but now that his capture served a political purpose, the Baron himself had come looking—and who better to send on that errand than the blackguard who'd set Will up in the first place? The only one who'd know him on sight? But then Townend had recognized Cybil, and everything had changed.

Ach, Cybil. The picture of her terrified, gagged and bound to a chair would be forever pressed into Will's mind. He'd go through a thousand trials, be transported a hundred times, submit himself to the gallows if only it would make her safe.

But it wouldn't. He'd purposely dropped the haversack with the ladder and the bit of money, in the hopes she might recover it and escape, but the chances of that happening were blastedly low. No, she was at the mercy of her husband. And what he might do—what he *would* do. Will couldn't bear to think of it. Even if Townend wasn't ready to follow through on the Baron's plans, some other man surely would be.

He'd failed her. He'd failed their unborn babe. His own children. Emily. *Faugh*. He could only pray that Sommerbell and Jane would take his bairns in, that the Baron wouldn't make good on his threats to hurt Luke, Emily or Ewan.

Instinctively, Will flexed his wrists, testing the bonds. But they held firm.

Townend glanced at him. Even in the gloom, Will could make out the smirk tugging at the man's lips. "My brother was a sailor. Taught me how to tie knots." Then his eyes tracked back to the window, he took a long pull on his cigar and there was silence once more.

⸻◈⸻

The quiet after the men left was deafening. Cybil sat unmoving, as if she were still tied to the chair. Her blood pounded through her veins, her breath seemed to rip through the still air, ragged and panicked, yet her body was paralyzed.

They had Will. They knew of his past, of everything. He could be transported or hanged. And it was all Cybil's fault.

Margaret's pale, tragic countenance floated into Cybil's mind. Margaret, who had lost her sweetheart, her future, to the Stirling Tollbooth gallows. Emily, whose husband had been sent away forever.

That couldn't happen. She couldn't allow it, just as she couldn't allow Ernie to steal their child. *She must do something.*

The room, the dim candlelight, the night, all of it dilated, crowding in upon her. Her body was tense, her gaze darted around the chamber, looking, searching for—

Cybil's wild eyes fell on the bag that still lay in the shadows where Will had dropped it by the door. It was made from rough woven linen. Two wooden buttons held it closed, and a long shoulder strap extended from it. It was the kind of bag a soldier might carry, or a thief.

Something bulged inside it. Something Will had brought before, when he thought they'd—no, she couldn't think of it. Their plan, the life that, for one enchanted day, she'd dared to dream possible.

An ache rose in her throat, and she finally found the will to move. She crossed the room and bent to pick up the bag. This was all she had left of him. A plain, ugly, rough cloth sack. She held it to her face, inhaling the scent. It smelled nothing of Will, but even still . . . it had been close to him.

She swallowed back the tears, slipped the crude wooden buttons through the fabric, then reached inside. Her fingers met something rough and fibrous. Rope. She pulled it out. It was knotted at intervals. A ladder. It was how he'd planned for her to make her escape. They'd talked of it the night before. He'd said the method he'd used to get to her room would be too treacherous, and he'd make a ladder instead so she could descend more easily from the window.

There was something else too, a small sack of coins.

Cybil's eyes darted to the window. The ends of the ladder were looped. She'd need to secure it to something, something sturdy and large enough to span the window frame—that chair perhaps . . .

If you try anything, he dies. Ernie's whispered words crept into her mind, but she banished them. Will might die anyway. He'd want her to *try*, or at least to get out, for the sake of their babe.

A quarter hour later, her feet touched the ground below her window. It was cold, and she could see her breath in the clear air. The moon had set, but the stars shimmered brightly above, like pinpricks in a tin lantern.

Thanking heaven that she still had the fur pelisse and sturdy half boots she'd been wearing when she was accosted in Strathaven, Cybil walked softly around the house.

All was dark, except a small light that came from Ernie's chambers on the main floor.

Where would they keep Will? The cellar perhaps? Or the stable? The stable seemed more likely. It was out of the way of most of the servants, and he could be spirited out more easily in the morning. If that was their plan.

As she neared the stables, a coach appeared from the yard and stilled in front. Cybil darted back and crouched in the black shadow of a gnarled oak tree. She stood frozen as the stable doors opened and two shadowy footmen emerged, pushing Will ahead of them. They forced him into the carriage, then

Townend climbed in behind. The door shut, then the coach jolted forward and the clip-clop of horses' feet rang out as It picked up speed, rolled down the drive, through the gate and onto the main road.

He was gone.

The two footmen watched the coach go, then they quickly disappeared into the main house, talking quietly. Cybil stood frozen, listening, but there was no sound beyond the static rustling of the dried leaves that still clung to the old tree's branches. A sleek stable cat prowled past, ignoring her in his nighttime pursuit of prey.

She glanced at the clock tower that crowned the stable roof. Half-past two. At least four hours until Phoebe would come to build Cybil's fire and discover she wasn't in her room.

Four hours to—to *what*? Rescue Will? Was that really her plan?

They were taking him to Glasgow to be prosecuted, of that she had no doubt. But what could she possibly hope to do about it? It wasn't as if she, a woman alone—a woman who was herself hunted, could free him. If he were in prison . . . The image of Will locked behind iron bars in a filthy, rank cell, awaiting his fate, was too much to bear.

And it was all because of her. There had to be something she could do—

Emily. Emily was in Glasgow, at Will's house. Will had intended to go there as soon as Cybil was on the boat to New York, to warn Emily of the danger. He'd talked of temporarily moving his family and hers to a hotel, and even of suggesting Emily leave Scotland with them.

But if Will couldn't . . . then it was up to Cybil to warn Emily away from Will's house, and to ensure his children were safe. She could take them to Percy and Jane, say her goodbyes, then make her own escape. It was what Will would have wanted. What she had to do.

The breath squeezed out of her lungs as the responsibility settled on her shoulders, a yoke, not unlike the one Emily used, except instead of simple, clear water, lives were in the balance.

At least Ernie would never suspect her going to Glasgow. It was the most dangerous, most foolhardy place she could go. And perhaps she could find a way to see Will, to disguise herself and enter whatever prison he'd be held in, to say goodbye.

Cybil swallowed the lump in her throat. There was no time for such things. How would she get to Glasgow? That was all that mattered now.

Her eyes wandered to the stables. In the early days of her marriage, she'd spent some time riding in the countryside around this house. She knew the terrain. But there were a host of stable boys and grooms sleeping in the upper floor of the building, perhaps even one or two in the empty stalls . . . The chances of finding a suitable horse, saddling the beast and making her escape without waking anyone were poor at best. And she couldn't ride all the way to Glasgow, especially in her condition.

She'd need to get a mail coach, or a stage.

Her mind raced to remember the surrounding towns. Leeds to the west was the largest, but it was ten miles away. Ernie might catch her on the road. The highway that led to Newcastle ran just north of the estate. There was a town she'd ridden through whenever she'd traveled from here to home . . . *Wetherby*. That was it. It was only a few miles distant, and if she remembered right, there was a coaching inn. Perhaps more than one.

Thank God for the money in Will's sack.

A plan began to form, a plan that hinged on a few bits of good luck. If she cut through the fields, it would be a short walk to Wetherby. And from there, she could surely get a stage to Newcastle, then north to Edinburgh and Glasgow. She could only hope there'd be an early coach to whisk her away before Ernie discovered where she'd gone, and that she might arrive in Glasgow before Townend or Ernie could get to Will's house.

The babe shifted in her womb. Rolling over in his sleep perhaps, or stretching.

Cybil put a hand to her belly. *Hang on, little one. We've got some business to attend to, but you're going to be safe. I will keep you safe.*

She pushed away from the tree and began to walk.

It seemed to Will that he didn't sleep, though he must have, because before he knew it, the horizon had turned from black to grey, allowing a faint light into the carriage.

His arms ached from being tied behind his back for so long, and he did his best to stretch them without sliding off the slick leather seat—not an easy task—all while ignoring the thirst pulling at his tongue and the fullness of his bladder.

Wilcox—or Townend—Will's mind was groggy—was sleeping across from him, his long legs stretched out, chin tucked to his chest. Strands of greasy blonde hair fell over his brow and onto his face.

Will studied him. In slumber, he appeared harmless. Peaceful even, if it hadn't been for the double-barreled flintlock he still gripped against his chest.

When he'd turned up at the factory looking for work, he'd seemed a nice enough fellow. Down on his luck but cheerful. Will had been one of the first to befriend him. He'd had little time for carousing back then with the children at home, but Wilcox had somehow found his way into their life. He'd met the bairns, brought them sweets just after payday once. He'd been interested in politics and in righting the wrongs of the world, so Will had convinced Davey to let him come along with them to meetings at the King's Head.

Faugh. He'd known solidarity with this scoundrel. He'd trusted him . . . and had walked right into his goddamn trap. And now, just as unaware and mutton-headed as he'd been four years ago, Will had walked into a second trap.

And yet, Townend was only a servant. A faithful cur doing his master's bidding. Perhaps if Will played his hand right—and managed to somehow choke back the hate—he'd be able to find a chink in the man's armor. Perhaps there would be a way out of this yet.

Townend stirred, then jolted awake. His blue eyes darted about the carriage, then focused on Will.

"Mornin'." Will reined his tone into something resembling civility.

Townend blinked, still obviously not quite awake.

"'Tis daylight." Will nodded toward the window.

Townend grunted.

"We're to Glasgow, then?" Will didn't expect an answer, but if he could somehow get the man to lower his guard, put a wedge between him and the Baron . . . "Must be exhausting, all this travel." He waited a beat. "How long did he have ye sniffin' around Strathaven before Cybil turned up?"

Townend stared at him through narrowed eyes, but his thin lips stayed clamped shut, drawn into a tight line.

"Must have been quite the shock to find the Baron's wife when you were lookin' for me."

Townend's eyes widened, almost imperceptibly, then his tight expression returned.

So it was true. He had been looking for Will.

"That's quite some predicament he put you in, eh? A known spy. If you'd been seen by the wrong man, even in Strathaven, it coulda been your head."

Townend's brows lowered. "I was careful."

Will nodded. "I'm sure you were, but even still, 'twasn't a good position to put you in. You, a faithful servant. I'd think he'd show a bit more care for your wellbeing."

Townend's jaw tightened. Will could see the muscles working.

He was on to something.

"What kind of hold does he have on you anyway?" Will continued, allowing his eyes to narrow. "Surely, you could—"

"Shut your gob."

"But—"

"I said. Shut it." Townend reached into his pocket again, pulling out the gag. So much for chinks in the armor.

"No need for that." Will jerked his chin at the fabric. After a long moment of tense silence, Townend put it away.

Sighing, Will sat back as best he could and directed his gaze out the window. Then another idea occurred.

He waited about a quarter hour, then spoke again. "I have to piss," he declared. "Surely, you'll let a man piss, willna you?"

Townend's eyes slid open. "When we change horses." He closed them again.

The carriage went over an abrupt bump, bouncing both of them off their seats. Then a smaller bump.

"Surely, it's better here than an inn with people about. I'm bound after all." Will held up his hands. "It'd be hard to—"

"Alright, already, I have to piss too," Townend muttered. Then he knocked on the roof with the butt of his pistol, and the coach slowed to a stop.

"I'll need use of my feet," Will pointed out. Townend stared at him for a moment, then reluctantly stooped to untie the knots.

"And my hands. Unless you're going to hold my tool for me?" He raised a brow.

"Not yet." Townend grasped Will's elbow and poked the cold metal of the pistol into his back. Then the door opened, and he pushed Will out.

They were in beautiful country, with rolling hills to the horizon, touched with yellow and green by the rising sun. The air felt fresh and clean after all the rain, and a low mist hung in the narrow river valley that spread below them—a *dale*, the Yorkshiremen called it. The only sign of human habitation was a straight stone fence bordering a field in the distance.

Will took it in as quick as he could, noting each tree, the gentle swell of land before them, the small, misted valley. The coachman, corny-faced and barely old enough to be called a man, was standing awkwardly before them. How much did the lad know of Will? Anything?

Townend handed his piece to the driver, with low instructions to keep it trained on the prisoner. The boy eyed the flintlock warily, then his gaze shifted to Will as Townend paced away, turned his back and unbuttoned his falls.

At the sound of Townend's piss hitting the dirt, Will grinned at the lad, then winked. As he'd hoped, the boy's expression went from guarded to confused. Will raised a brow and made another face, one he'd used on the bairns when they were small, to make them laugh. The boy flushed, not amused but clearly bewildered by the display.

By the time Townend was back and untying Will's hands, he had the boy thoroughly befuddled. And distracted. When his bonds fell loose, his hands came around and his shoulders hurt like the devil. He winced and rolled them out.

But still, he waited. Townend still stood behind him, alert, and he wanted both of them as off guard, and as unprepared, as possible. Nonchalantly, he tugged on one of his gloves, pulled it off. Townend began to turn, going to retrieve his piece from the lad. Will moved his hand to the other glove, as if to pull it—

He lunged, kneeing Townend in the stomach and unbalancing him mid-stride. In the same motion, he paced toward the coachman, but he didn't look at the lad. Instead, he kept his eyes trained just beyond him, as if he intended to dart past and make his escape. Just as he came near enough, Will reached to the side and grabbed for the pistol, easily wresting it from the boy's thin grasp.

The lad cried out, but Will didn't wait to see what he did next, or how quickly Townend recovered. He took off down the slope, away from the road and toward the thick, mist-enclosed valley below. It was easy running downhill, and the ground, still wet from the rain, was spongy, almost springy under his boots. His strides widened as he grew accustomed to the movement.

There were shouts behind him. He dared not look back, but surely, at least one of his captors was pursuing him. Thank God he'd gotten the pistol.

He crossed into the mist, and his foot fell half on, half off a stone. His ankle twisted painfully. The next stride hurt like the devil, but he ignored it as he splashed through the small stream that creased the valley, then sprinted up another rise, dodging and weaving between boulders and tree trunks.

He paused at the top of the hill, listening. Heavy footfalls thudded up the rise behind him.

He turned and ran down into the next dale. He had the pistol if need be, but ye gods, he didn't want to use it.

Finally, after what seemed years but was probably only a half hour of hard running over hills, down dales and through brambles, fog and woodland, he stopped, crouched behind a stone fence and listened.

Silence.

He poked his head up, scanning the landscape.

No one.

He was free.

TWENTY-FIVE

WILL REACHED THE CREST of the next hill, the fifth? The tenth? He'd lost count. The sun was past its zenith, and he had no idea where he was. His trouser legs were torn from running through the brush and wet from crossing more rivers and streams than he could remember. His right ankle throbbed with each step. His stomach was rumbling with hunger, and his muscles were trembling with fatigue.

He'd been walking for hours, and though he'd seen plenty of sheep and a few crumbling stone fences, the landscape had been devoid of people and habitations—till now.

He crested the hill, and a farm came into view. Not a large one, just a cottage, a barn and a tidy little garden, all tucked snuggly into a glen. A thin trail of smoke rose from the chimney, and he could hear the lowing of cattle.

A more welcome sight had never been seen.

Most of the money he'd had was in that damn sack, but there were a few coins tucked away in his waistcoat. He could pay for a crust of bread and cheese and perhaps some fresh milk, then bed down in a loft for a few hours of much-needed sleep. Most importantly, he could get some idea of where the devil he was, and how he might find transport out of here.

But where to go?

The question had been rolling around his mind for the last hour or so, once the panic had worn off.

Every instinct told him to turn around, to go back to the Baron's house and to Cybil. To finish what he'd started. That image—of her tied to the chair, terrified—it haunted him. And Lord only knew what the Devil would do to her now. He might not harm her body, but he'd make her life a living hell.

But . . . Will's eyes tracked to the north, toward Glasgow. Nat and Rosie were in danger. Emily and her bairns were in danger, even more so now that he'd escaped. He'd been a fool to think his house a safe place. It was only a matter of time before the sheriff's men came knocking, or worse, the Baron's.

Ach. If the Devil got to them before Will did . . . He might kidnap them to lure Will in, hurt them, or—Will couldn't let his mind go any farther down that road.

But what if he went to Glasgow, only to find Cybil had been whisked away somewhere beyond his reach? Lost to him forever?

Will scrubbed his face with his hands. *Christ's teeth.* These what ifs would tear him to pieces, rip him clean apart at the seams. He had to act, do *something*, but he had no idea what—

Promise me. She'd said. *Promise me you won't sacrifice yourself.*

The memory landed like a lead weight in his mind, heavy, painful and real. All too real. He had promised, and he'd sworn he wouldn't disregard her again. And so there really was no choice. Now was the time to make good on that promise.

His children needed him. And Cybil—if he loved her, truly loved her, he must put them first and trust her to look after herself.

Will looked South again, toward his love. He *would* get her. He would. But he'd go to Glasgow first. Once he was sure Rosie and Nat, and Emily and her children, were safe, he'd find Cybil and they'd leave for America right away.

He took a long, steeling breath, then limped down the hill toward the cottage.

The stage stopped to change horses in Dunbar. It was early, just past sunrise, but even after spending an entire day traveling, Cybil hadn't found sleep the previous night—or, if she had, it hadn't brought any of the restorative properties of true slumber. The rattling and jostling of the coach, the chattering of passengers, the anticipation and dread roiling in her gut, had all made true rest impossible.

It was like, yet so unlike, the last time she'd traveled to Dunbar. That memory, as bleak as it was, seemed almost . . . comforting. She'd not thought anything could be worse than having to tell Will of her pregnancy, or the pain of keeping the truth from her family. How wrong she'd been.

But, at the same time, she had much to be thankful for. There'd been an early mail coach departing Wetherby just as she'd walked into the innyard, almost as if it had been waiting to whisk her away. She'd transferred to the private stage in Newcastle, which, though more crowded, was faster than the mail and familiar. And though she was a bit lightheaded from the lack of sleep, and her body ached, she'd not been physically ill during the journey.

But true gratitude was hard to find. She was exhausted, restless and impatient. Her task was underway, but far from complete.

And always the questions, the wondering, the worry. Would she be too late? Were Emily and the children safe? Where was Will? What had they done to him?

The coachman opened the door. "Twenty minutes, no more," he barked at the six drowsy passengers within.

Cool air and sunlight streamed into the dark space, piercing Cybil's skull. She'd known she was tired, but the pain of the sudden light was surprising, almost overpowering. She winced, wanting nothing more than to crawl back into the dark hole of the carriage. But she needed to relieve herself, and she should procure some food, if not for herself than for her son. He'd been bouncing about for the last hour with unbelievable energy. Cybil had no idea where he found it. Certainly not from her.

Following the other passengers, she moved toward the light, squinting to keep it at bay. Then the driver's outstretched hand was before her. She took it, and climbed down.

The white columns of the George Hotel loomed before her.

Her legs grew weak. She swayed and attempted to blink away her daze. Somehow, she managed to stumble up the steps and into the hotel, to drop into a seat. But visions of Will were everywhere. Sitting across from her. Ordering food at the bar. Helping her to the stairs.

The proprietor approached, wiping his hands on his apron. "Mrs. Oliphant, so nice to see you again. Would you be wantin' some breakfast?"

The man, the room, began to blur.

"Will your husband be joining you?"

Cybil closed her eyes, then opened them again. He was still there, looking at her expectantly, if somewhat concernedly.

"Is everything alright, ma'am?"

"I think . . . Do you have a room?" she stammered. Just a few hours rest, then she'd be on her way.

"Surely. Will your husband be—"

"No."

Thankfully, the innkeeper didn't ask any more questions. He offered his arm and walked Cybil to a room—not the same one she and Will had shared, thankfully. It was quiet and peaceful, though Cybil's body still felt as if it were being jostled along in the coach.

Without even bothering to remove her shoes, she fell onto the bed and slipped instantly into a deep sleep.

The mail coach rattled over the wooden planks of the Rutherglen Bridge. The River Clyde flowed beneath, a thin, early-morning fog rising from its surface.

Will stared blankly out the window, looking at, but not seeing, the suburban scene. Glasgow, or the outskirts of it. Almost home.

His mind was bleary and slow, and he was in sore need of some sleep. It had been two days since he'd closed his eyes in the loft of the farm in Yorkshire. Sowerby, the farmer, and his wife had been more than hospitable—but even then Will hadn't really slept. His mind had been too occupied. After that, it had been two hours' walk to the nearest village, more than half a day's wait to get the mail coach, then a series of dark and uncomfortable rides that eventually brought him here.

But at least he'd had time to hatch a real plan. It was harebrained, to be sure, with more holes than a leaky sieve, but if it worked . . . *Ach*, he wouldn't think of it. As Cybil had taught him, those kinds of happy endings never happened in real life.

They didn't. She was bloody right. And yet, once he'd thought of it, he couldn't help but request pen and paper from the innkeep of that tiny inn in Yorkshire, couldn't help penning the four identical letters as he sat in the barroom and waited for the mail coach to arrive. He didn't know when, or how, or even *if* he'd make use of them, but if the opportunity arose, he'd be ready.

Now all he wanted was to go straight home, kiss his bairns, then tumble into bed, but he daren't go near the house without making a thorough check of the neighborhood first. There was no telling if it might be watched. Even if the Baron or his man hadn't yet arrived in town, they could have easily sent word ahead to the authorities.

He'd take a hack as near as he dared, then creep up on the place.

He stepped down from the mail coach at the Avondale Arms, a large inn just over the bridge, wincing in pain as his foot hit the pavement and the weight went onto his ankle. Goodwife Sowerby had wrapped it for him, and the swelling was down, but it still hurt like the devil.

The Avondale was near to the city, but not quite city itself. A dyeworks had been built nearby, but there were still trees growing along the Clyde and a few fishermen tossed their lines through the early morning mist.

Will stood on the pavement, resting his ankle and assessing the scene. A beggar was stretched out in front of him, snoring into the tattered hat that covered his face. A group of laborers, lunch pails in hand, made their way over the bridge. A man who appeared to be a gentleman came out of the inn and got into a private carriage. None of them paid him any mind.

A woman holding a basket came into view behind the laborers, a wench of middling age. A farm wife probably, or the wife of a weaver walking to market.

She looked nothing like Cybil, yet in the dim light . . . her hair was dark, her skin pale.

What was she going through back in Yorkshire? What was that devil doing to her? Would she still be there when Will arrived? Had he made the right choice?

Christ. Where had his mind gone? These questions had no answers. They weren't even worth asking. He'd told her he'd mind her wishes from now on, and so he would, even if it killed him. He owed her that much.

But if she were harmed—

Enough. He shook himself, then hobbled up Borrowfield Road. It was busier up ahead. Surely, he'd find a hack.

⚬

Cybil had never been to Will's house, but she would have known it anywhere. It was new, on the Western outskirts of the city and at the top of a steep hill. The neighborhood appeared wealthy, though the house wasn't elaborate in any way—two stories with a slate roof, made from the same yellow brick that was typical of the town. It faced east, and the morning sun lit up the bricks as if they were bars of gold. Around one side was a yard, fenced, with several dogs romping in the grass. A garden stood in the back, bordered by a low stone wall. Even in winter, it was as tidy a plot as Cybil had ever seen with straight, clear rows, cleaned of all brush and rubbish from the season before. Two carved wood columns flanked a freshly painted white door that was adorned with a plain brass buckle knocker.

It was a beautiful house, restful and clean. Simple in every detail, but well made. Looking at it . . . her heart, her soul ached for Will.

But, of course, Will wasn't here. He was—Cybil wouldn't begin to ponder where he was.

She'd thought to be here the day before, but instead she'd let her fatigue get the better of her and unwittingly slept most of the day in that quiet room in Dunbar, waking just in time to catch the late stage to Glasgow. She'd arrived in the city just before midnight, and she'd wanted to come directly here to find Emily, but navigating the foreign town in the middle of the night proved too daunting and, as the coachman had dutifully informed her, too dangerous. She'd been to Glasgow several times, to visit her aunt and uncle and to attend family gatherings, but she'd never had to learn the city, and certainly never traversed it on her own.

So, she'd reluctantly secured a room at the coaching inn, and as soon as morning dawned—a beautiful, bright, cloudless day—she'd gotten a hack and directed the driver to take her to Will's address, the address she knew by heart, the same one she'd sent her missives to back when they were carefree lovers . . .

She grew suddenly nervous as she pushed past the gate and into the small yard. What if Emily wasn't here? What if it was only Will's children? How would she explain herself?

What if no one was here?

If no one was here, she'd go to Aunt Cynthia and explain everything. She'd beg her forgiveness and her help. It would be agony, embarrassing beyond words, but she'd have no choice, and surely her aunt wouldn't turn her away.

A movement caught Cybil's eye. One of the curtains on the first floor moved, and a small face peered out. Ewan.

The boy's countenance lighted at the sight of Cybil. His mouth opened as if he were shouting, then he disappeared and the curtain fluttered shut.

Cybil's heart skipped. She flew up the two stone steps and lifted the knocker, but before the brass struck wood, the door opened.

"Cybil." A stern voice, not Ewan's or Emily's.

How—Cybil backed up a step, staring in disbelief. "Percy?"

TWENTY-SIX

CYBIL STOOD FROZEN ON the step. Percy looked so like Father, irritated and loury, one dark eyebrow raised in flinty disapproval.

The silence hung between them until, finally, she summoned the courage to speak. "Wh-what are you doing here?" she stammered.

Percy's brow lowered. "I was—"

"Mrs. Smith!" Whatever he'd been going to say was cut off by a jubilant Ewan Flemming. He barreled past Percy, nearly knocking him down before colliding with Cybil's skirt. "You're here!"

Cybil embraced the boy. "I'm so sorry to have worried you."

"Cybil." Cybil looked up to find Emily standing beside Percy on the threshold. An expression somewhere between relief and confusion lined her face. "Is Will . . ." She peered past Cybil.

"No. I— I'll explain."

"Of course." Emily seemed to suddenly remember where they were. "Come in. Have you eaten?"

———◆———

Ten minutes later, Emily was pouring tea in Will's sitting room, while Percy looked on and Cybil devoured a scone laden with butter.

It was a small room, but comfortable and warm. It smelled of Will. Sunlight poured through the front window, pooling at Cybil's feet.

Ewan had been banished to the nursery where the children were taking their breakfast. Cybil was relieved not to have to confront Luke just yet. Not that she blamed the boy, really, but . . . Dealing with her brother was difficult enough.

Percy sat on an armchair to Cybil's right. Emily was to her left, sharing the sofa. Her brother had remained silent as they'd gathered in the room, but he'd glared at her, his dark brows raised in disapproval. The only time he opened his mouth was to answer in the negative when she asked, hopefully, if Jane or Mother was with him.

They were, of course, home with little James and the twins, who were still just two months old.

Two months. It had only been two months since Cybil had left home. It seemed an eternity.

She accepted a cup of tea and blew on it lightly, watching the ripples race across the dark liquid.

"So, you escaped Leeds," Percy said.

"Yes. I took the mail coach here, bu—"

"And you're with child." Her brother's eyes flicked to her stomach. His voice was tense, flat and judgemental.

The scone stuck in Cybil's throat. She took a quick sip of the scalding tea. It burned her mouth. Ignoring the pain, she set the cup down and slowly raised her gaze to meet her brother's. Her heart pounded. "Yes."

"It's Chisolm's." His dark eyes sparked, as if he were looking for a fight.

Cybil took a breath. "Why are you here, Percy?"

"This." Percy pulled a folded letter from his waistcoat, Will's letter. "I came as quickly as I could."

"But why *here*?"

"Your—lover didn't give any details of your whereabouts, or the situation with your husband, only your *condition*. And his part in it. I didn't know where else to go." He shook his head. "I'd hoped *you'd* be here, to be honest." He let the missive fall to his lap. His head dropped to one side. "Cybil. Why didn't you tell us?" His eyes searched her face, and she was suddenly uncertain if it was, in fact, accusation behind them. Perhaps it was closer to hurt.

"I—you told him everything?" She swallowed, her eyes darting to Emily. There were so many secrets Will had kept from her brother—not just his relationship with Cybil, but Emily as well, the whole truth behind what had happened on that fateful day by the canal.

Emily nodded. "I thought it for the best, given the circumstances."

"I was to leave for Leeds this morning." Percy's eyes were back on Cybil. He sprung up from his chair and paced to the window. "You've been lovers since my wedding." He exhaled, looking out at the street. "There was no Lilian Smith, was there?"

"Well—she really *was* a friend of mine at school, but—" Heat flared in Cybil's cheeks. "No. I never traveled with her. She lives in Cornwall, I think."

"I would have helped you." Percy turned back, his voice thick with emotion. "I don't know how, but I would have." He scrubbed a hand across his face. "You should have seen Jane. When this came"—he held up the letter—"she was beside herself." He paused, took a long breath, then gazed at her with dark, wounded eyes. "Am I so like Father that you couldn't trust me?"

Cybil's breath caught. She stared at her brother and saw, really *saw,* him for the first time in years. Percy, the small, irksome she'd tormented in her youth. The lovestruck swain she'd counseled to follow his heart. He was right. Somehow—somehow, he'd taken the place of Father in her mind. Her jailor. But he was not Father. How had she thought that?

Bitter guilt. Hot shame. "Percy, I'm so sorry."

"But what of Will?" Emily's solid voice broke the spell between Cybil and her brother. "He came after you. Did you see him? In Leeds?"

Cybil blinked back the tears. "They have him. And they may come here. You need to—"

"*Who* has him?" Emily demanded.

"Ernie, and his man Townend." She eyed her brother, who was still standing by the window, studying her, his brows drawn into a tight line. "You remember him?"

"Townend?"

"Yes. He's the steward at the Leeds estate."

Percy shrugged. "Vaguely."

Cybil took a steeling breath, then looked at Emily. "Townend was the spy who called himself Wilcox. It was he who betrayed Will and Davey all those years ago. The bridge, the canal . . . 'twas his doing." Emily's eyes widened at her husband's name. "I saw him, near your house, just a week after I arrived. I didn't think it was possible at the time. I thought I was mistaken, but—it was him. I believe he was watching your house, intending to apprehend *Will,* when he recognized me."

"That's how he knew to threaten the law on Will," Emily murmured.

Cybil nodded.

"'Twas a trap." Emily's voice hardened. "They knew Will would follow."

"Yes, and no. I think, in the end, Ernie was more interested in my child than in Will. He needs an heir."

Emily went white. "He'd—he'd take your child? Pass it as his own?"

Cybil couldn't answer that question, not in words. She nodded.

"Wait." Percy, clearly confused, held up a hand. "Townend is Ernie's man. And he's the same who called himself Wilcox, a spy working for the Home Office. But wasn't he in Ernie's employ before—since your wedding, at least?"

Cybil forced her eyes to meet her brother's. "He never worked for the Home Office, not directly, at least. He worked for Ernie." She took a breath. "It wasn't just the money that kept Ernie away, Percy. He and Father—it seems they had an arrangement to allow Ernie's man into the factory. To pose as a worker, and try to draw the others toward violence." Percy blinked once. Twice. Understanding dawned. Cybil forced herself to continue. "It was because of *me.* It was *my* fault Will was shot. My fault Davey—"

"Where is Will now?" Emily spoke slowly. Forcefully.

Cybil shook her head, helpless. "They have him." Her lip trembled. She held it taut. "I think he's here—in Glasgow somewhere. In a prison perhaps. I—I don't know—I thought you might—"

The door opened behind them. The maid probably, back with more scones. Cybil closed her mouth and let her gaze drop to her hands, using the time to collect herself.

"Praise God." Emily's voice. Full of . . . *relief?*

Cybil turned to follow her friend's eyes. Will was in the doorway. He was wearing the same clothes he'd had on when she'd seen him last—but his trousers were torn and dirty. He only had on one glove, and a dark shadow of a beard covered his face, but he appeared unharmed.

Cybil was to him before thought could form. His arms folded around her, his scent enveloped her—sweat and leather, wool and soap. For several heartbeats, he said nothing, just held her as she leaned into his chest. Then he pulled away and gazed into her face wonderingly. "You got away."

"I told you I would." She nodded, smiling, but unable to speak through the tears.

"Thank heaven." He exhaled.

He tugged off his glove and set it on a side table, then his hand found hers, and together, they came into the sitting room. Will was limping, Cybil realized, but before she could remark on it, Percy spoke.

"Chisolm." All emotion had left her brother's face.

Will nodded tightly. "Sommerbell." He looked quickly to Emily. "The bairns?"

"They're upstairs. They'll be right glad to see you." Emily's gaze flicked from Will to Percy, as if she could see the tension stretching between them. "I'll fetch them." She darted from the room.

The door closed behind her, and Cybil drew Will onto the sofa, ignoring her brother. "Are you hurt?"

"A sprained ankle is all. Cybil, how did you—"

"You escaped." She still couldn't believe he was here. Safe.

"Aye. In Yorkshire. I took the mail coach—but how did you get away?"

"I used the ladder." She smiled. "The one you'd brought. I was there when they—I saw the coach pull away, but I was too late."

Will's face brightened. "I'd hoped you'd find it. And the money too?"

She nodded. "I walked to Wetherby and got the mail coach, then took the stage from Newcastle."

"Through Dunbar." He reached out with his free hand, and his thumb brushed across her cheek, still wet with tears.

Cybil's eyes flooded as she nodded, then she leaned into his hand. So warm—

Percy cleared his throat.

"Sommerbell." Will turned his attention to her brother, but his hand tightened on hers as he spoke. "I owe you an apology."

"Several. Apologies." Percy eyed her lover, then looked away and shook his head.

"I'll be resigning my post, of course," Will broke in. "And I have a plan to set this all right. I—"

"That's not what I meant," Percy snapped. "Damnation, man, what were you thinking? She's my *sister*. To keep this secret all these years, then to not even tell me when—"

"Stop." Heat rushed Cybil's cheeks. "You will not turn Will into the villain, Percy. Everything I did—everything *we* did was my choice. Not his. *I* chose not to tell you."

"But—"

"My. Choice. Are you so virtuous that you can't understand that, brother?" Cybil stared daggers at Percy.

His shoulders fell. "Of course not." Then his eyes darted to Will. "But to not even tell me where she was when she was in such danger, it—"

"'Twas wrong of me," Will interrupted. "I misjudged you. I thought you'd sack me if you knew."

"You're the father of my sister's child. Of course, I wouldn't—"

Before Percy could finish, the door opened and Rose Chisolm streaked into the room, followed by her brother, Emily and Ewan. Luke was noticeably absent.

"Da!"

Will released Cybil's hand and stood up just in time to catch his daughter as she launched herself at his chest.

"We were so worried." She craned her neck to look at Will's face. "Is it true we're to have a little brother?"

Will glanced hesitantly at Cybil. She nodded.

"Aye, lass, 'tis true. Or a sister."

Rose's face broke into a wide smile, and her arms went around her father again. She buried her face in his chest.

After a time, Will peeled Rose away, set her down and faced his son. He held out a hand stiffly, warily. "I'm sorry, son. I did what I had to. But it wasna right or fair of me to lie—" He was cut off by Nathan's rough embrace, and when they finally broke apart, Cybil could see the tears in both their eyes.

Will shifted his weight and winced.

"You're hurt." Rose's voice was full of concern.

"Just my ankle, pet, nothin' to worry about."

Rose settled her father on the sofa while Cybil drew up a chair to prop his foot. Then, with his daughter curled on his lap, Nathan sitting on one side and Cybil the other, he told them of his capture, of his escape over hill and down dale, of sleeping in a hay mow in Yorkshire before his long, painful walk to the village where he got the mail coach.

"I got off at the Rutherglen Bridge, then took a hack to the bottom of the hill," Will finished. "Then I walked up and crept in the backdoor, quiet as a cat." He grinned.

"Why, Da? You're safe now, surely? You got away from them," Rose said.

Will smiled at his daughter, a not very convincing smile, but a smile nonetheless. His eyes tracked to Emily. "I'm safe, aye, but we must all leave here today. I'm afraid those men will come fo—"

As if on cue, a loud pounding sounded from the front hall.

Emily darted to the window. She peeked out. "To the nursery. Now, children." Her voice held iron and fear.

"But—" Rose and Ewan spoke in unison.

"Do as she says." Will's tone did not allow for argument. He pulled his foot off the chair and stood, pushing the children out of the room.

"You should go. Hide." Cybil was frantic. It was inevitable that Ernie would find *her*, but if he were to find Will—

"No." He took her hand and brought it to his lips. "No more hiding." His hazel eyes flashed gold in the sunlight. Then, without breaking eye contact, he raised his voice. "Sommerbell. Take these." He reached his hand in his coat pocket and took out a fistful of papers.

Percy rose hesitantly, then crossed the room and accepted them. He scanned the writing, then glanced up at Will, clearly confused. "What's this about—"

"Keep them safe." Will's eyes flicked to her brother, and there must have been something convincing in his look, because without further argument, Percy nodded, then tucked the papers away.

Will took a breath. "Now, would you answer the door?"

"You're sure?" Percy didn't move. "We could get you both out of here. Hide you somewhere, then—"

"I'm sure." Will squeezed Cybil's hand, and though she had no idea what he had planned, she was suddenly sure as well.

"Let them in, Percy," she said.

Percy left the room. There were several moments of thick silence filled with only the tick of a clock, the warm rays of the sun, the firm grip of Will's hand in hers and the glimmer of certitude in his eyes. Emily sat, pale, her gaze fixed on the door.

Will leaned in. "I love you," he whispered.

Their eyes connected, and she could only nod assent.

Then the door opened, and Percy entered, an uncomfortable frown creasing his face. He was followed by Ernie, Townend and two burly men in tall hats and high-collared blue coats with shiny brass buttons—the uniform of the Glasgow Police.

TWENTY-SEVEN

THE BARON WAS JUST what Will had expected. A fleshy bag of tripe, with drooping eyes and a cruel mug.

"That him?" The taller of the two bluecoats nodded at Will.

"Yes. Take him," the Baron ordered.

Townend circled the room, then came up behind Cybil and Will. He rested his hands on the back of the sofa, on either side of Cybil's head.

Will could feel her tense beside him. Her hand tightened in his as the policemen advanced.

"Up you get, then," the tall one said, speaking again, his tone polite. He was obviously trying to keep things seemly for the ladies.

Will ignored him and looked past the bluecoat to the Baron, who was skulking in a corner, clearly pleased with himself. "You're sure about this, Falstone?" he said loudly, to be certain everyone in the room heard.

The Baron sneered. "I've never been more sure of anything. With your record of running, you're sure to swing."

Will nodded knowingly while keeping his eyes trained on the man. He had to appear confident, that was the only way this would work. "It'll be a long, public trial, willna it?" He spoke slowly, as if he were telling a story to a bairn. "The press'll love it. It'll stir people up and prove the radicals are still a threat." The Baron's eyes narrowed, but he didn't answer. "And if the radicals are still a threat," Will mused, "the Tories'll have a much better chance of stayin' in power, willna they?"

The Baron's neck flushed. He opened his mouth to retort but stopped himself.

"Sommerbell. Stay where you are, but take those letters out of your pocket, if you would." Will looked away from the Baron just long enough to ensure Sommerbell did as he asked, then he flicked his eyes back to the Devil and continued. "I had a few hours to myself on the way here, so I wrote a letter. Or—a few letters, I suppose."

"You're wasting time," the Baron growled. He nodded to the policemen. "Just take him."

"Wait." Sommerbell held up a hand, stopping the men. He spoke with the tone of someone used to being obeyed. The bluecoats hesitated, and Sommerbell nodded to Will. "What's in these papers, Chisolm?"

"An account of what happened four years ago," Will replied, grateful for the man's help. "Names, dates, witnesses. How a spy named Wilcox came to work in the factory where I was employed, and how he drew me and Davey Flemming into a plot he'd hatched."

Townend, still standing behind them, let out an audible gasp.

Sommerbell scanned the writing. "So it is," he murmured. "It names Earnest Bythesea, Baron Falstone, as Wilcox's employer, and it gives your real name," he said, glancing at Townend, "what you look like, and that you're from Leeds."

Will didn't dare take his eyes off the Baron, but he felt Townend's fingers dig into the sofa's plush fabric and heard a low, almost inaudible growl.

"There's . . . four copies." Sommerbell paged through them. "Identical?" He looked at Will questioningly.

"Aye," Will said. "One for the *Herald* in Glasgow, one for the *Leeds Mercury*, one for the *Times of London*, and one for the *Dundee Advertiser*." He paused and glanced over his shoulder at Townend. "I thought it important that all the radicals of England *and* Scotland know the identity of the scoundrel who sent an innocent man to Botany Bay." As he'd hoped, Townend's eyes went wide, his face white. Will directed his attention back to the Baron. "And that all the citizens of this country know what Sidmouth and his Tory cronies were up to four years ago."

The Baron crossed toward Sommerbell and lunged for the letters, but Sommerbell was too quick. He moved to put the policeman between himself and the Devil, while at the same time tucking the letters back into his pocket.

"Get those letters," Ernie commanded the police. The two men looked at Percy uncertainly, and he met them with a challenging glare, daring them to approach. The flush on Ernie's neck crept up to his face. "I said, get them! It's a matter of national security!"

But the policemen didn't move. Sommerbell was a wealthy mill owner. That meant something in Glasgow.

"*Get them,*" Ernie screamed to Townend. But the manservant, clearly shaken, didn't move either.

A silence came over the room, and after a few moments, the bluecoats glanced at each other, then nodded in agreement. The shorter of the two stepped up. "I don't know what's goin' on here, but it appears to be a matter for the courts to sort out. Why don't we—"

"What's your price, Chisolm?" The Baron's voice was low again. Controlled yet full of hate.

"A pardon for Davey," Will answered quickly. The Baron opened his mouth, but Will continued, "and divorce. You go to London, divorce Cybil and leave her, and her child, alone."

Ernie looked at Will, stunned, then his eyes darted to Townend who still stood frozen behind the sofa. The Baron studied his servant for a long moment, considering, then suddenly his face relaxed, as if he'd won something.

"I could never divorce my beloved wife." He shook his head. "She's with child. 'Twould be a cruelty to leave her in such a state." He approached the sofa, then stopped before Cybil and spoke smoothly, as if he were the most caring, loving husband in the world. "Cybil, darling, let's go home." He put a hand on her shoulder, and Will could feel Cybil tense at his touch. "This man's a criminal, and a liar. There's a warrant out for his arrest, you know. He's been running from the law for—"

"He is not a criminal, and you know it." Cybil jerked away. Her hand gripped Will's, impossibly tight. "Ernie. Don't. Please."

"Ah, but I have no choice, do I, love?" Ernie paused, a tight condescending smile on his lips. His gaze never left Cybil as he barked to the bluecoats, "Take him."

"No—" Cybil cried out, and Will wanted with all his being to turn to her, to comfort her, hold her, give her the happy ending she so deserved.

But he couldn't. the police approached, and this time, Will stood, released Cybil's hand and allowed himself to be taken. Just as the bluecoats marched him through the door, Sommerbell shouted, "I'll send the letters, Chisolm."

Then Cybil's mournful wail pierced the air. "Will!"

But Will couldn't even turn to look at her. He'd failed. It was over.

<hr />

Cybil sat and watched as Will allowed himself to be handcuffed. This had to be part of his plan. Any second now, he'd speak, pull away, claim his victory. But the seconds ticked by. The iron of the cuffs clicked into place. The two policemen led him away. Percy shouted after him. But Will did nothing.

"Will!" she cried out as he passed through the threshold. He didn't even turn to meet her panicked gaze.

The door closed behind them, cold, hard wood. Her hand was still warm from his touch, but she could feel nothing. See nothing. Hear nothing. He was gone.

"Cybil, it's time to go." Ernie, too near. She shuddered.

"Falstone." Percy's voice was grim. "Don't do this. Leave her with me. I'll pay. I'll—"

"No, no," Ernie crooned. "We're past that now. No amount of money can replace my wife's presence, or my *child's*, in my life. I've been lonely, you know." His hand crawled across her cheek. "Let's not make a scene, my dear." He gripped her arm.

Will hadn't fought, and neither did Cybil. She clenched her teeth, raised her chin and allowed her husband to pull her up, to lead her out of the room past a stricken Percy and Emily, out the front door, down the steps and into his carriage.

TWENTY-EIGHT

THE NUMBNESS DIDN'T FADE as Ernie's coach made its way down Will's street.

Perhaps later, tomorrow or the next day, she would summon the strength to move, to care, but for now, it didn't matter where they were taking her or what might happen next. All she could do was breathe. It took every bit of her will just to survive.

She barely registered when the carriage stopped moving, or when the door opened and she was pushed into the bustling light of St. Andrew's square. She felt like a puppet—limp, unable to move without the strength of its master.

Ernie. He was her master.

He looped her limp arm in his and began to walk. Townend, silent as ever, fell in behind.

A stiff shiver went through her as they turned toward the steps of a hotel, a familiar hotel. The same one she'd stayed at with Mother, Percy, Jane and little James just a few months before, when they were here for Cameron and Letty's wedding. She could still see her nephew scampering out the heavy door, grinning in anticipation of an outing, and Percy running after him, waving the boy's hat.

"Don't make a scene, my dear," Ernie murmured as they crossed the threshold. "I do wish I'd a better place for you, but for tonight, this must do." They ascended the large, grand stairway, then he silently led her down a hall and unlocked and entered a room.

All pretense of civility was dropped as soon as the door clicked shut. Ernie released her arm and advanced on her, menacing. Cybil backed away, but the cold wall stopped her retreat.

"I'm disappointed, Lady Falstone." He raised a gloved hand and struck her, one calculated blow to the face. Pain shot through her cheek, her lip, and reverberated through her nose.

"Ernie, pleas—" Cybil cried out, but he did it again, and this time his white glove came away stained with blood, just a speck.

Ernie's angry gaze stayed fixed on her, the corners of his nostrils white and flared as he removed his gloves and held them out for Townend, who was still standing by the door. Oddly, the servant didn't move. He just stood there, observing, his eyes narrowed. With an irritated sigh, Ernie turned away and dropped his gloves on a side table, then he spoke in that low, grating voice she hated so much. "I've made arrangements for your new home in Cornwall. It's a suitable place, I'm told. Remote and secluded. They provide the latest treatment for disturbed women such as yourself, and the security is impeccable."

"But what about the—"

Ernie continued as if she hadn't spoken. "You will bear the child there. They'll alert me when its arrival is imminent, and I'll send someone for it."

"But—"

"We depart in the morning." He turned abruptly away, dismissing her, then spoke to Townend. "I've business to attend to."

Townend startled, as if he'd been daydreaming. "Aye, sir. I'll watch 'er"

"My gloves, Townend." Ernie glared as his servant.

"Of course." Townend jerked into motion, darted into an adjoining room, then returned with a pair of fresh gloves. Ernie donned them, then left.

Cybil's back was pressed against the wall, as if her husband still held her there. She could taste iron on her tongue—her lip must have been split.

Townend eyed her. Once again, he'd been relegated to her keeper, but there was something else in his visage, besides the usual unaffected annoyance. his face was flushed, his lips crimped tight. He was scared, or angry, or—something.

"In there." He jerked his head toward the room he'd fetched the gloves from. "There's a bed. I'll order food later."

She peeled herself from the wall. She could feel the blood dripping down her chin, but she couldn't—she *couldn't* give up. Not without one last, desperate attempt. "Please," she implored the servant. "You saw him. He's—he's going to blame it all on you. He'll find a way to cast himself the victim, and you'll be—"

"I said. Go. In. There." He stalked toward her, and Cybil gave up. She turned and scurried past him into the dark room. Townend closed the door behind her.

She stood for a moment, not knowing what to do. The drapes were closed, and the chamber had a leaden, stifling feel. There was a bed, a chair and one door that led to a tiled room with a tub and a washbasin, but that was all. Cybil eyed the exterior door, but all thought, all hope of escape was passed. Townend was on the other side, and tomorrow—no, she couldn't think of tomorrow.

Cybil removed her shoes, then stretched out on the bed. She tried to cry, to rage, to plan, to care, to feel . . . but nothing came. It was over. It was all over.

———⟡———

She awoke from a heavy slumber to the far-off sound of knocking. Not the door to the room where she slept, but one farther—

Everything came rushing back. The hotel. She was in the hotel, in Glasgow. Townend was out there, guarding her.

She waited for him to answer the knocking. But he didn't. It continued, more insistent.

Was he asleep?

Cybil rose from the bed, pallid and bleary, then winced at the pain in her face. Her lip had scabbed over, and it stung when she moved it. Her eye was achy and hot.

The knocking sounded again.

She tested the bedchamber door, expecting it to be locked or barred. It wasn't. She pushed it open, cowering into the darkness behind her, eyes scanning the room. There was barely enough light to see by. The day was finished, and the light outside was a periwinkle blue, as if the sun had just gone down and night had not yet fallen. Townend had to be asleep on the sofa or—somewhere, but he wasn't. The room was empty. It looked just as it had this morning. Tidy, Ernie's blood-spattered gloves were the only thing marring the hotel décor.

But where was Townend? There were no other doors, or rooms. Where could he—

"M'lady!" a voice sounded on the other side of the outer door, demanding, almost alarmed. Then, softer, "Should we knock it in?"

A different voice. "Na, the keep'll have a key if we've need of it. Try again. She's probly asleep."

More knocking, then louder again, "M'lady. Are ye in there?"

As if moving through a liquid dream, Cybil strode to the door, unlocked it and pulled it open.

Two uniformed policemen stood on the other side. Not the ones who had taken Will.

"Lady Falstone?" The older of the two spoke. Both men eyed her face, clearly noticing her wounds, but they didn't say anything of it. They took off their hats and nodded, as if she were someone to be respected.

"Y-yes?"

"May we come in?"

Cybil hesitated, but surely if they'd come for her, they'd be acting differently. She moved aside.

"Ye may want to sit down," the older policeman said. He had greying hair and kind eyes. "We've news for ye." He spoke gently, but there was something ominous in his tone.

Cybil sat.

The grey-haired man looked to his younger companion, as if for support, then back to Cybil. "Your husband is dead, m'lady. He died this afternoon."

TWENTY-NINE

WILL WAS AWAKENED BY the faraway echo of metal banging against metal. It was black as pitch in his cell. What little light filtered through the one, dirty pane had long since disappeared with the sun.

He listened for a bit, but the sound didn't come again. There was only the regular drip of water—from where, he didn't know—the soft snore of the inmate in the next cell, his own breath.

It was cold, and the stone floor was punishingly hard. He sat up and pulled his coat closer about his shoulders, then laid back down on the scrap of smelly, damp carpet they'd given him for a bed. Then he closed his eyes. Waited.

Faugh, it was a miracle he'd fallen asleep at all. It was only because he was so bloody tired after the last few days. Now that he was awake, he'd never get back to sleep. No, now the worries would close in, as they had all that day.

There was no sense in worrying, really. He'd known what must happen as soon as the irons were clapped on his wrists—he'd been waiting and planning for this moment for four years. It was just a miracle it hadn't happened sooner.

After seeing Sommerbell earlier, he was relatively sure the man would still agree to act as guardian for the bairns. Will would need to send a letter to his man of business to transfer funds for their care, and some to Emily. He should probably also direct the solicitor to sell his house, and quickly, for there was always the chance the government would try to seize his property after he was sentenced.

His children would be cared for, as would Emily and her bairns. His responsibilities would be fulfilled.

Except for one. And there was the worry. No, it wasn't a worry. It was horror. A nightmare that wasn't a dream. Christ. Where was she now? What was she doing—or, what was being done to her? He'd give anything, *anything*, to go to her. Not even to change things, just to see her. To hold her. To say goodbye.

A flicker of light reflected on the blank wall beyond the bars of his cage, and he could hear low voices. They must have been bringing in a new man. Duke Street Prison never slept, it seemed.

Will had tried not to hope for his plan to work. Tried, and failed. He'd alarmed Townend, that was for sure—the terror on the man's face had been clear enough, and rightly so. Townend knew enough of the radicals to know his life would be in danger if his part in the plot was known. But the Baron hadn't gone for it. He'd considered the threat, sure, but Townend would be too easy a scapegoat and the Baron had too much sway with the government to have any real fear . . . *Ach*. Will had been a fool even to try it.

The light grew brighter as whomever it was got nearer. Then the clear flame of a candle came into view, though he still couldn't see the figures around it. He expected them to pass by, but they didn't. The light stopped. There was the scrape of a key in the lock.

Will sat up, squinting in the dark.

"Will?" A female voice. It sounded like—like *Cybil*. That couldn't be—

But it was. She was there, kneeling beside him, touching his face, smoothing his hair. "You're free," she whispered. Then her lips were on his. His arms were around her. This made no sense. It couldn't be happening, really, and yet, it was . . .

She pulled away, and Will could see her brother behind her in the dim light. A thin-lipped prison guard hovered nearby, holding the candle.

"You're free," Cybil repeated.

Will stared at her, unable to make sense of the words. But—she was hurt. Her lip was split, her eye puffy and swollen.

"What happened?" He reached out to her.

"It's nothing." She shook her head, then smiled. "Ernie's dead. Townend's disappeared. Percy went to the sheriff, and—and you're free."

"The Baron's—?" Will blinked at her.

"Dead," Sommerbell confirmed. "Shot in the head. They found him under the wooden bridge in the Green this afternoon."

"And Townend's gone." Cybil clasped Will's hands, then kissed them. "He was to guard me at the hotel where they took me. I fell asleep, and when I woke, he'd left, and the police were there to tell me of Ernie's death. We thought we'd have to wait until morning to get you . . ." She looked back at her brother. "But Percy went to the sheriff—to his house—and talked him into setting you free."

"How?" Will still couldn't believe this was happening.

"I can be convincing when I want to be," Sommerbell replied slyly. "I *am* the owner of the Fulton Company Mills after all." His voice took on an authoritative, mocking tone.

"But, that's not—"

"Technically, it's only bail." Sommerbell's usual voice was back. "The sheriff's got a mess on his hands. A murdered English peer on the streets of Glasgow. His manservant the main suspect, *and* a known spy." He shook his head. "It's lucky you were in gaol, or they'd think it was you. But now you're just making everything more difficult, and given that Townend and Ernie were the only two who could identify you . . . honestly"—he shrugged—"I think the sheriff is glad to be rid of you."

"Did Townend really—?" Will broke off. The man had been terrified by the idea of his name being known, sure, but terrified enough to—

"Kill the Baron?" Sommerbell finished the thought. "No way to know for sure. He's not shown his face since the body was found, but . . . it *did* appear as if Falstone was planning to shove the blame on him . . . He'd have been blind not to see that." Again, Sommerbell shrugged.

"Your plan worked, my love." Cybil's eyes were sparkling in the candlelight. "'Twas delayed a bit, but it worked."

And just like that, from one second to the next, the weight of four years lifted. The worry, the fear, the guilt . . . it was gone.

"My God."

Cybil's smile broke through the darkness. She leaned down and kissed him. "Let's go home."

⚊⚬⚊

It was well after midnight when they got back to the house. Cybil woke Emily, to tell her all was well, then they went to bed.

Will couldn't bear to be apart from her, and she seemed to feel the same way, so they slept nestled together in his bed, too weary to make love but content in one another's arms. Will was careful to lock the door, since Rosie was certain to rush in as soon as she heard her father was safe.

And sure enough, they were woken just after sunrise by the pounding of a small fist. "Da! Let me in. Da!"

Cybil stirred in Will's arms, blinking at him sleepily. "Should I—?"

"Stay. You're our family now."

"But I'm not decent."

He handed her his dressing gown to put over her chemise. "You're more than decent." He pressed a kiss to her lips, swallowing down the emotion that rose at the sight, the feel of her warm, happy and in his bed. "You're perfect."

Cybil beamed at him.

The morning was marked by happy reunion after happy reunion. First Rose, who didn't seem at all put out by Cybil being in Will's room—though she did insist on doctoring Cybil's face—then Nat, then Emily and Ewan at breakfast. Luke came down alone, after the rest, obviously nervous. But Cybil didn't hesitate. She swept him into a tight hug, absolving him of any blame.

"I'm right sorry, Mrs. Smith—" Luke stopped himself. "I mean Lady Fal—"

"No." Cybil chuckled. "We'll need to find a better name. How about Cybil?"

A name. Yes. Cybil would need a new name, and Will couldn't wait.

⚊⚬⚊

It wasn't till after dinner that Will had a chance to speak with Emily alone. The children were all in bed, and Cybil, Emily, Percy and Will retired to the sitting room. Percy was itching to get home, and he planned to leave for Northumberland the following day. Cybil cornered him on the sofa, peppering him with questions about the new babes. The way he answered—the smile on his face—made Will warm inside. The man was an excellent father.

Emily sat alone by the window, looking past the reflection of the warm room and into the night. Will went to her, finally able to offer the apology he'd been wanting to give all day.

"I'm sorry."

She looked up, surprised. "Sorry? Whatever for?"

"For—I'd hoped to see Davey pardoned, but now—"

"You tried. That means something." She smiled bravely, then turned back to the window. After a few beats, she spoke again, slowly, as if she were testing the idea. "I've thought of going to him, in New South Wales."

"Going to him." Will couldn't hide his surprise.

"Aye. People do that, you know. We could settle there. He's in service, but he has rooms of his own, or—he shares them with another convict. Anyway, he said there's space for us. We could be together."

"You'd bring your bairns?"

"Of course."

Will studied her in the window's reflection. "You're serious."

"Aye. I've been thinking of it for some time now, and Davey is for it. I just—'tis a long trip."

"It is that." The voyage to New South Wales was at least four months.

"Would you—?" She turned again to look at him.

"Of course. I'll buy your passage as soon as you like."

"Thank you."

THIRTY

TOWNEND WAS NOT FOUND that week, nor the next. He'd exchanged the fear of being known as a spy for the terror of a man wanted for murdering a peer. Neither a good position, but perhaps, in the end, killing Ernie was the only way he'd seen to be free.

And he wasn't *just* a spy. Cybil played the grieving widow to the police and learned that Townend had, in fact, been arrested in Leeds fifteen years prior for horse theft. He'd been sentenced to hang, but Ernie had seen him pardoned on the condition he work as a servant in his house, doing whatever his master bid him.

And after everything Ernie had put him through—it was no wonder he'd wanted to see Cybil's husband dead.

Will suspected he'd left the country, and Cybil hoped he was right. For as much pain as the man had caused, it wasn't really his doing, and in the end, he'd saved them all.

Emily, Ewan and Luke went back to Strathaven to begin preparations for their journey. Emily would need to sell the house and all their belongings, and she hoped to leave by the early spring. Cybil would miss her friend, but she couldn't help but be happy for her. She found herself daydreaming of a new novel . . . A wife who sacrifices everything to join her exiled husband in a faraway land. It would have the epic feel of Homer's *Odyssey*, but with the genders reversed. Yes, there was a story there.

Cybil, Will, Rose and Nat traveled to Grislow Park a week after Will's release, once Ernie's body had been shipped back to Leeds and Will's exoneration was finalized. Jane and little James, with Henri at their heels, came rushing out of the house as soon as the carriages were within view. Mother and Percy weren't far behind. The driver handed Cybil down, and Jane was there—pale and tired, but smiling. She swept Cybil into a hug as Henri danced around their legs.

"I was so worried." Her friend's eyes glistened.

"I'm sorry—" Cybil began.

"No. None of that. You're safe. That's what matters." Jane pulled away, and her gaze floated to Cybil's belly. "And I'm going to be an aunt." She beamed, wiping her eyes with the back of her hand. "Our children will grow up together, Cyb—" She sniffled and wiped her eyes again. "I'm sorry. Since the twins came, I've been crying at every little thing."

But Cybil was crying too. They looked at each other and laughed through their tears.

"You two." Mother shook her head, but a lightsome smile was creasing her lips. She embraced Cybil. "Welcome home."

"Miss Jane!" Rose was down from the carriage now. She hugged Jane's knees. "Can I meet the babies?"

"Of course. They're going to love you." Jane drew them into the house.

<hr />

"It's finished. Do you want to hear it?"

It was late. They'd had a jovial welcome dinner with Mother, Jane and Percy, then the women had retired while the men stayed up drinking. But Cybil hadn't slept. She was sitting on the bed, her lap desk settled on her lap.

"Aye. Give me a minute, lass." Will chuckled and shut the door behind him. He shrugged out of his jacket, sat and slowly took off his boots.

"Are you ready?" Cybil eyed him impatiently.

"The words arena goin' anywhere." He unwound his cravat.

She sighed. "You're going to like it, I promise."

Grinning, he unbuttoned his waistcoat. One . . . two . . . three . . . four buttons, then he slipped it off. He patted the pockets of his trousers, checking to see if there were anything in them before taking them off. Then, without warning, his face broke into a gleeful grin. "Ach. I almost forgot." He pulled out a small silver box, and held out to her, his brows arched meaningfully. "This is for you."

Cybil's stomach dropped. She hadn't expected this—no, of course she had. She'd known it was coming, just not *when*. She could only pray she wouldn't hurt him too badly.

She stared at the proffered box, and slowly, Will's cocky, expectant grin gave way to worry. Cybil took a long, shaky breath and met his eyes. "I love you, Will. Always. But I—I don't want to marry."

Will let the box drop. "What?" His golden hazel eyes, suddenly full of fear, searched hers.

"I want to be with you, and our child of course, and *your* children, but—I don't want to marry. After the first time . . ." She attempted a smile. "I don't think I could do it again. Not so soon."

"Oh." Will's expression seemed to be somewhere between doleful and confused.

"It's just, to give anyone—even *you*—so much power over me. I trust you, completely, of course, but . . ." She implored him with her eyes. Surely, he could understand.

Will thought a moment. "It's just the marryin' part you dinna want to do?"

"Yes, just that part."

"You'll still live in Glasgow?"

"Of course."

"With me?"

"Yes. I hope we can visit here often, but . . . my home is with you." She cradled his cheek. It was rough with day-old whiskers. "I love you."

Will's brows furrowed. "The child—"

"He'll be Ernie's heir, not a bastard." The idea was so odd, that their child would grow up to be the next Baron Falstone.

"Aye, but if there's another one, I wouldna want my child growing up a bastard."

She'd expected this, and really, she didn't either. "Then we'll marry, I promise. I think I just need—some time."

She held her breath as Will gazed at her a moment longer, then, at last, he sighed and nodded. "I dinna ever want to be your jailer, Cybil." He hesitated, then continued. "If you change your mind . . . I'll be here."

Then he leaned in and kissed her.

When they finally broke apart, Will's eyes wandered to the box he still held. "Do you still want the ring? 'Tis pretty."

Cybil laughed. "Yes, I want the ring, but first you must hear the ending."

"Alright then." Will tucked the ring away, then settled beside her on the bed. "Go on."

Cybil took a breath, then began to read.

The fervent coal hit the still water and hissed, then all was silent. I gazed into the depths of the well as a puff of gentle steam floated up and caressed my disparaging visage—the last kiss of Tam Lin. Then the smooth clear ripples gave way to glassy tranquility, and he was gone.

My hand burned. My soul, my heart were stultified by the shock, unable to comprehend the darkness that loomed before me. And in that moment, that bleak, defeated moment, I stared into the black water and I wished that I'd never loved. That I'd never met, or known Tam Lin. I yearned to return to that blissful, miserable ignorance of the life I'd known before. For this, the knowing of love, only to have it wrenched away, was too much. Too much to bear.

The fairy queen cried out in triumph. "You fool!" she shrieked. "You thought to best me, but I have won the day!"

My husband, who had so stealthily followed me to the crossroads, laughed with her—a deeper, more villainous sound, one that portended pain and the most depraved cruelty.

With a hollow heart, I turned to face them, to face the truth of my inevitable defeat . . . And there, before me, stood Tam Lin.

He was naked as the day he was born, his body pale in the purple light of the dawn—but the curl of his chestnut hair, the golden flash of his eye, the strength of his brow and the warmth of love on his lips—my beloved. My Tam Lin. He was free!

I'd let him go. I'd trusted him, as he trusted me, and I'd thought all was lost. But in that release—in that desperate, burning, heartrending release—was freedom.

The fairy queen bellowed her rage. She howled and seethed, burning with fury. Her terrible gaze fell on the cowering figure of my husband. "Tam Lin is lost to me, but I must have another," she cried.

My husband cowered in her sight. He turned to run toward the safety of his house, but the moon had set, the sun was rising, and with the first glint of gold on the horizon, the fairy queen swept him onto her fiery steed and they disappeared together in a great thunderous flash of light.

Then all was silent once more.

The enchantment was broken. Yet the bond—the sacred bond of love and trust and understanding that entwined Tam's soul with mine—it held fast, stronger and truer with each breath we took.

Tam came to me, shivering in the cold early light. I covered him with my mantle, and together we made for home.

Cybil looked up. "That's it. That's the end."

Will blinked. His mouth was hanging slightly open. "But—it's happy."

She grinned.

"You don't write happy endings, Cybil."

"I do now."

Will scratched his head, sudden concern creasing his face. "There's only one problem that I can see."

"What?"

"I'm not naked." He raised his brows and smirked at her, then grasped the hem of his shirt and started to lift it over his head. But at that same moment,

Cybil's stomach lurched as the babe inside jumped with greater force than she'd ever felt.

"Wait." She stopped him, then drew his hand to her belly. "Can you feel it? He's dancing in there."

Will's expression went inward, as if he were listening. Cybil's belly lurched again, even harder this time, and slowly, his father's face lit up in the biggest, widest grin Cybil had ever seen.

Will sat as if frozen, feeling the life inside her, then with one smooth motion, he picked up her lap desk and set it aside. He brought his face down, till he was only inches from her swelling womb.

"Hellooo, wee one," he crooned to her belly. "I canna wait to meet you. I canna wait."

Epilogue

Ten Months Later

WILL HAD BEEN PACING the foyer for the last hour, stopping only occasionally to peer at the clock in the sitting room. If they'd left The George at daybreak as Cybil had promised, they should be here—

The sounds of horse's feet clipping up the hill came through the open window. Will was out the door just in time to see the top of his new traveling carriage come into view. The last hundred yards seemed to take forever, but at last, the driver pulled the reins and the coach stopped. The muffled sound of a wailing infant came from inside the transport.

The door opened, and Rosie's head poked out. Henri, Cybil's aged dog, was in his daughter's arms, and a bully was at her feet. "Da! We're home!"

The bully hesitated, then leaped to the ground. "Toby!" Rose called to him, but he paid her no mind. Obviously wanting to follow her dog, she glanced at the driver, who was just starting to descend the perch. Then she braced herself, preparing to jump.

"Hold on, lass." Will bounded down the walk and put the steps down.

In two seconds, Rosie was in his arms. He hugged her tight, then stepped back so she could usher the dogs into the yard to do their business. Nat descended the steps next, followed by two more dogs, then finally Cybil with wee Nimue in her arms. The lass was wailing at the top of her little lungs.

Their eyes met. Cybil had a tired, enduring look. Dark circles rimmed her eyes, which seemed a bit glazed, but her expression lightened when she saw Will. And she smiled. Will felt an answering grin spread across his own face.

He held out his arms and accepted his almost five-month-old daughter, noting how much heavier she was than the last time he'd lifted her, just two weeks before. He held the squalling bairn in the crook of one arm as he extended the other to help Cybil down.

"Ah . . ." She sighed, rubbing her eyes. "It's good to be home."

Will craned his neck over the crying child to give Cybil a quick kiss, then he bent over the red-faced babe, breathing in the milky scent of her curls as he planted a kiss on her forehead.

They'd been so certain she'd be a boy, but now that she was here, he couldn't imagine such a thing. Nimmy was herself—a loud, lusty lass who knew exactly what she wanted and stopped at nothing to get it. She was perfect.

"Now then, ye wee hell-raker, what are you givin' your ma such a hard time for?" Will asked with mock severity. The babe's eyes grew wide, then without warning, the tears gave way to a bright smile. Will's heart near exploded as she cooed and reached out with her wee chubby hands. He offered his index finger, and her tiny fist wrapped around it, holding tight.

"Jane and Percy send their regards," Cybil murmured. She was also watching Nimmy, or perhaps watching Will watch Nimmy. "She's been smiling so much of late. She has your dimple, I think."

"The twins are walking, Da," Rose piped up from behind him. Will turned to let her into their circle.

"Really?"

"Aye. And you should have seen Nimmy watching them. She wants to learn so badly, but—she's a bit scared. I've been teaching her."

"Have you now?"

"She has," Cybil confirmed. "And you should have seen your son, Will. He and that stallion jumped everything that could be jumped in all of Grislow Park these last weeks. A born horseman."

Cybil and the children had spent four weeks in Northumberland. Will had stayed the first two, then returned home to see to business and attend a series of political meetings he'd helped organize. Nothing illegal, just a group of re-form-minded men and women gathering in private. On Cybil's urging, before he left, he'd given Nat leave to ride the spirited stallion in Sommerbell's stables, praying his son would stay safe.

And he had.

Will looked at the lad, who was beaming under Cybil's praise. He nodded. "I was thinkin', perhaps in a day or two we'd go to the horse fair and look for a new horse for you to ride. Somethin' with a bit more spirit than the ma—"

"Really?" Nat's eyes lit up, and his grin widened. "Can I pick it out myself?"

"Aye lad, you may." A lump formed in Will's throat, and he swallowed it down. His son was growing up.

<hr />

Later that night, after tucking the bairns into bed, Cybil and Will retired to Cybil's study. The room used to be Will's, but he'd given it over to her for her writing since he had an office in town and could do work in the sitting room if need be.

He showed her Emily's letter, which had arrived only the week before, post-marked from Sydney. Davey had met their ship at the dock, she said, and they'd taken up residence in their own apartments. Davey still had to work for little pay, of course, but his position as a clerk in a government office was a good one and would probably lead to paid employment when his sentence was finished. Emily could take in washing to make ends meet in the meantime. It wasn't ideal, but they were together.

"She sounds happy." Cybil set the letter down.

"Aye. Another happy ending." Will shot her a look.

They fell silent as Cybil began sorting through the correspondence piled on her desk, setting some letters aside, opening others. Will watched, holding his breath.

She read the address on one, then opened it quickly and scanned the page. She looked up, her eyes sparkling. "The Tam Lin book is going for a second printing."

Will shrugged. "I'm not surprised."

"I am." She beamed at him. "The critics hated it."

"Critics be damned." Will snorted. "'Tis a good story."

Another long silence as she went back to the pile. Will watched intently, waiting for her to get to the bottom.

"What's this?" She scanned his note, then glanced up inquisitively. "It's in your hand—"

But Will didn't wait for her to finish. He grinned, then darted from the room, letting her read in private.

———— ◆ ————

Will went to his office the next day, as usual. Just after luncheon, Cybil left the house, telling Nimmy's nurse that she had shopping to do and would be back before dinner.

She would usually have taken one of the carriages and a footman, but today she waved them off, descended the hill on her own, then hailed a hack.

It seemed to take an eternity, but at last, the coach stopped, and the Avondale Arms stood before her, the Rutherglen Bridge just beyond. The inn was an old establishment, built in the previous century, crisply whitewashed with a half-thatch, half-slate roof. As she stepped down from the hack, Cybil's stomach began to flutter.

A sign hung above the door, and as she drew nearer, she recited the familiar verse to herself.

All ye that pass through Gallow Moor
Step inside Helen Whitehead's door
She's what will cheer man in due course
And entertainment for his horse

Cybil didn't have a horse, but she *was* here for entertainment. And after two days in a coach with a screaming infant, it was entertainment that was sorely needed.

She climbed the slate steps and opened the heavy wooden door. The inside was cool and dark. A few laborers finished their meals at the worn wooden tables. The smell of ale and roasted meat hung in the air.

"Mrs. Oliphant." Mrs. Whitehead, the portly, red-cheeked innkeeper, bustled toward her, wiping her hands on her apron. "'Tis a pleasure to see ye. How's your sister?"

"She's better, thank you." Cybil smiled politely, trying to keep her eyes on the woman, not the dark stairway behind her that beckoned—

"I was sorry to hear of her illness, but glad it brought ye back our way."

"Yes." Cybil nodded. "Always a pleasure." She swallowed. "Has my husband arrived yet?" The fluttering in her stomach sped up.

"Aye, he said he was wantin' a wee nap while he waited. Room 6."

"Thank you." Cybil started toward the stairs.

"Would ye like me to send up some food? Or a bath? I'm sure you're weary, and you've a ride ahead of ye."

"That won't be necessary, thank you."

"Very well."

Finally free of idle conversation, Cybil crossed into the darkness and slowly climbed the wooden stairs, worn smooth with time. The fluttering spread down from her belly to between her legs. Her nipples were two hard points of sensation, and her fingertips tingled. By the time she reached the door of Room 6, her earthly body seemed incapable of containing the churning energy within.

She held her breath and pushed the door open.

The chamber was dark and still. Just a small bed, a battered armchair and one narrow window with the drapes tightly closed.

Ruthven sat staring into the cold hearth. His profile was stark in the dim light. Dark, brooding brows, strong chin, serious, unyielding lips—yet there was a curve to them. A seduction. A draw that Effie was powerless to resist.

He glanced up when she entered, but he didn't stand.

"You came." He raised a brow.

"You summoned me." She bit her lip, then released it. "My lord, I—"

"Come here."

Slowly, eyes wide with apprehension, she put one foot before the next, drawn forward as a moth to the flame. When she reached his chair, she hesitated. "I should not have come. Please, my lord—"

"Yet, you did." His eyes flashed. He inclined his chin toward her. "Take off your gloves, Effie."

She had no choice but to obey. Trembling, she pulled one glove off, then the next, letting them fall to the floor. The sensation of newly exposed skin sent a shiver through her entire body.

"On your knees."

Slowly, she complied. Her breasts heaved. Her lips parted, and the breath came between them, a whisper of heat. She could feel his eyes on her flesh—hot and hungry.

He lifted a hand and lightly traced her lips.

Effie's eyes closed at the touch. She leaned in.

Then he was gone.

She nearly fell forward, and her eyes flew open, looking for him—

He still sat before her, watching with fiery interest. He'd sat back, and there was a bulge in his trousers—a dangerous wanting lurking below the surface. Waiting to strike.

Effie swallowed.

He caught her looking, and a small, wicked smile curled at his lips. "You want that, dinna you? You want it buried deep in your quim, or your mouth, Fucking you hard, filling you, till you forget who you are. Till you forget all else but me."

She gasped in shock at his crude words. "No, of course not. My lord. How could you—"

"Don't play games with me, Effie." He grasped her arm and pulled her close—his fingers pressing into her flesh like a vise of iron. Then he bent forward and whispering in her ear. "I know what you want. And you will not have it. Not till I say." The hair on her nape stood on end.

Then he released her, pushing her backward as he did and almost making her lose her balance. "Give me your hand," he growled, impatient.

Mesmerized by the golden light in his eyes, Effie held out a pale, shaking hand. He took it, his touch warm and firm.

Her eyes fluttered shut again at the feel of his lips on her skin, starting at her wrist where the pulse beat fast and hot, then moving up to the soft flesh of her forearm, the inside of her elbow.

She gasped, her head listing back as Ruthven rose from his chair and knelt over her, pulling her toward him as he continuing his line of kisses. Her upper arm. Her neck. His teeth grazed at the sensitive flesh below her ear, gentle at first, then harder, until she bit her lip to stifle a cry, pain balancing pain. "My lord, Ruthven. Mercy. I'm but a—"

But she never finished the sentence. He crushed his lips against hers in a scorching, rapacious kiss, then without allowing her to even come up for air, he lifted her—as if she weighed nothing at all—and carried her to the bed.

HISTORICAL NOTES

A Radical Affair is a work of fiction. However, the fabric of this tale was woven using many real, historical threads.

The Early Gothic

I drew inspiration for Cybil's biography and writing style from the late-eighteenth/early-nineteenth century novelists, Mary Wollstonecraft, Charlotte Dacre and Mary Wollstonecraft Shelley—three women who were not only extraordinary writers, but who led extraordinary lives.

- **Mary Wollstonecraft** (1759-1797) is well known for her proto-feminist essays and philosophical works, but she was also a novelist. Her unfinished work, *Maria, or the Wrongs of Women,* is incredibly moving, and served as a catalyst for the development of Cybil's views on marriage and motherhood. Wollstonecraft's biography is astounding for her day, and though I don't have space to recount it all here, I should mention that, like Cybil, she chose to bare (and be mother to) a child fathered by a man she did not marry.

- **Charlotte Dacre** (1771-1825) pioneered a new type of Gothic fiction (and shocked the British reading public), by writing strong-willed, lusty heroines who stopped at nothing to get what they wanted. This might not seem out of the ordinary now, but compared to the submissive, passive heroines that came before, Dacre's women were a revelation. Dacre also had a long-lasting affair with her publisher, a married man, with whom she had three children. *Zofloya* is Dacre's most famous work, though I also drew quite a bit of inspiration from her lesser-known novel, *The Libertine*.

- **Mary Godwin Shelley** (1797-1851) Shelley was Mary Wollstonecraft's daughter, though, tragically, she never knew her mother. (The elder Mary died from complications following her daughter's birth.) Shelley would have been a contemporary of Cybil's, and I gleaned quite a bit of Cybil's writing style from Shelley's work, particularly her short stories, and her novel, *Mathilde*, which was written in 1820 and published posthumously in 1959.

The Radical War

The plot to destroy a bridge and block the flow of coal into Glasgow's factories is a work of my imagination, however, the Scottish 'Radical War', which took place in Glasgow and the surrounding towns in the spring on 1820, was a very real event.

In the aftermath of that insurrection, twenty men were convicted of sedition and transported to New South Wales (current day Australia). And three men, Andrew Hardie, John Baird and James "Purlie" Wilson, were executed as traitors. Most historians now agree that these "radicals" were incited to violence by provocateurs working for The Home Office under the direction of Viscount Sidmouth. Though much has been lost to history, it's thought that (in order to remain secret from liberal members of Parliament and the public), many of these spies were not directly on Sidmouth's payroll, but instead worked for local magistrates and officials. And many were convicted criminals who had been given a reprieve from execution or transportation in exchange for their services.

One of the most touching things I came across as I was researching all of this, was a series of Andrew Hardie's letters to his friends and family, written from Stirling Prison just before his execution, including a heartbreaking love letter he penned to Margaret, his sweetheart, the day before he died. I have no idea if Margaret attended her lover's execution, or what happened to her afterward, but I couldn't help but put her in my story. Callie ('Purlie' Wilson's daughter), is also based on a real person: she and her niece did indeed sneak into a Glasgow cemetery and exhume Purlie's body from his unmarked "traitor's grave" in order to bring him home to Strathaven for a proper burial.

After The Radical War, there was a period of relative peace that eventually led to the repeal of the Six Acts, the draconian laws that were put into place in 1820, as well as the election of more liberal politicians. Though the "Ultra Tories," (a group of conservative Tory politicians), fought to stop this liberalization, it continued until, at long last, voting reform was passed in 1832. This fixed many problems in the British electoral system and gave the vote to a large swath of the British public who had never had that right before. Though it's important to note that women, and many in the lower classes were still left out.

Acknowledgements

Whoever said that writing is a solitary endeavor never self-published a novel. This, and all of my novels, are truly collaborative works.

First and foremost, I'd like to thank my support network of author friends and readers, without whom I would have given up well before publishing this, my third novel. There are too many to list here, but I'm particularly indebted to Alivia Fleur, Jane Hadley, Helen and Caitie.

Thank you as well to my editor, Isabelle Felix, my cover designer, Hallie and my beta reading team, (Jane, Maureen, Brendon, Patrick and Mom) all of whom, in one way or another, helped make this book what it is.

It was a class that I took with Dr. Sam Hirst that first sparked my interest in the early nineteenth century Gothic, and Sam gracious provided me with a reading list of titles that would have influenced Cybil and her writing. If you are at all interested in Gothic romance, you absolutely must check out Sam's site, romancingthegothic.com

And lastly, thank you to my children, for putting up with an (at times) incredibly distracted mother. And my husband, Mr. Mayberry—the love of my life, my alpha reader, my rock—who makes it all possible. I love you!

Thank you, readers!

Thank you for reading this book.

Let's stay in touch!

To stay in the loop on upcoming releases and other goings-on (as well as discounts and freebies!) head over to my website to sign up for my mailing list: www.louisemayberry.com. You can also find me on Instagram and Facebook. My email is louise@louisemayberry.com.

Reviews

If you enjoyed this book, I hope you'll consider sharing your thoughts with like-minded readers by posting a review. It may seem like a small thing, but reviews and word of mouth recommendations are incredibly important. It would mean the world to me!

ALSO BY LOUISE MAYBERRY

The Darnalay Castle Series

Book 1: Roses in Red Wax

JANE STUART HAS LOST everything, her betrothed, her ancestral castle in the Highlands, and her life's work—the orchard where she ran her apple tree crossbreeding trials. But after a year of exile in smoke-filled Glasgow, she's gone numb to the loss, indifferent to her lonely, grey future.

Then *he* comes along.

Percy Sommerbell is a musician, a free spirit who holds nothing but disdain for his industrialist father. But when familial duty forces Percy to travel to Scotland to inspect his father's holdings, he's confronted with an uncomfortable truth. His fortune—the money that funds his aimless wandering through all life's pleasures—is generated by the exploitation of people, *children*, in his father's spinning mills.

There's something else in Glasgow, a mysterious Highland beauty whose sad eyes and luscious curves promise temporary distraction from his growing sense of guilt, and inspiration for his music.

Against her better judgement, Jane finds herself falling for this man's charms. But when the mills become the first spark in a violent radical insurgency and old enemies threaten, everything changes. Can Jane and Percy's connection survive as the world catches fire?

Book 2: Swept Into the Storm

Yucatan Peninsula, Mexico, 1824.
Ever since he unexpectedly inherited his father's earldom in the Scottish Highlands, Cameron Dunn's been searching for something, *anything,* to bring meaning to his new life—a search that reaches an abrupt end when he's washed up, alone, on a deserted beach in Mexico.

Or at least the beach *should* be deserted. There's no village for hundreds of miles. So who's that beautiful woman walking toward him over the sand?

Letty Monro has a business to run, a plan for her future. Rescuing a ship-wrecked earl wasn't on the agenda. But the man's desperate, so of course she'll bring him to the British Settlement—for fifty pounds. And his signet ring for collateral. She's even prepared to look past the fact he's a peer, part of the system of oppression she despises.

As they begin their journey, sailing south through the Caribbean sea, Cameron finds himself falling for this guarded, stubborn businesswoman, and the heat smoldering between them threatens to burst into flame. Keeping her distance from the Earl of Banton will prove one of the greatest challenges Letty has ever faced. Especially when she notices, in the distracting warmth of his brown eyes, the one thing they have in common . . . How lost they both truly are.

Book 3: A Radical Affair

Cybil Bythesea is imprisoned in a marriage that ended ten years ago. That's when she fled the cruelty of her husband, Lord Falstone, and took refuge at her father's estate in Northumberland. Since then, her family's money has kept the villain at bay, and she's been able to pursue her creative passion—writing. But freedom, true freedom, has been beyond her grasp.

Except for her clandestine liaisons with Will.

Will Chisolm is haunted by the past, the tragedy of his family's eviction from their ancestral Highland farm, then his own foolish descent into political radicalism. Even now that he's gained wealth and respectability as the manager of a set of spinning mills in Glasgow, he's burdened with more responsibility and guilt than anyone knows.

But there's something about Cybil—a lightness, a kinship that, at least temporarily, makes all Will's troubles fade away. It's a dangerous game. Cybil is his employer's sister, the wife of his political enemy and for the last four years, his lover.

She's also with child. Will's child. And their world, their lives, will never be the same.

Available from all major book retailers, or purchase directly from Louise's website: <u>www.louisemayberry.com</u>

Sign up for Louise's newsletter to receive 30% off your first order.

ABOUT THE AUTHOR

Louise Mayberry lives with her family in the Upper Midwest, where she savors the summers and survives the winters. When not writing, she can be found wandering in her garden, attempting to talk her her kids into eating healthy food, or curled up in a pool of sunshine with a cup of tea and a good book.

Made in United States
Orlando, FL
22 April 2024

46075321R00159